SIGNS OF LIFE

SIGNS OF LIFE

M. John Harrison

St. Martin's Press ⚹ New York

ISBN 0-312-15656-1

First published in Great Britain by Victor Gollancz,
an imprint of the Cassell Group

First U.S. Edition: September 1997

10   9   8   7   6   5   4   3   2   1

SIGNS OF LIFE

1 · LEARNING TO FLY

My name is Mick Rose, which is why a lot of people call me 'China'. Choe Ashton never did. That was one of the differences between him and Isobel Avens. Isobel was hooked from the word go. She would hold my face between her hands in the night and whisper dreamily over and over – 'Oh, China, China, China. China.' But it wasn't my name that attracted her to me in the first place.

The year we met, she lived in Stratford-upon-Avon. I walked into the café at the busy little toy aerodrome they have outside the town and there she was, serving meat pies and Kenco coffee. It was an old-fashioned café, full of mismatched wooden furniture, cracked melamine trim and the hot steamy air of an era before true fast food. Glass ran the full length of one side, so that you could watch the aircraft landing and taking off. Exhausted young mothers from Stratford favoured the window tables. There they could fill themselves with cigarette smoke while their children smeared jam on one another or stared out at the strip of grass and sky between the runway buildings opposite, hoping to see a helicopter.

'Mummy, can we have another cake?'

'No.'

Isobel was twenty-five years old then: slow, heavy-bodied, easily delighted by the world. Her hair was red. She wore a rusty-pink blouse, a black ankle-length skirt with lace at the hem. Her feet were like boats in great brown Dr Marten shoes. When she saw me looking down at them in amusement, she said: 'Oh, these aren't my real Docs, these are my cheap imitation ones.' She showed me how the left one was coming apart at the seams. 'Brilliant, eh?' She had a nice smile and she smelt of

7

vanilla. She had a way of handing over a cup of coffee with both hands which made it seem a desperate gesture, precarious and fraught.

'I'd love to be able to fly,' she told me.

She laughed and hugged herself.

'You must feel so free.'

She thought I was the pilot of a little private Cessna she could see out of the window. In fact I had only come to deliver its cargo, an unacknowledged load for an unacknowledged destination, one leg of a journey that would end at some private medical research centre in Zurich, Budapest or the Near East.

I said, 'It isn't so hard to learn.'

'Flying?'

'It isn't so hard.'

She laughed again.

'I don't know,' she said.

She came back two or three minutes later and leant over me to wipe the table, rearrange the place setting.

'It won't be a minute now,' she said.

'No rush,' I said.

'I'm not used to waitressing.'

The deft movements of her hands, the sudden smell of perspiration beneath vanilla, the quick soft touch of her left breast on my shoulder, filled me first with excitement, then a strange, hypnotized calm.

'Is there much to do in Stratford?' I asked. 'Apart from the theatre?'

'Not a lot,' she said.

I watched her walk off between the tables to take another order. She called back over her shoulder:

'You'll never get into the theatre, anyway.'

'Listen to your heart . . .' Radio 1 was advising the mothers by the window. I wondered what they would hear if they did. Not Radio 1; or two children arguing over half a Mars Bar. '. . . It's gonna tell you what to do.' They knew what to do already. A

8

milky opaqueness passed across their eyes and was gone. When Isobel came back with my egg and chips, she said:

'I'm going to a wedding reception tomorrow evening.'

Behind her the Cessna was taking off. I watched it go. Tomorrow was Saturday and I was due back in London.

She smiled.

'You could come to that.'

'I'd love to,' I said.

She looked down at my plate.

'Egg and chips,' she said. 'You've just reminded me how brilliant it is to have a fried egg for breakfast.'

I began to eat.

'Where will it be,' I asked, 'this reception?'

'I'll write it down for you,' she said.

Saturday, I woke early. It was a cold, damp winter morning. Over by the theatre the tourists were already telling one another: 'Look how swollen the river is.' I hadn't slept well, but I was excited and restless. I went out and bought the *Daily Express*. I went into the theatre foyer, where I picked up a lot of leaflets; then into the theatre restaurant to sit drinking hot chocolate with dark rum while I tried to read the paper. Yeltsin was visiting the West, in the wake of 'a new Star Wars offer'. The UN was pulling out of Yugoslavia, the UN was staying in. No, there, it was pulling out after all. Here at home, a 50 per cent rise in auto-crime. I couldn't settle to any of this. Every minute or two I found myself looking out across the Avon, which was a sullen brown colour and running quite fast between low muddy fields, its surface chopped and herring-boned by the east wind. Crows stumped about on the far bank. A kittiwake hovered above the water. The willows leant uneasily into the wind.

'Let's look at auto-crime,' a spokesman was quoted as saying. 'Let's take auto-crime. The public can do a lot more.'

Every figure in the distant gardens caught my eye: every oiled cotton jacket, every cyclist, every couple walking their labrador

9

dog over the bridge. Suddenly I realized why. I was hoping to see Isobel Avens among them.

I turned to the TV pages.

Auto-crime, I thought: crime against the self.

By half-past eleven I had found my way to a pub called the Green Dragon. The Green Dragon was part of some other Stratford, noisy, smelly, unreconstructed, full of boys in grey jeans or scuffed motorcycle leathers, with their student girl-friends, drinking bottled lagers while they listened to a curious mix of music from R.E.M. to the Bryan Adams hit 'Everything I Do'. I felt comfortable with them, perhaps because my attention span had become as short as theirs. I talked to the girl behind the bar. I found 'Raindogs' on the jukebox and played it twice.

All morning I was aware of the scrap of paper Isobel had given me at the aerodrome café. Once or twice I took it out and looked at it. 'Woodcotes Country Hotel,' she had written; adding a tiny aeroplane in blue felt-tip pen. 'Don't be late!' Her hand-writing was careful, decorative, self-conscious.

'You shouldn't read that stuff,' said the girl behind the bar.

I stared at her.

'What?'

'The *Daily Express*,' she pointed out amiably.

'I never buy the *Daily Express*,' I said.

I never do. I folded it up carefully and put it on the bar.

'It'll rot your brain.'

'True.' I tapped the front page. 'We can always do a lot more auto-crime, though,' I told her. 'Is that a man's haircut?'

It was fifties-retro, dyed a harsh yellowy white above her ears.

'I like it,' I said.

'I'm flattered. Do you want another Holsten?'

'Yes, please.'

Later I drove the van about in the damp Warwickshire lanes for a bit, then parked it with the engine running, in a lay-by a little way down the road from the main gate of the aerodrome. Every four or five minutes I would remember something about

Isobel – the smell of vanilla, the way she pushed her hair away from her face – and find myself looking up with a shiver of anticipation. For the briefest moment there she was, walking towards me down the empty lane. I turned up the radio. R.E.M. again, 'Can't Get There From Here'.

It was two o'clock in the afternoon. I had no idea how I would fill up the rest of the day.

Woodcotes Country Hotel, just off the A40 about five miles out of Stratford. I don't know what I expected, but it turned out to be the ideal venue: a profoundly self-satisfied sixteenth-century house with heavily ornamented wooden beams. In the dining room you could see some famous wall-paintings, done in 1720 in 'vegetable dyes and blood'. They were kept covered now with little plum-coloured velvet curtains to stop them from fading. I arrived late and squeezed my van into the gravelled car-park between a sixteen-valve Golf ragtop and a steel-coloured V12 Jaguar. The dining room and the lounge adjoining it were packed and smoky. Everybody there had been successful at something in early middle age. They were still uneasy with it. They had finished eating – plover's eggs, a sorbet and then saddle of lamb with rosemary, followed by a Belgian chocolate mousse – and they were ready to enjoy themselves. You could hear the younger single women, who lived in Putney and had come up for the day wearing a Harrods' hat, ask one another loudly:

'Have you ever had mussels cooked on a fire of pine needles?'

'Now that's an experience I've been waiting for all my life. You don't get that over here, do you? Where do you get that?'

And then, shouting and waving across the room:

'Debbie! Debbie!'

'It's Jane.'

'Jane. I'm good with faces but so bad with names. We're going to see you tomorrow evening, I hear. From John.'

'Are you? Are we? Oh.'

I was relieved to find Isobel Avens, sitting on her own

underneath the wall paintings. As soon as she saw me she got up and said:

'I thought you weren't coming.'

At exactly the same moment I asked, 'Did you get your egg?'

She stared at me.

'For breakfast?'

'Oh.' She laughed. 'Yes, I did.'

She led me back into the crowd.

'Come and meet Colin,' she said.

Before she left the house, her hair had been caught up for the evening in a big bow like a butterfly, black velvet to match her dress. But it had already escaped, and was falling in long untidy wisps round the freckled nape of her neck. Her shoes were patent leather, with very high heels which shortened her long, considered stride. In the black velvet dress, with its low square neckline and puffed shoulders, she looked older than she had in the aerodrome café. At the same time she looked vulnerable and young. I would have been content to follow her anywhere just to be surrounded by the smell of vanilla. All the tension had gone out of me as soon as I saw her.

'You'll like Colin,' she said.

Colin was the groom.

'Great,' he said vaguely, when we were introduced. 'Where have you come from?'

Tenerife, I told him. I had a business just back from the beachfront at Los Cristianos: African leather tourist goods. When he asked me how the journey had been, I replied, 'The flight was crowded, but they always are.' He was so nervous he said:

'Good, good.'

Colin bought print, but talked mainly about local cricket. He loved close fielding. By midnight he was kneeling on the floor of the hotel bar with his head up the front of his wife's skirt. A dozen guests egged them on. Earlier I had overheard her saying, 'I've just spoken to my ex on the phone and he managed to yawn twice in the first five minutes. I'm not used to being yawned at.'

Then, about a spray of orchids and stephanotis: 'They've gone up a bit. I must have paid ten pounds for each orchid in that.' Her name was Jennifer. She was toppling over into her forties, toppling over into Colin's close dependable hands. At the buffet in the corner her twelve-year-old son by the other marriage was learning how to pour beer. He stumbled about in his little bow-tie and neat black trousers begging, 'Would you like a Grolsch? Would you like a Grolsch?'

Isobel watched me watching them.

'Why did you tell Colin you'd come from Tenerife?' she asked.

'I honestly don't know.'

'I mean I thought it was brilliant, but I know you haven't.'

She thought for a moment.

'You don't like this much, do you?'

I shrugged.

'I wish you'd worn your Doc Martens,' I said.

She looked down at the black velvet dress, then back up at me.

'With this?'

'With that. Look, let's—'

'What?'

And then before I could answer: 'They're staying here for the weekend, Colin and Jenny. They're working too hard to have a honeymoon. Do you want to see their room? It's full of the most marvellous flowers.'

I stared at her.

'Very much,' I said.

It was cool in there. The flowers, made up into careful arrange-ments like frozen fireworks, were still wrapped. A faint breath of florists' cellophane hung about them, later to become confused for me with vanilla essence and the smell of sex.

'I'll just put the table lamp on,' she said.

By now we were frantic. I started to say something like, 'What are we going to do about one another, then?' But as soon as I touched her she murmured, 'Oh,' in a surprised, musing voice and sat down on the edge of the bed. The black velvet bow fell out of her hair. She put her hand up to the side of her head. Suddenly she began to struggle with her dress.

'Here,' she said, when I tried to help.

She said: 'Here. The zip. No, the zip.'

In the end we couldn't do it, and she had to lie down and raise her bottom an inch or two off the counterpane so that I could take the dress by its hem and pull it up round her waist.

'Christ,' I said. I was shaking.

'Quick,' she said. 'Quick.'

She had her arms so tightly round my neck that I had to struggle away to get my trousers off. Entering her, I thought I would faint. Her legs went round me, her eyes snapped open, she opened her mouth silently and rolled her head from side to side on the pillow.

'Oh,' she said. Then:

'Fuck me.'

Fuck me, in a small panicky voice.

As if she meant, *Save me from falling*.

By the time we got back down to the party, it was over. One or two red helium balloons hung among the beams of the old hallway, but Woodcotes was quiet, empty, intent on itself. The hotel staff had tidied the dining room and were setting tables for breakfast, two or three middle-aged women talking in quiet local voices. Isobel waved at them as we went past; one of them laughed and waved back. In a hotel at night, things are comfortably in abeyance. All the odours are kind: carpet, floor polish, central heating. You feel warm, you feel tended. None of this, you think, takes place in the real world. Because of that, it can never end. Isobel smiled every time I looked at her. I walked with my arm round her waist, because I already loved to feel her hip roll and sway under my hand.

'I've got to find Colin and Jenny before we go,' she whispered.

14

I looked at my watch.

'We've been up there for three hours.'

We stopped and stared at one another in horrified delight.

'Oh no. Three hours . . .'

Colin and Jenny were in reception. Jenny had passed out on a chintz sofa with her mouth open. She had flung one arm up over the back of the sofa in the middle of some gesture. Her legs sprawled awkwardly: Colin had covered them with his jacket. There was no need to look closely to see the Yves Saint Laurent foundation caked into the laugh-lines round her mouth. Colin was staring down at her, pulling at his bottom lip in a puzzled way. At first I thought he was simply working out how he could get her upstairs. Then I saw that his eyes were full of wonder. There was some mystery for him in all this; how a print-buyer like himself, nothing much more than a useful pair of hands, had managed to capture someone so beautiful, so intelligent, so . . . Well, you saw that he could get no further, would always have difficulty getting further. As we went past, he looked up defensively. 'Ssh,' he said. The flesh under his eyes was grey; his cheeks were bright red, lacquered with the effort of remaining conscious. He had rolled up his sleeves and taken off his patent leather shoes. There were two great saddles of sweat underneath his arms. Isobel went up to him and kissed him on the chin. I saw her tuck something into the pocket of his dress shirt.

'Colin, it's half-past two,' she told him.

He looked down at his wife. I saw him *think*: My wife.

'Have a Glen Morangie,' he invited us.

He said: 'We're having one.'

'Bye bye Colin.'

Outside, the air was cold and sharp. The car-park had emptied itself of Audis and BMWs an hour before. Only a faint smell of money remained – unleaded fuel and sophisticated catalysers, German iron. 'Look up there,' Isobel said. 'How brilliant. All those stars.' Then after I had unlocked the passenger door for her and we were sitting waiting for the heater to clear the windscreen: 'Colin and Jenny deserve to have the best time they can.' I shrugged. I switched the headlights on. Beyond the car-park, through a dark fringe of hedge, I could see an empty field. 'You mustn't feel superior to them.'

Instead of replying, I asked her:

'What was that you gave Colin?'

She blushed.

'The room key,' she said.

'They all knew?'

She said: 'None of them knew.' Then: 'Jenny knew.'

I peered out into the car-park, put the van into first gear.

I admitted: 'I'm not a pilot.'

Isobel smiled.

'I guessed that,' she said.

'Don't you care?'

'No.'

I knocked the van out of gear again and leant over.

'Kiss me then.'

'China.'

Before six months were out we were inventing one another hand over fist. I went back to see her every weekend. Spring came early. It was an extraordinary summer. You have to imagine this:

Saturday afternoon. Stratford Waterside. The river has a lively look despite the breathless air and heated sky above it. Waterside is full of jugglers and fire-eaters entertaining thick crowds of Americans and Japanese. There is hardly room to move. On a patch of grass by the water, two lovers, trapped in the great circular argument, are making that futile attempt all lovers make to get inside one another and stay there for good. He can't stop touching her because she wants him so. She wants him so because he can't stop touching her. A feeding swan surfaces, caught up with some strands of very pale green weed. Rippling in the sudden warm breeze which blows across the river from the direction of the theatre, these seem for a moment like ribbons tied with a delicate knot – the gentle, deliberate artifice of a conscious world.

'Oh look. Look,' she says.

He says: 'Would you like to be a swan?'

'I'd have to leave the aerodrome.'

He says: 'Come and live with me and be a swan.'

Neither of us had the slightest idea what we were talking about. But by the end of July I had persuaded Isobel to leave Stratford and come down to London with me. On the morning of her last day at the aerodrome, she woke up early and shook me until I was awake too.

'China,' she said.

'What?'

'China.'

I said: 'What?'

'I flew!'

It was a dream of praxis. It was a hint of what she might have. It was her first step on the escalator up to Brian Alexander's clinic.

'I was in a huge computer room. Everyone's work was displayed on one screen like a wall. I couldn't find my C-prompt.' People laughed at her, but nicely. 'It was all good fun, and they were very helpful.' Suddenly she had learned what she had to know, and she was floating up and flying into the screen, and through it, 'Out of the room, into the air above the world.' The sky was crowded with other people, she said. 'But I just went swooping past and around and between them.' She let herself fall just for the fun of it: she soared, her whole body taut and trembling like the fabric of a kite. Her breath went out with a great laugh. Whenever she was tired she could perch like a bird. 'I loved it,' she told me. 'Oh, I loved it.'

How can you be so jealous of a dream?

I said: 'It sounds as if you won't need me soon.'

She clutched at me.

17

'You help me to fly,' she said. 'Don't dare go away, China. Don't dare.'

She pulled my face close to hers and gave me little dabbing kisses on the mouth and eyes. I looked at my watch. Half-past six. The bed was already damp and hot: I could see that we were going to make it worse. She pulled me on top of her, and at the height of things, sweating and inturned and breathless and on the edge, she whispered, 'Oh lovely, lovely, lovely,' as if she had seen something I couldn't. 'So lovely, so beautiful.' Her eyes moved as if she was watching something pass. I could only watch her, moving under me, marvellous and wet, solid and real, everything I ever wanted.

2 · LOST IN SOHO

Choe and Isobel disliked one another the moment they met. It would be easy to say that she felt threatened by him; that he felt displaced by her. But things between them were more complex than that. They were more alike than they seemed. I loved them both, but you could hardly say which of them was the more dangerous.

To begin with, you would have thought it was Choe. I had known him for about two years. Between us, we were running a courier service we called Rose Medical Plc. Our fleet comprised a single Vauxhall Astravan into which Choe (you pronounce it as in 'Joey' or 'Chloe') had dropped the engine of a two-litre SRi insurance write-off. We specialized. If it was small, we guaranteed to move it anywhere in Britain within twelve hours; occasionally, if the price was right, to selected points in Europe. Choe kept the fleet operating. I touted for business. We shared the driving. We would move anything – transplant organs in ice, small runs of a new drug, diagnostic technology designed to bolt on to existing computers. But we preferred the really profitable loads. Recombinant DNA; viruses at controlled temperatures, sometimes in live hosts; cell cultures in heavily armoured flasks. What the stuff was used for we had no idea. I didn't want an idea until later; and that turned out to be much too late.

The day I met Isobel Avens, it was Choe's turn to drive. I had phoned him repeatedly the night before: no answer. I did the job myself, then rang him again. Nothing. He was away for three or four days. I began to worry. Finally he picked the phone up.

'Where have you been, Choe?'

'What can I say? I went to France.'

'What?'

'I met someone I knew in a bar, Mick. We went to France.'

'Choe, you unreliable fucker.'

'I know. It was real, though.' He laughed. 'What's happening?'

'Weird stuff, Choe. I'm still in Stratford—'

'It's a girl,' he said. 'Isn't it?'

'Choe, you don't know that.'

'Ho, ho. Oh yes, I do. Brilliant. Is she a tart, Mick? Is she a *real fucking tart?*'

This was Choe's highest form of praise.

'I bet she is,' he said. 'I bet she's a real fucking tart.'

'Stop trying to talk me round, Choe. It was wrong of you to go to France.'

'I know. I *know* it was wrong. But I can't seem to *care.*'

'Choe—'

'Do you forgive me? I bet you do. I bet you forgive me . . .'

I had been forgiving him one thing or another since December 1989, the weekend Bush talked to Gorbachev on the *Maxim Gorki* in half a gale in Valetta harbour. In those days I still worked for other people.

Ten past ten on a Saturday night. The upper rooms of a media drinking club in central London. In the East, governments were going over like tired boxers – saggy, puzzled, almost apologetic. Here, we were celebrating the birthday of an agency boss called Andy Dawes – 'Ada' to his friends. I knew him vaguely, the rest of the people in the room hardly at all. The women were in PR: the last of the power dressers. The men were in advertising, balding to a ponytail. Men or women, they all had a Range Rover in the car-park at Poland Street. They were already thinking of exchanging it for one of the new Mazdas. Soon they would be giving Dawes a cake in the shape of his nickname, on which had been iced the words 'Just Do It'. Meanwhile they were eating pasta.

'Now that's *two* thousand calories.'

'So far I've had cheese but not much else, which is interesting...'

'Are we going to get that fettucini we've paid for?'

'How much more do you want?'

I moved away and went to stare out of the window. Over towards Trafalgar Square the sky looked like a thundery summer afternoon. The buildings stood out against it, and against one another, like buildings cut from cardboard. I followed an obscure line of neon. A string of fairy lights slanting away along the edge of a roof. Then cars going to and fro down at the junction by St-Martin-in-the-Fields, appearing very much smaller than they were. I had been there about a minute when someone came up behind me and said:

'Guess what? I was just in the bog.'

'That's interesting.'

'No, come on. I switched the hand-drier on and it talked to me.'

I stared at him as flatly as I could.

'I expect it did,' I said.

He was delighted.

'Why do you say that? Has it happened to you, too?'

He was in his forties, short and wiry, full of energy, with the flat-top haircut and gold ear-ring of a much younger man. His 501s were ripped at the knees. With them he wore a softly tailored French Connection blouson, which made his face, reddened as if by some kind of outdoor work, look incongruous and hard one moment, shy the next.

'"Choe, I really like drying your hands." I'm not kidding you, you know. It talked to me.'

I shrugged.

'You don't believe me, do you?'

'No.'

'OK. Give us a fag then, if you don't believe me. Eh?'

'I don't smoke,' I said.

'Come on,' he wheedled. 'Every fucker smokes. Dawsie only knows people who smoke. Give us a fag.'

I laughed.

'I honestly can't help you.'

'All right then,' he said. 'Let's fuck off to Lisle Street and have a Chinese. Eh?' He gave me his sly, beautiful smile, just an ageing boy in a French Connection jacket. 'Come on, you know you want to.'

I did. I was bored.

As we were leaving, they brought the birthday cake in. Ada made several efforts to blow the candles out, to diminishing applause. He ended up pouring wine over them until, fizzing and bubbling grossly, dripping thick coloured wax down the sides of the cake, they blackened and cooled. There was a loud cheer as he cut inaccurately into the first A of Ada. Then an odd thing happened. The candles, which had seemed to be completely extinguished, began to burn again. Blinking happily around, Dawes took this as a powerful metaphor for his own vitality. He poured more wine on them.

'Did you see that?' I asked Choe Ashton.

But he was halfway out of the door.

At first we walked rapidly, not talking. Head down, hands rammed into the pockets of his coat, Ashton paused only to glance at the enormous neon currency symbols above the Bureau de Change on Charing Cross Road. 'Ah, money.' But as soon as he recognized Ed's Easy Diner, he seemed content to slow down and take his time. It was a warm night for December. Soho was full of the most carefully dressed people. Ashton pulled me towards a group standing outside the Groucho, so that he could admire their louche haircuts and beautifully crumpled chinos. 'Can't you feel the light coming off them?' he asked me in a voice loud enough for them to hear. 'I just want to bask in it.' For a moment after he had said this, there did seem to be a light round them – like the soft light in a seventies movie, or the kind of watery nimbus you sometimes see when you are peering through a window in the rain. I pulled him away, but he kept yearning back along the pavement towards them, laughing. 'I love you,' he called to them despairingly. 'I love you.' They moved uncomfortably under his approval, like cattle the other side of a fence.

'The middle classes are always on watch,' he complained.

We dodged briefly into a pick-up bar and tried to talk. The only free table was on a kind of mezzanine floor on the way to the Ladies. Up there you were on a level with the sound system. Drunken girls pushed past, or fell heavily into the table.

'I love them all!' shouted Ashton.

'Pardon?'

'I love them.'

'What, these too?'

'Everything they do is wonderful.'

Actually they just sat under the ads for Jello-shots, Schlitz and Molson's Canadian and drank Lowenbrau: boys in soft three-button shirts and Timberland boots, girls with tailored jackets over white silk trousers. I couldn't see how they had arrived there from Manor House or Finsbury Park, all those dull, broken, littered places on the Piccadilly line; or why. Eventually we got sick of bawling at one another over the music and let it drive us back out into Cambridge Circus.

'I was here this afternoon,' he said. 'I thought I heard my name called out.'

'Someone you knew.'

'I couldn't see anyone.'

We ended up in one of those Lisle Street restaurants which specialize in degree-zero decor, cheap crockery and grudging service. There were seven tables crammed into an area smaller than a newsagent's shop. The lavatory – with its broken door handle and empty paper roll – was downstairs in the kitchens. Outside it, on a hard chair, sat a waitress, who stared angrily at you as you went past. They had a payphone: but if you wanted to use it, or even collect your coat from the coat rack, you had to lean over someone else's dinner. Choe Ashton, delighted, went straight to the crêpe-paper shrine mounted in the alcove to show me a vase of plastic flowers, a red and gold tin censer, from which the stubs of old incense sticks protruded like burnt-out fireworks, two boxes of safety matches.

'See this? Make a wish.'

With considerable gentleness he put fresh incense in the censer and struck a match.

'I love these places . . .' he said.

He sat down and rubbed his hands.

'. . . but I'm bored with Hot and Sour.'

He stared away from the menu and up at the industrial ceiling, which had been lowered with yellow-painted slats. Through them you could still see wires, bitumen, ventilator boxes. A few faded strings ejected from some exhausted Christmas party-popper still hung up there, as if someone had flung noodles about in a claustrophobic fit or paddy.

'Let's have some Bitter and Unfulfilled here,' he called to the waitress. 'No. Wait a minute. I want Imitation Pine Board Soup, with a Loon Fung calendar. But it has to have copulating pandas on it.'

After that we began to drink Tsing Tao beer. Its packaging, he said, the pale grey ground and green, red and gold label, reminded him of something. He arranged several empty cans across the table between us and stared at them thoughtfully for some time, but nothing came of it. I don't remember eating, though we ordered a lot of food. Later he transferred his obsession from the Tsing Tao label to the reflections of the street neon in the mirror behind the bar. SOHO. PEEP SHOW. They were red, greenish-yellow, a cold blue. A strobe flickered inside the door of the peep show. Six people had been in there in two minutes. Two of them had come out again almost immediately. 'Fucking hell, sex, eh? Why do we bother?' said Choe. He looked at me. 'I fucking hate it,' he said. Suddenly he stood up and addressed the people at the nearer tables. 'Anyone who hates sex, stand up,' he tried to persuade them. 'Fucking sex.' He laughed. 'Fucking, fucking,' he said. 'Get it?' The waitresses began to move towards us.

But they had only come to bring the bill and offer him another beer. He smiled at them, moved his hands apart, palms forward, fingers spread.

'No thanks,' he said shyly.

'The bill's in Chinese!' he shouted. He brandished it delightedly at the rest of the diners. 'Hey!'

I agreed to drive him home. For the first few minutes he showed some interest in my car. At that time I owned an Escort RS Turbo. But I didn't drive it fast enough for him, and he was silent again until we were passing the Flying Dutchman in Camberwell. There he asked in an irritable voice: 'Another thing. Why is this pub always in the same place?' He lived on the other side of Camberwell, where it nudges up against Denmark Hill. It took him some time to find the right street. 'I've only just moved in.' I got him upstairs, then consulted my watch. 'I think I'd better sleep on your floor,' I said. But he had passed out. It seemed like a nice flat, although he hadn't bought much furniture.

I woke late the next morning. Ten o'clock. Sleet was falling. A minicab driver had parked his Renault under the front window, switched its engine off, and turned up Capital Radio so that I could hear clearly a preview of a new track by the Psychedelic Furs. Every thirty seconds he sounded his horn. At that, the woman who had called him leant out of a fourth-floor window in one of the point blocks on the other side of the road and shrieked:

'Cammin dahn!'

Beep.

'Cammin dahn!'

Beep.

'Cammin dahn!'

Beep. Beep. Beep.

'Cammin dahn! Cammin dahn!'

The back of the flat overlooked a row of gardens. They were long and narrow and generally untended between walls of sagging, sugary old brick; so choked, some of them, with bramble, elder and buddleia stalks, that they reminded you of overgrown lanes. In the bleaker ones, you knew, a dog would trot restlessly all day between piles of household or builders' rubbish, under a complex array of washing lines. Choe Ashton's garden had once been kept in better order. There was a strip of lawn and a patio of black and white flagstones like a chess board, a few roses pruned savagely back to bare earth, a little pond full of leaves. Suddenly I saw a fox sniffing round the board fence at the bottom of the garden.

At first I thought it was some breed of cat I had never seen before: long-backed, reddish, brindling towards its hindquarters and long tail. It was moving a bit like a cat, sinuously and close to the ground. After a minute or two it found the pond and drank at length, looking up every so often, but too wet and tired, perhaps too ill, to be wary or nervous.

I watched with my heart in my mouth, afraid to move, even behind the window, in case it saw me and ran off. Choe Ashton came into the room.

'Fucking hell,' he said. 'Are you still here?'

'Sssh. There's a fox in your garden.'

He stood beside me. As he watched, the fox wandered into the middle of the overgrown lawn, pawing and sniffing at the earth. It yawned. I couldn't see anything there it might eat. I wondered if it had smelt another fox. It sat down suddenly and stared vaguely into the sleet.

'I can't see anything.'

I stared at him.

'Choe, you must be blind—'

He gripped my arm very hard, just above the elbow.

'That hurts,' I said.

'I can't fucking *see* any fucking fox,' he said quietly.

We stood like that for thirty or forty seconds. In that time the fox went all round the lawn, not moving very fast, then crossed the low brick wall into the next garden, where it vanished among some elders, leafless laburnum bushes and apple trees.

'OK Choe.'

People like Choe are like moths in a restaurant on a summer evening just as it gets dark. They bang from lamp to lamp, then streak across the room in long flat wounded trajectories. We make a lot of their confusion but less of their rage. They dash themselves to pieces out of sheer need to be more than they are. It would have been better to leave him alone to do it, but I was already fascinated. I spent the rest of the day phoning everyone who might have something to tell me. No one knew the whole story. But they all agreed that Choe was older than he appeared and, as Andy Dawes put it, 'Career-wise at least, a bit of a wimp.'

He was from the north of England. He had taken one of the first really good media degrees – from Sussex – but never followed it up. He did occasional design jobs for the smaller agencies that operate out of top rooms above Wardour Street. In addition, he had some film work, some advertising work. But who didn't? The interesting thing was how he had filled his time until he appeared in Soho. After Sussex he had moved back north and taken a job as a scaffolder; then joined a Manchester steeplejacking firm. He had worked in the massive stone quarries around Buxton, and out in the North Sea on the rigs. Returning to London, obsessed with motorcycles, he had opened one of the first courier operations of the Thatcher boom. He never kept any job for long. Boredom came too easily to him. Anything hard and dangerous attracted him, and the stories I heard about him, true or not, would have filled a book. He told me some of them himself, later:

Stripping old render near the top of a thirty-storey council high-rise in Glasgow, he found himself working from scaffolding fifty feet above a brick-net. These devices – essentially a few square feet of strong plastic netting stretched on a metal frame – are designed to catch dropped tools or bits of falling masonry. With a brick-net, you don't need safety bunting or a spotter on the ground to protect unwary pedestrians. Ashton quickly became interested. He thought about the brick-net in his digs at night. (Everyone else was watching *Prisoner Cell Block H*.) During the day everything that fell seemed to go down into it in slow motion. Things were slow in his life too. One cold windy Monday, ten minutes before lunch, he took a sly look sideways at the other jacks working on the scaffolding. Then he screamed and jumped off, turning over twice in the air and landing flat on his back. The breath went out of him – boof! Everything in the net flew up into the air and fell down again on top of him – old mastic tubes, bits of window frame, half bricks.

'I'd forgotten that stuff,' he said with a grin.

'Were you injured?'

'I walked a bit stiff that week.'

'Was it worth it?'

'It was a fucking trip.'

Later, induced by money to take a long-running steelworks job, he decided to commute to Rotherham from London on a Kawasaki 750. Each working week began in the early hours of Monday morning, when, still wobbly from the excesses of the weekend, he pushed this overpowered bright-green monster up the motorway at a hundred and fifty miles an hour in the dark. He was never caught, but quite soon he grew bored. So he taught himself to lie along the Kawa with his feet on the back pegs, wedge the throttle open with a broken matchstick so that he could take both hands off the handlebars, and roll a joint in the tiny pocket of still air behind the fairing. At the right speed, he claimed, Kawasaki engineering was good enough to hold the machine on track.

'The idea,' he said, 'is not to slow down.'

I wasn't sure boredom was entirely the issue. Some form of exploration was taking place, as if Choe Ashton wanted to know the real limits of the world, not in the abstract but by experience. I grew used to identifying the common ground of these stories – the point at which they intersected – because there, I believed, I had found Choe's myth of himself, and it was this myth that energized him. I was quite wrong. He was not going to let himself be seen so easily. But that didn't become plain until later. Meanwhile, when I heard him say, 'We're sitting on the roof one dinner time, and suddenly I've poured lighter fuel on my overalls and set myself on fire,' I would nod sagely and think of Aleister Crowley's friend, Russell, discharged from the US Navy after he had shot up forty grains of medical-grade cocaine and tried to set fire to a piece of glass by willpower alone.

'I just did it to see what people would do,' Choe said. 'They had to beat me out with their hands.'

In a broad fake-northern accent he added:

'I'm scared of nowt, me.' Then, in a more normal voice: 'Do you believe that?'

'I think I do,' I said, watching with some interest the moth on its flat, savage, wounded trajectory.

He gave me a look of contempt.

But that didn't stop him from flirting with me all winter. I don't know why. Perhaps he had sensed something changing as the eighties slipped inexorably into the nineties. If I remember being dissatisfied with what the decade had shown me, how much more might Choe feel it, who was always looking for something new? I pursued him, and he slipped away – although never too far – between the sets of a comically complex personality. He was always waiting for me to catch up, or catch my breath. 'You can't make me out, can you?' he boasted. He was like a conjuror or a tart, always revealing something hidden – a taste for expensive food or difficult books – always keeping something back. He was a member of the ICA, the British Film

Institute. He would telephone me late at night to recommend a photographic exhibition, invite me to some performance event in Princelet Street or sneer at the *Late Show* coverage of 'virtual' art. 'I'm not kidding,' he once insisted, arriving at the ENO dressed in an immaculate designer two-piece with baggy trousers and immense shoulder pads: 'I'm into Philip Glass, me.' And then announced:

'I've got the Kawa parked round the corner.'

'I'm sure you have, Choe.'

'You don't believe I came on it, do you?' And again, appealing to a foyer full of people who had arrived in 8-series BMWs:

'This fucker doesn't believe I came on me bike.'

To see how far he would go, I took him to a dance version of *Beauty and the Beast* at the Royal Opera House. He sat there quietly, entranced by the colour and movement, quite unconcerned by the awful costumes and Persil-white sentimentality, until the interval. Then he said loudly: 'It's like the fucking fish tank at the dentist's in here. Look at them!' He meant the audience, who, gorgeously dressed and vaguely smiling, had begun to come and go in the depopulated front stalls like moonlight gourami or neon tetras nosing among the silver bubbles of the oxygenator. Quiet, aimless, decorative, they had come, just like the dancers, to be seen.

'They're a bit more self-conscious than fish, Choe.'

'Are they?'

He stood up.

'Let's go and get some fucking beer. I'm bored with this.'

3 · PICTURES FROM CHINA

Isobel and I bought a tiny, one-bedroomed flat in Peckham. Though it was quite empty when we viewed it, it took three months to buy. We loved its two skylights, its proximity to the park. We were less certain about the plump, ear-shaped growths at the junctions of the bathroom walls. 'It must be the cheapest flat in London this summer,' our solicitor said uncertainly. 'Is it really that cheap?' He remained calm when the freeholder tried to charge us for the right of way over the pavement outside. We bought a copy of Muriel Spark's *The Ballad of Peckham Rye* to read while we waited for the land searches to come through.

'My God,' Isobel said, the day we moved in. 'Why have we done this?'

Round the kitchen, at the height of a young child or a biggish dog, ran a gluey black dado impregnated with hair. Above it three layers of wallpaper were peeling stiffly off the plaster. The gas cooker alone had taken all afternoon to clean. In its grill pan I found three-quarters of an inch of solid fat with a whole fish in it – a complete fossilized fish, with the silver skin and black, intelligent eyes of a fish in some old Russian story.

'We'll soon have it finished,' I said. I hugged her. 'This is nothing.'

But she was already staring away from me, down into the street, where a firm of contractors had been working since nine that morning to make an irregular hole about a foot deep, now filling rapidly with brown rainwater. A British Gas engineer bent over it as we watched. He began baling with a two-litre plastic container, while a lime-green JCB went busily back and forth behind him, bouncing on its suspension like a toy.

'They'll never put the gas back on,' said Isobel. 'I know that.'

*

I loved her sudden despairs because they were so rare and – unlike my own – so easy to divert. At that time I loved everything about her. She was a resource, densely stratified, embedded with objects whose significance I might never understand. 'Oh, I've had *that* for years,' she would say dismissively of a record, an old menu, a faded pink satin camisole. But as soon as she had left the house to go windowshopping at Compagnie Internationale Express, I would play the record; let the underwear run through my fingers like cold water; glance over the menu, trying to imagine how Isobel had looked as she ordered from it before I met her. 'Did you *really* like Marillion?' There would always be something new to find out. Isobel, delighted at first, soon became impatient.

'Why are you courting my mother so hard?' I remember her saying suspiciously, after we had been together for some months.

'Because she knew you before I did.'

'You don't even like one another much.'

'True.'

Margaret Avens was a broad, muscular woman of about sixty, who had retired, on the death of her husband, to a cottage conversion in Gloucestershire with extensive views of Cleeve Hill. This she shared with three noisy, affectionate Burmese cats. She took the *Daily Telegraph*, claimed to find Nigel Lawson sexually attractive, and brought home her weekly shopping from Cheltenham in an F-registered maroon Daimler.

'Everyone calls me Maggie,' she had encouraged me the afternoon we met. I could never bring myself to do that. But if we had nothing else in common we had Isobel, and I soon persuaded Margaret to lend me a shoebox of crumpled Instamatic snaps, the earliest of which – summer 1968 or 1969 – showed a curved beach, an ebbing tide, a small, naked, sturdy toddler, her features washed out by the light.

Isobel stared emptily at this version or abandoned prototype of herself.

'Give me that,' she said. 'I'm warning you.'

I moved it out of reach. 'Tell me what you were up to, then,' I bargained.

She thought for a moment.

'I'm going to kill my mother for this,' she said. She said: 'I was three before I would walk. They tried everything, but I just sat there and looked at them. I wasn't a "late walker"; I knew quite well what to do. I just didn't need it for anything.'

'What made you change your mind?'

'Give me the photo back now. You promised you would.'

'Tell me,' I said. I was intrigued.

'I had to be able to walk to steal toys from the beach.'

'What?'

'The beach was mine. I was there the whole year round: the other children were just visitors. If I liked what I saw, I took it. See that rubber swan? It's a swimming ring. I hit the girl to get it.'

She laughed.

'They went mad about that.'

Her first memories were of a café owned by her parents at Sennen Cove. 'We had an ice-cream cabinet, and about five tables inside. My father cleaned and set them every morning.' He had decorated the walls with local paintings of fishermen in yellow oilskins. 'They were as stiff as Woodentops. Do you remember the Woodentops, China?' What Isobel remembered best was looking out of the window at the grey Atlantic waves smashing against the base of Aire Point. 'There was always a man walking two dogs on the beach.' Whenever the wind changed, she said, or the air pressure fell, the window pane gave out a soft, distant booming sound. 'At the end of the day the clouds parted for a moment. They sent down great sheaves of light to the west over the water.' Caught suddenly in that light, so that they looked like seabirds in a water-colour, the young herring gulls picked about on the tideline until dark; or, bracing themselves against the sky, turned impassively out to sea and let the cold air slip by them. Most of her childhood had been spent like that. Beaches had seemed to stretch away from her forever. 'We always lived in Cornwall.'

'What did you like best about it?' I asked her.

'I hated it all.'

'Isobel! No one really hates anything at that age.'

'Don't you believe it.'

'I do believe it.'

She shrugged.

'More fool you,' she said. Then: 'At least the gulls could get away.'

Her father, already in late middle age, surprised perhaps to find himself a father at all, had moved his family steadily north along the Penwith coast, urged on by vague commercial dissatisfactions. 'He liked anything new,' Isobel recalled. 'He liked everything to be new.' The way she put this made me imagine the two of them, staring out of the café window in Sennen. While the young Isobel willed herself away – 'I didn't know where, just anywhere.' – her father willed the future towards him, bearing its extraordinary freight of possibility. It was a future not just of tourists, but of surfers, divers, sailboarders, hanggliders. All those fluorescent plastics to sell. Black lycra from America, violet neoprene from Australia, hotfoiled with names like Gul and Quicksilver. Open-topped Japanese offroaders, bouncing on their huge polished alloy wheels down the narrow lanes to the bay. Whole new ways of being by the sea. His own father had been a butcher in Cheshire, hidebound and smug. Determined to live differently, he stared out of the café window, and took a flying lesson every Wednesday afternoon at the St Just aerodrome, and Isobel was perhaps the last thing in his mind.

'So after that,' I said, 'you moved to Newquay.'

'After Sennen we moved to St Ives. *Then* eight years in Newquay.'

'Tell me something else.'

'When I was young I kept hamsters.'

34

'Something else.'

'I lost most of them behind furniture and up chimneys. I lost a rabbit.'

'How careless. Something else.'

'I read a lot.'

'Something else.'

'China!'

'Something else.'

'I believed that books had feelings. I was afraid to say I didn't like a book in case I hurt its feelings. Now that's enough.'

'One more thing.'

Isobel sighed.

'One more thing and you can give me the photographs back. Promise me, China.'

'I promise.'

'After we left Cornwall we moved to Wales. My parents bought a huge, run-down old guest house above the A5 in Gwynned. They built it up from nothing into a good business. I had a room in the roof, with a Velux window. Every night I would stick my head out and watch the mist creep down the valley towards Betwys. I felt magical and exalted. After about three years my father died. He was sixty-eight years old, I was eighteen. We sold the house the following autumn.'

She was silent for some time.

'Hello?' I said.

'There was an overgrown orchard on the sloping ground at the side of the house. The day we moved out, my mother decided to pick all the apples. When I asked her why, she said, "It's a shame to let them go to waste."'

For an hour or more the two women had scrambled about in the damp leaf mould and the growing darkness. Their faces alight and excited, they had shaken the upper branches of the trees with a long pole, pounced on windfalls, run backwards and forwards to the house for cardboard boxes. Leaves had floated down. Apples had thudded on the soft floor. Then quite suddenly the night had enveloped them, and they were puzzled to find themselves there, tired out, staring at the old house which hung emptily above them, one big window yellow with light. Eight years later, Isobel was still puzzled.

'We'd never bothered with the apples before,' she told me. She laughed. 'Two grown women as impulsive as children.' Then she said:

'It was a harvest.'

I had seen photographs of the house, pebbledashed and four-square on its damp Welsh hillside. I could imagine the road from England rumbling endlessly past in the bottom of the valley.

I said: 'I don't understand.'

'Neither of us would be going back there. Picking the apples was the last thing of that kind we could have together. My parents had worked hard for so many years, and my father was dead, and soon enough my mother would be too. It was the harvest of their whole lives together.'

She shook her head.

'That isn't it, either,' she said.

She said: 'It was panic. Have you got any idea what I mean?'

'No.'

'The whole thing was on and off like a tap. Don't you see? Twenty minutes later the boxes were packed in the boot of the car and we'd forgotten them. The next day we drove off and never saw the place again. She was a widow and I was going away to university: we picked the apples out of pure panic. Give me the photographs now, China.'

Isobel had a love of anything odd or old or cheap; anything that seemed exotic. This led her to furnish the Peckham flat with reclaimed pine bought under the railway arches at Camden Market, ancient velvet-covered sofas from Austin's on Rye Lane, lace curtains and kitchen chairs she had found one Friday afternoon in Camberwell. She liked chenille, in deep reds and purples, burnt orange. She was drawn to the colours of unfinished wicker, tarnished brass and Afghan carpets. She painted the front-room walls a pale terracotta and covered them the same afternoon with art posters, favouring anything warm, anything Klimt, anything Pre-Raphaelite. She bought little African tables, draped coloured shawls over them, scattered the shawls with jackdaw things, shells and pebbles, a dried starfish, ceramic roses, broken ear-rings, bits of leather and hessian, cheap brass bowls, Moroccan pottery, Chinese fans, painted plaster suns and moons, fake icons, and mirrors the size of postage stamps in heavy moulded frames. She uncovered the bedroom fireplace (which turned out to be Victorian), enamelled it gold and filled it with dried flowers. From the bedroom ceiling, by invisible nylon thread, she strung her collection of birds: strangely articulated wooden parrots in sombre colours from Indonesia, an ancient paper mobile of hummingbirds that looked like a shoal of small fish, owls and hawks and seagulls assembled from thin card, whose wings curled and curved in realistic shadows on the walls. Red and blue balsa-wood macaws perched on the windowsill. The eastern light fell through a peacock's tail of stained glass which scattered the headboard of the bed with oblique lozenges of cobalt, cadmium yellow and green.

It was like living with Kate Bush.

'Wouldn't you like a real bird?' I suggested.

'China, they *smell*.'

She lived in the moment. She woke to find you beside her and that was enough, whoever you had been before she met you. We were quite different in that respect. I was glad, because I hadn't kept much of anything to show her. 'At fifty,' I told her, 'you've left all your snapshots with your ex-wife.' Luckily, Choe Ashton was the only part of my past that made Isobel in the least curious. By then I'd known him for two years, perhaps a little longer. While I was always willing to talk about him, I didn't always know how to begin.

37

'When I first met him,' I would say tentatively, 'he was talking to a hand-drier.' Or: 'Choe's the sort of person who will set fire to himself if he gets bored.'

Isobel wasn't sure how to take this kind of thing.

'Is that supposed to be clever?'

'Well . . . funny, anyway.'

'Boys will be boys.'

'Look, do you want to hear about him or not?'

'I'm sorry, China.'

I thought for a moment. 'What can I tell you?' I asked, more of myself than Isobel. And then: 'I know. We once went to the Mumbles for a weekend, with a friend of Choe's called Stevie—'

'The *Mumbles*? You're making this up.'

'No I'm not. Listen . . .'

The universe, I remember reading, simply knitted itself together one day, out of numbers. One moment there was nothing. The next, this. What we have. All of it. Just numbers, knitting themselves together because their rules left them no option. A compact, elegant idea. If you want to know why it's wrong, go to the Mumbles for a weekend. The Mumbles, stamping ground of Dylan Thomas and other Welsh drunks, lines the western curve of Swansea Bay like hair in an armpit. Rain swings in over the grey arc of water, and through the rain you glimpse the cooling towers of Port Talbot across the bay. You note seven churches in half a mile. If the Mumbles was knitted out of anything, it was the strangled howls of Perry Como in a breakfastroom full of pensioners, something that calls itself 'SAS Coffee' and two Welsh salesmen talking in the Foreshore Café.

'Fresh mackerel,' one of them says. And: 'Get some fresh mackerel off it.'

Off what? You won't ever know.

Choe and I arrived late one Friday afternoon. Though the weather was good, endless motorway roadworks had given Choe a pinched, resentful look. The first thing he saw on the

Mumbles seafront was an old woman in a white mac, dragging her reluctant Cairn terrier along the pavement parallel to the slow-moving traffic. After a moment, she encouraged the dog to squat down and, staring straight at Choe, waited for it to extrude one small perfect chalk-white turd. Then she slipped a plastic bag over her hand to pick the turd up, wiped the dog's bottom with a bit of Kleenex, and tottered off.

'Christ!' said Choe.

He said: 'I wish we hadn't come here.'

'It was your idea, Choe.'

'Did you see that?' he said.

He said: 'She wiped the fucker's arse!'

He stopped my car so suddenly it stalled.

'This is the pub here,' he said.

'Bloody hell, Choe.'

It was whitewashed. It was half-timbered. Inside, it smelt of dust, mice and microwaved pie-filling. It was crowded. Choe bought two beers and sat down at a table already occupied by a woman of about thirty wearing a Mickey Mouse sweatshirt, black trousers with plaid turn-ups and black shoes on which had been appliquéd, just in front of the arch of the foot, a design of small red, green and yellow flowers. Pale lipstick gathered in the corners of her mouth, and a liquid redness at the rims of her eyes. In front of her on the table stood four empty glasses and one still half-full. All five had some kind of sediment crusted on to the rim. Choe stared at her for a moment, gave her a brief, empty grin and then said loudly to me:

'All over Europe women go into the sea with bare tits. Here they don't feel right without a swimsuit. And even then they have to pull a Snoopy T-shirt on over it before they can bring themselves to walk across the fucking beach.'

'Choe,' I warned him.

'Yet they'll shriek and run out into the fast traffic at the slightest excuse. You know? Especially at night when crossing an unlit road from one pub to another.'

He grinned at the woman.

She smiled uncertainly back.

'Had a nice time today?' he asked.

'Oh, lovely, thanks,' she said.

'Lev-ly,' mimicked Choe. 'Buy anything nice?'

'Choe,' I said.

'I bought some lovespoons,' the woman said. 'At the Love-spoon Shop.'

Choe stared me down.

'I reely lev levspoons,' he said.

'Would you like another drink?' the woman asked us. She got up unsteadily. 'I'm having margaritas,' she explained.

'No shit,' said Choe. 'Beck's.'

On the way to the bar she changed her mind suddenly and veered towards the Ladies.

Stevie turned up wearing patched 501s and a dirty white T-shirt. He was a slim, depressed-looking man, just out of his twenties, with big feet and bedraggled shoulder-length hair the brown side of blond. He had spent most of his life in Chorley or somewhere like that, and he had the indescribable snuffling Lancashire accent which goes with those places. He and Choe had done steeplejacking together up there, before Choe moved to Soho in search of other kinds of work. They had once been around a lot together. He came over to our table and began kicking morosely at the legs of Choe's chair. The little finger of his left hand was splinted and wrapped in a wad of bandage.

'This is Stevie,' Choe told me, not looking at him.

'Fuck off, Choe,' Stevie said, not looking at me.

He scratched his armpit and stared vaguely into the air above Choe's head. He said:

'I want the money first.'

Neither of them could think of anything to add to this, and after a pause Stevie wandered off to the bar.

'He's always like that,' Choe said. 'You don't want to pay any attention.' All week he had been promising me, 'You'll get on well with Stevie, though. You'll like him. He's a mad bastard.'

'You say that about all the girls.'

'Oh, Stevie should be in a strait-jacket.'

Stevie came back from the bar with a pint of Guinness. He sat down facing away from Choe and spoke only to me. If you said anything that impressed him, Stevie replied: 'That's through the other side.' What he meant by it I have no idea. He had been up the coast all that week, he said, at Pembroke Dock. He was working on one of the cracking-plants there.

'There's always a lot of that kind of work down here,' he said. 'Oil work. Chemical work.' He asked me, 'You getting plenty of work?'

I said I was.

'What kind of thing?'

'TV advertising,' I told him. 'That kind of thing.'

'What?' he said. 'You—'

'I write the adverts,' I said.

'Yeah? Through the other side.'

'I don't know about that.'

Choe said: 'For fuck's sake, Stevie.'

He took four or five notes out of his pocket and offered them across the table.

Stevie grinned suddenly.

'I've got some E back at the bed and breakfast.'

Choe laughed.

'It had better be *fucking* good stuff.'

I stared up at the clock above the bar. Not yet seven. I could see what sort of weekend we were in for. We would eat at the Quo Vadis, just along the front, a restaurant so uncertain of its own identity that it displayed next to its tariff board, as an idealization or dream of itself, two or three colour photographs of the Acropolis. Choe and Stevie, having dropped the E at Stevie's bed and breakfast – some warren with asbestos fire doors, locks that didn't work and heavy-duty plastic covers on the mattresses – would annoy the other diners by telling them how beautiful they were, and how much they ought to love one another. Full of the benign language of the drug, as energetic as toddlers out of a playpen, seeing the world as if for the first time in every broken seashell, they would run about on the beach all night, calling to one another, 'I love you Choe.' 'I love you too, Stevie. Have you ever honestly *looked* at your own hands?' and eventually be trapped by the tide at Caswell Bay.

But this time Choe had other ideas.

'Down the coast,' he said, 'there are some fucking fantastic limestone caves that *look just like cunts*. You think I'm joking, don't you? But they do. They look just like cunts a hundred feet high.' He said, 'We get in the van and drive over there in the dark – fucking brilliant empty lanes – and drop the E in a giant cunt.' He laughed delightedly. He said: 'Get it – ? Drop it in a giant cunt.' He said: 'That's the plan.' He said: '"Love is the plan. The plan is death."' Stevie began to laugh too. 'Fucking hell, Choe. Right through the other side.'

'I'm not sure I can be bothered with this,' I told them.

'Don't be a wanker, Mick,' Choe said.

'No, come on Mick,' said Stevie. 'Don't be a wanker.'

The woman in the Mickey Mouse sweatshirt came back from the toilet. She had been to the bar and was carrying a tray with two Beck's and a pint of Guinness on it.

'There,' she said.

'Ask her to say "pub",' Choe advised me.

'Go on,' he urged. 'What do you bet me it comes out "peb"?'

'That's right through the other side, Choe,' I said.

'Don't be a wanker, eh Mick?'

He laughed.

'Not all your life.'

It was late before we got away. By midnight the seafront was alive with psychotic middle-class teenagers from Swansea: two hundred would-be estate agents and aerobics teachers – the boys and girls of summer – all trying to manoeuvre their mid-range GTIs and white Suzuki four-tracks out of the car-parks at the same time, in a fog of alcohol, bad blood, missed gears and lead-free exhaust. Choe's brilliant empty lanes weren't much better. Chains of high-intensity fog lamps glittered across the black emptiness of the peninsula, as if to anchor Mumbles Head to Rhossili. It was one-way traffic, windsurf traffic, jet-ski traffic, Caravan Club traffic, coming in bad-tempered and wiped-out after a hard drive down the M5 from the suburbs of Manchester and Birmingham. Stevie's vehicle, an ex-post office delivery van bought at auction and with only one functioning brake light, bobbed and weaved among them, lurching on its fucked-up shock absorbers and smooth tyres, brushing the vegetation on the wrong side of the road every time he tried to pass. He was successful twice in every five attempts. Through the rear windows of the van I could see three silhouettes against the bald glare of oncoming headlights – Stevie hunched over the wheel, his elbows sawing up and down energetically like the wings of some badly planned bird; Choe turned in profile, mouth opening and closing; and the Mickey Mouse woman, staring rigidly ahead. I wondered what she was thinking.

Failing to take off, Stevie changed his mind and plunged into the narrow back roads around Penrice and Hangman's Cross, hoping to find a way through to the B4247. I kept up with him for about five minutes. Then he turned right so suddenly that ten inches of air appeared under his offside rear wheel and I couldn't brake fast enough to get round after him. I wasn't going to rack my Cosworth up just to stay with a drunk in a dented post office van. I let them go. By then it was half-past one at night, and I didn't have much idea where I was. Gusty onshore winds had brought the rank smell of the sea to the whole peninsula. The lanes were like dark tunnels. I drove up and down the coast road from Rhossili to Scurlage, to see if they had already parked the van somewhere. Nothing. I went back into the lanes and drove around slowly in case I met them coming the other way. Nothing.

'Fuck it,' I said.

I was lost. I was ready to give up. I came round a blind corner to a T-junction about a mile east of Llanrhidian, and there they were. Stevie had driven straight across the junction into a steep grassy bank planted with rhododendrons. In his anxiety to avoid the local telephone box he had knocked down a road sign. The impact had crushed the bonnet of the van and popped all its doors. It looked deformed but at the same time opened up, like a rare species of moth in the moonlight. Stevie, who looked nothing like a rare moth, had banged his face on the windscreen and was leaning against the back doors, sniffing and wiping his nose with the back of his hand. Whatever he did, blood continued to pour out. The woman in the Mickey Mouse sweatshirt was vomiting freely into a drain she had found by crawling carefully along the interface between the road and the bank. I got out of the Cosworth to look at her. There were some cuts around her mouth and neck. Between each spasm she shivered and whispered to herself, 'Oh dear. Oh dear me.' When she felt my hand on her upper arm, she said, 'I'm sorry,' as though she had failed me in some way.

'You're OK,' I said. 'You're OK.'

Choe eyed me from the front passenger seat of the van, where he was fiddling with the radio as if nothing had happened.

'I can't get this fucker to work,' he called.

'Don't be a wanker all your life, Choe,' I advised him.

I decided to telephone 999. Nothing. A brief warm squall of rain blew in from the south, buffeting the rhododendrons. I held the receiver tightly to my ear and stared at the stone wall behind the telephone box. In the yellow wash of light I could see several brown spiders, some of them quite large. Despite the rain they were running in and out of the crevices between the stones. They had orange marks on their legs. I decided to drive the Mickey Mouse woman to Swansea hospital.

44

Behind me, Stevie began laughing.

'Look.'

I put the handset down and watched him walk uncertainly round to the nearside door of the van, using the edge of the roof as a handrail. He urged Choe out into the road.

'Look,' he said. 'Fucking look at this.'

'What?' said Choe.

'The sign! The fucking road sign!'

The road sign said: 'De Gwyr.'

'More like de pits,' said Stevie.

Suddenly they were both almost helpless with laughter.

Stevie said: 'De fucking pits. Get it?'

4 · BURN WITHOUT OPENING

That was only the first of many attempts. Choe and Isobel had no common ground. There was no language that would describe them to each other. Despite that, they swam around in my head like bits of the same unfinished fish. Every time I told her some anecdote, Isobel asked in a bemused way: 'Why are you laughing – ? You're talking as if you think it's clever to act like that.' Then, getting out of her chair and walking away across the room: 'It just seems like bad behaviour to me. It just seems childish.'

'I suppose you had to be there.'

One day she said: 'I'm sorry, China.' She said: 'I just don't want to think you're the same kind of person.' She said: 'I know you're not.'

When I didn't answer, she said:

'Tell me some more.'

'About what?'

'Tell me about Rose Services.'

'There wouldn't be a Rose Services without Choe. It was his idea.'

She sat on the sofa, leant forward and put her arms round me. 'Don't be defensive,' she said. And, eyeing me closely: 'Sometimes I don't quite know what to make of you, China.' I pulled her legs across mine and began to stroke them.

'I love that,' she said.

She curled round me like a shell.

'When I met Choe he still had all the connections he'd built up as a motorcycle courier.'

'Yes, do that,' said Isobel. 'Oh.'

'He knew someone who wanted some waste moved. It wasn't difficult. None of that stuff is particularly bulky or heavy. I hired

46

the van. It didn't cost much. Choe drove it to some brand-new trading estate in Bermondsey, just off Rotherhithe New Road.'

'I love you to touch me.'

'We loaded the stuff and took it to a dump.'

There was a silence.

'I can hear you breathing,' I said. 'Inside.'

'That's how you started?'

'That's all there was to it.'

I didn't tell her where we had dumped the waste, or what it had turned out to be. I didn't tell her I'd been in two minds about the whole thing from the start.

'It was a cold night in November,' I said.

'Touch me like that again. Yes. That's . . . Yes.'

'Choe came without a coat.'

We got there early in the evening. Fog and dog shit lay in the hollows of the bleak strip of parkland south of Millwall football ground. We could hear a floodlit game in progress – meaningless roars, a loudspeaker playing current hits at half-time. We could smell hamburger, puddles full of leaves, industrial disinfectants leaking out on to the local roads from the legal tip under the railway arches off Bolina Road. Choe huddled between a stack of pallets and a Biffa waste tub, shivering patiently in his old cap-sleeved T-shirt and grey Italian army trousers. Under the halogen lamps, his upper arms looked varnished with the cold. He kept consulting his watch. Every so often a train would rattle past on the embankment above us, while we waited, on its way to London Bridge from the quiet, ordered life of East Sussex.

'For God's sake, Choe.'

'It won't be long.'

He was right. A dark blue diesel Transit pulled into the parking area and rolled to a stop about ten yards away. It was a site vehicle from some small construction firm – bald tyres, a mass of dents in every panel, rust breaking out round the inexpertly welded sills, engine rattling as unevenly as dice in a cup. Choe walked over and spoke quietly to its driver – their voices were thick, hesitant; there was a sudden laugh. Then he went round to the back. The doors creaked open.

'Good enough,' I heard him say to himself.

He jumped in and began moving things about.

'Come on Mick,' he called.

The load was packed in a dozen high-impact cardboard boxes, unmarked, ordinary-looking, a bit battered as if they had been used before: very light to carry. Someone had sealed them carefully with yellow biohazard tape. In five minutes we had moved everything across to our own van, stripped off the blue rubber gloves Choe insisted we wear and taken our money in cash. An hour later we were ploughing up the M1 like a barge on a freezing canal.

'I think I'll have game casserole with a spicy dumpling,' Choe told the barmaid, who had dressed for the evening in jeans and a promotional T-shirt for some old horror novel, Chinese red on black and yellow. When she spoke it sounded as if she was eating what she said, dipped in glutinous sauce from a Morecambe chippie. Choe rolled his eyes at her. 'Fucking hell! Savoury dumpling, eh?' He stared at the menu again. 'No. No I won't. I'll have steak, Guinness and Stilton vol-au-vents.'

He warned me: 'I'm paying.'

'With a smile like that,' the barmaid said, 'you can have it for free.'

We had ended up in the lounge bar of a 'country' pub tucked up among leafless oaks and little brown valleys under an arm of the Pennines south-east of Preston. The Boar's Head: maroon carpet, tan velvet seat covers, ceiling beams; the usual collection of fake firearms, horse brasses and cheap copper jugs. In addition, the walls were hung with landscapes, all by the same artist. He had painted something wrong and sentimental into the light – something unsuitable and at the same time lucid, as though the moors and fells, the little Lake District crags and tarns, were embedded in a clear, gel-like substance. Despite that, or perhaps because of it, you wanted to run away into them and hide.

Outside it was heavy rain, low cloud. While we were waiting for our food, three local men arrived, pink-faced with cold and shaking out the Barbour jackets they had worn over suits and ties to cross the car-park. You couldn't tell whether they were upper-class farmers from the Trough of Bowland or middle-class accountants fresh from the trough in Bolton. Between them they ushered in a frail-looking woman, perhaps seventy years old, wearing a red silk shirt tucked into her white wool skirt. She had thrown an expensive American raincoat loosely over her shoulders. Her face was heavily lined, especially round the mouth, where tiny vertical creases intersected her upper lip so that it looked like a badly stitched seam. Articulate and attentive, they settled her down at the bar. Did she want a stool? Or would she prefer to sit down by the fire? (Here they looked vaguely in our direction in case we might want to help, perhaps by giving up our seats.) They bought her a large G&T and a foil bag of dry-roasted peanuts.

'Oh,' she said. 'What a lovely idea.'

She pronounced it 'aydeah'.

When he heard that, Choe raised his head and said distinctly:

'Ay up! Fox and chips!'

'Actually I was trying to find you some cashew nuts,' apologized one of the men. The foil bag being just too clever, she smiled helplessly at him until he opened it for her. 'I know how fond you are of cashew nuts,' he reminded her.

'Still, it's a lovely idea.'

Aydeah.

'Fox and fucking chips!' repeated Choe, raising his voice in case they hadn't heard.

'Eat your vol-au-vents, Choe.'

He stared emptily past me.

'When I woke up this morning,' he said, 'I could 'ave sworn there were a maggot on me face. I were that depressed.'

He emptied his glass.

'Aren't they delicious, these nuts?' said the woman in the silk blouse.

Her voice carried. Choe's voice carried too.

'Fuck me, a maggot on me face, I thought I'd had it. But it were only a dream.'

'I've often thought they'd do well with cashews in these places.'

'Fact were, I just needed a piss.'

'Aren't they delicious?'

'*I just needed to piss.*'

In an attempt to divert him, I asked Choe:

'What's in the boxes?'

He had the grace to look amused. 'We don't want to know,' he said. He consulted his watch. 'Soon be time to drop them.' He pushed his chair back. He looked directly at the woman in the silk blouse and called over in his idea of a cut-glass Cambridge accent:

'Actually, I *am* off for a piss, this awfully moment.'

If it's glib to claim 'By the time you're fifty you've left all your snapshots behind with your ex-wife,' what should I have told Isobel? That when I was tired it still seemed inconceivable I could escape the frustration, the depression, the cloudy rage I had dragged around with me until I met her? That by simplifying my life to a place, a glance and a voice whispering, 'Fuck me, fuck me,' in the night, she had returned to me the optimism eroded by what seemed a long and ordinary life?

I don't know.

I could have explained: 'You took me away from someone else and I can't pretend I never loved her.' I could have told her: 'Some people marry young to hide.' I could have said: 'My whole generation had an obsession with authenticity we found it impossible to shake, and so we were always old but never grew up.'

I could have admitted:

'I let Choe Ashton persuade me to illegally dump fifteen cardboard boxes of low-level biological waste because it was a way of breaking with everything I had ever been.'

Would that have been any less glib?

In a cabinet in a corner of the Boar's Head lounge, someone had assembled a collection of real and yet meaningless bits of brass machinery – parts of old engines, beautifully turned valves and cylinders – whose origin and purpose was now completely lost. If I stared at it I became so puzzled I had to focus my attention somewhere else. I was tired out. When I closed my eyes I could still feel the M6 winding past me as if the van was stationary and the landscape moving, bridge after bridge, at seventy or eighty miles an hour. I could still see Choe's sharp, unreadable face next to me in the feeble dashboard illumination, and hear the roar and rattle of the Luton van. I tried to let the warmth of the Boar's Head seep into me. I tried, without turning round, to separate a single voice out of the babble at the bar—

'So that's the connection, then. Frederick North was her father.'

'Ah, the Shuttleworth connection. Yes.'

'Marianne North. She's the daughter of Frederick North. His second wife was a famous Shuttleworth. Her work—'

'Yes, please. Some more of that and another drink.'

'Her work ... all of it in Kew Gardens, and some of it ... the book explains ...'.

'Food, that is.'

'Oh yes?'

'... the book explains ...'

'My father inherited two tied cottages on the estate. He was so softhearted he could never put up the rent. Two families at three pounds a week, and we're paying that in rates. More than that. They must think my father is a complete idiot.'

'... never seen by the public!'

51

'Excuse me. Excuse me. Could I have one of those? What is that? Oh good, I'll have one of those.'

'Sometimes I wake up in the night, thinking of all that money.'

All that money. Choe had returned from the lavatory. He was shaking my arm. I stared up at him dry-mouthed, barely able to remember who he was, while he looked down into my face with an amused, almost tender expression.

'Ay up Mick, tha's bin asleep.'

'What's in the boxes, Choe?'

'You'll love this,' he said. 'There's a sign in the lavatory, "CONTINENTAL EXCITER CONDOMS – USE FOR FUN ONLY".'

'Choe, what's in the boxes?'

He shook his head.

'Rubber johnnies, I suppose. I didn't *buy* any.'

He said: 'It's time we got on.'

'Where are we going?'

'You drive. I'll tell you when to stop.'

Outside, he seemed to wince for a moment in the wind and rain. Then he hunched his shoulders; walked over to a bottle-green Daimler V12, the only other vehicle in the car-park; and, in one long, sensuous motion, dragged his keys down the side of it to leave a deep scratch curved like a wave. 'There,' he said simply, ignoring the *wah-wah-wah* of the Daimler's alarm – which sounded, as he put it, just as piss-pointless as the fuckers in the bar – 'They'll love that, won't they?' His eyes were quite blank.

'For God's sake, Choe.'

'Go left out of here. Left.'

After a mile or so, he made me take the narrow gated road of the local North-West Water catchment area. There, a bulky Victorian architecture of revetments, ramps and spillways petered out among broken vernacular walls, eroded gritstone earth, unsurfaced tracks: as if, anxious to warn his audience about the natural world and its encroachments, the architect had designed a steady, homiletic movement from order to chaos.

Soon we were bumping along two ruts, hardcored with brick and crushed tarmac, which wound up steeply beneath black rock outcrops. I couldn't see much. Rain flew into the headlamp beams like insects. Wind tore through the sedges and rocked the van on its suspension as it wallowed and strained against the gradient. 'Fucking hell,' complained Choe. 'I fucking hate the outside.' His face was pressed up against the windscreen. He seemed uncertain, nervy. 'Right! No, go right!' The rain stopped, leaving a few clouds to redistribute the moonlight, which had given them the colour of a fish's skin.

'Yes,' said Choe suddenly. 'Not bad for someone who's only been here twice.'

He made me stop the van. He got out. 'Wait,' he ordered. He slammed the door, then called: 'You can turn the engine off.'

To the left I could see as far as the faint, ghostly sweep of Morecambe Bay. To the right, beyond a stone wall in poor repair, the ground fell away steeply to open space and very distant street lights flickering on the eastern slope of the watershed – Blackburn, Burnley, perhaps Colne. All I could hear was the wind rumbling across some large obstacle; the ticking of the engine as it cooled. Choe was gone for some time. The rain started again, harder than before, rattling and booming on the back panels of the van. I turned up the collar of my leather coat and watched the big clouds rush across the moon. The moor smelt like cinders. The wall seemed to go on for miles in both directions, punctuated by empty gateways opening on to nothing but rough pasture and bog-cotton. Suddenly Choe was hammering on the offside window. When I opened it, he shouted:

'We'll not get the van near enough to tip the stuff over the top.'

I could hardly hear him. The rain had plastered his T-shirt to his bony chest. His cheeks looked as if they had been peeled for some cheap cosmetic enhancement. His nose was running, he

53

was shivering uncontrollably and his eyes were full of excitement.

'We'll have to carry it down.'

'What?'

'I said we'll have to carry it down.'

'I can't hear you.'

'Weather won't be so bad down there.'

He vanished. The back doors of the van burst open on a gust of freezing wind. He started to drag the boxes out.

'Come on Mick,' he said angrily. 'Don't fuck about.'

Then he was gone again.

I took a couple of boxes and scrambled awkwardly over the wall. Two feet the other side of it everything fell away without warning into a deep quarry choked with rhododendrons and young oak trees. It was a hundred and fifty foot drop into darkness. There was no wire, no sign. The edge was marked only by some crumbling red blocks of stone and two or three stunted birches. For a minute or two all I could do was teeter there in the wind, soaked to the skin, so close to falling I couldn't even speak. 'Choe!' I managed to call eventually. 'Choe, why don't we just throw them off the top?' But he had already started down, so I was forced to slither after him, clutching at the tangled rhododendron stems. Damp, friable brown soil soon caked my hands and feet. I dropped one of the boxes and had to feel about for it in the dark. Later, the whole episode would seem hallucinatory to me, a descent in more ways than one.

'Choe!'

At the bottom, worn aimless paths curved between heaps of spoil in the bluish, rain-dirty moonlight. Up under the steep sodden rock walls the earth was packed and hardened by years of use. Into it had been trodden a kind of light urban silt – layer after layer of smashed safety glass, broken battery cases, blue fertilizer bags, bedsprings rusted down to a powdery deposit, railway sleepers rotted and fibrous. Three or four burnt-out cars lay sprawled on their collapsed shock absorbers and rusty brake drums, as if they had maintained a perfectly straight and level stance during their fall from the ridge above, bounced once and come to rest. Burst laundry bags lay everywhere, children's clothes spilling out of them across the standing puddles and flooded ruts.

'Choe!'

I remember thinking, Who would want to do this? Who would want to do this? But the worst was still to come.

'Choe? Choe!'

A great frail wing of rock, like an eighty-foot razor blade, had caught itself years ago in the act of toppling from the main face and now, balanced precariously on a foundation of loose blocks, divided the quarry floor into two. When I walked cautiously round it, there was the real tip – one huge collapsing mound of plastic drums, bent strips of metal oxidized to white, cardboard boxes split and pulped by the rain, heavyweight plastic bags slashed open by the broken laboratory glassware inside, all resting in an expansive pool of water five or six feet deep and iridescent with escaped chemicals. There was a dead sheep in the shallows, bloated and grey. Around it floated literally hundreds of used latex gloves, their whitish transparent fingers ghostly as live squid in the dim light; swatches of asbestos waste like clumps of wool; detached biohazard labels the colour of willow leaves on a village pond. A thick, rotten smell came up, palpable as a touch, corrupt and chemical at one and the same time. But if I closed my eyes and listened to the rain, pattering straight down on half-submerged polyurethane and cardboard, it sounded as comforting and steady as rain on the roof of a garden shed.

'Choe?'

I couldn't see him.

'Choe?'

'What?' he said softly.

There he was – still as a lizard on a rock – impossible to separate from his setting until I had understood the shape and

55

size of it. He had got as close to the water as he could. His eyes were narrowed and one leg was tensed to bear his weight. The cardboard boxes rested negligently on his hip. I don't know if I can describe the way he looked to me at that moment. He looked as if he was watching something, some animal that might be frightened away if we spoke loudly. At the same time he had the musing expression of a professional sailor wondering how he would navigate some small, newly discovered sea.

'Choe?'

'What?'

And then, as if he had really said *Don't bother me now*:

'Be careful.'

Then he was turning towards me in swimmy slow motion from the edge, his mouth opening, his eyes widening in amazement and wild surmise.

'Choe?'

'Fucking hell, Mick! *Look* at it!'

He stopped, coughed, choked, clamped his hand over his mouth. With a violent, despairing overarm gesture he hurled the cardboard boxes into the water – they turned over and over in the air, yellow tape flickering – and stumbled towards me. He clutched wildly at my upper arms.

'Mick!'

I pushed him away.

'It wasn't like this before,' he said. 'It was nothing like this.'

I said: 'I'm not coming down here again.'

He grinned.

'Oh yes you are, Mick,' he said. 'Go on. You know you are. Eh?'

'I'm not.'

'You know you want to.'

'I don't.'

'I can't do it on my own,' he wheedled.

'Bollocks, Choe.'

I knew exactly what he was trying to do. But in the end I

would never be able to defend myself against him – Soho, 1989; ageing boy; French Connection jacket; sly, beautiful smile. 'Let's fuck off to Lisle Street and have a Chinese. Eh? Come on, you know you want to.' Somehow that would always pull me back, steady me down. Choe could always steady me down. He could always get on the right side of me. We made six trips between us, cutting a furrow in that soft, steep, unpleasant earth between the rhododendron roots: and an hour later we stood on the edge of the pool to toss the final box on to the great stinking tangled raft of stuff in the centre. We were filthy and exhausted. It was like standing on the shore of a completely unknown future.

'This water's *warm*,' Choe whispered wonderingly.

A faint, milky steam lay above it.

'Here we go,' I said.

'Wait,' he ordered. 'Look at this.'

Peeling a length of yellow biohazard tape off the box, he offered it to me. It was two inches wide and printed with bold black capitals.

'BURN WITHOUT OPENING.'

'Jesus, Choe.'

I hurled the box away from me as far as I could and blundered off across the quarry, straight up a short steep slope of half-stabilized spoil and into the stripped frame of a 1979 Vauxhall Chevette, which had once been pale blue. I hung on to it helplessly, panting and groaning and peeling off flakes of rusty paint like dry skin, repeating, 'Why would anyone want to do this? Why would anyone want to do this?' until I felt calmer. When I was able to look back, I saw Choe on his knees, his back curved like a foetus', throwing up into the pool.

'Choe!'

'*Fuck off back to the van. I'll catch you up.*'

I had the engine going by the time he reappeared. He stood swaying and retching into his hand as I turned the van round to face downhill. He opened the passenger door and then stood there gazing in at me like a drunk, unable to summon up enough strength to get into his seat. 'I'll need directions,' I said. And when he didn't answer: 'Choe, I'm just going to find the motorway, OK?' The van lurched forward, Choe's door swung open. He didn't say anything or do anything. He just sat looking tiredly ahead. He sat that way for thirty miles, then suddenly straightened up and looked around.

'Christ,' he said. 'Where's this?'

'It's the M6, no thanks to you. How do you feel?'

'Fucking desperate.'

'You should have stayed out of that water.'

'It wasn't the water.'

'What was it then?'

'Stop at the next services. I've got to drink something.'

'If it wasn't the water, Choe, what was it?'

He stared out of the side window.

'I had a look in one of them boxes.'

'Christ, you moron.'

It was raining again. From Chorley on south, both inner lanes had been jammed with vast ARC carriers hauling high-grade road materials from the great northern limestone quarries down to bypass projects in Sale or Oldham, daubed to their cab windows with white mud, shifting in and out of view in a groaning aerosol of water and red light. I moved into the outside lane to overtake; moved back. Lights flashed behind me out of chaos; flashed again.

Choe ducked his head and grinned suddenly.

'Aren't you going to ask me what was in it?'

'No, Choe, I'm not.'

He frowned at something: perhaps his own reflection in the windscreen.

'Well, I'll tell you anyway,' he said. 'It was full of dirty bandages. What do you think of that, Mick? Fucking dirty bandages.'

I looked sideways at him.

'We could have burnt them in your back garden and saved

the petrol money,' I said. Then it occurred to me to ask: 'You didn't touch anything, did you?'

With Choe around, it was always a wrong move to display anxiety.

'I fucking *licked* one,' he claimed.

I crossed all three lanes as quickly as I could, and pulled to a halt on the hard shoulder. Trucks rushed past, shaking the van on its suspension, spraying it with their sour emulsion of mud and oil and butyl rubber. I leant across Choe and opened the passenger door.

'If you as much as touched that crap,' I told him, 'you can fucking walk home.'

I was shaking.

Two weeks later I bought the Astravan from an advert in the north London edition of *Auto-Trader* magazine. When he saw it, Choe laughed.

'What's this?'

I was hurt.

'What does it look like?' I said.

'It looks like a shed.'

'It was cheap,' I explained. 'And I've got the offer of the engine from a newer model.'

'Take the brakes too,' was Choe's advice.

'Fuck off, Choe.'

He kicked one of the wheels.

'I'll see what I can do with it,' he said.

He uprated the suspension to handle serious loads, fitted big discs front and rear to stop them. He shook his head at the diesel engine I showed him and went off to find a two-litre petrol unit of his own. 'Fell out of an SRi,' he boasted. 'It'll go like shit off a shovel.' It did. Within a week we had used it to move our first live consignment, a thousand transgenic moths for release into a timber plantation in Argyll. Six months after that we were carrying anything we could lay our hands on, from cellular raw

59

materials to apparatus and computers (including a secondhand DNA sequencer, which we wrapped in an old mattress of Choe's in case it broke); from 'passive immunity' vaccines to artificial antibodies and speciality bloods designed in the US. We moved plant specimens shipped quietly in by air from the Third World so their seeds could be patented by self-financing university research departments in the Midlands. We had our foot in the door of the genetic supply industry. We were on our way.

5 · FOOD FOR THOUGHT

In the end Isobel never asked me why anyone would pay two thousand pounds to have some cardboard boxes taken to Lancashire. All she said was, 'It's a big boys' game to you two.'

I shrugged.

'I quite like it, really,' she said.

I knew I was giving her too simple a picture of Choe, but I couldn't seem to stop mythologizing him. He put an end to this himself, a week or two after I told her the Lancashire story. From then on, he was in charge of his own myth.

It was a cold November night, but he came on a motorcycle wearing one of his extraordinary Paul Smith suits, winding his way east from Chalk Farm, where he now lived with his girlfriend, into Mile End so he could take the Rotherhithe tunnel – where he tried to reach a hundred and twenty miles an hour along the deep interior straight with its 20 m.p.h. speed limit and Toytown carriageways – and into Peckham from the Jamaica Road. His right wrist was in a lightweight cast. 'This fucker got broken a couple of weeks ago,' he explained, as if the wrist itself were at fault. 'Throttle hand, too.'

We were standing in the sodium light on the pavement outside the house. 'You've just *got* to come out and see this bike,' he had told us when we answered the door. 'You'll kill yourself if you miss it.'

Isobel shivered.

'I've never broken anything,' she said.

She said: 'Did it hurt?'

'I felt nowt,' he reassured her.

He grinned.

'I won't tell you how I did it,' he said. 'But I'll tell you what I did after. Shall I?' And then: 'Shall I tell you?' as if he was really asking both 'Ought I to tell you?' And 'Do you want me to tell you?'

Isobel folded her arms under her breasts.

'I'm cold out here,' she said.

'Ask me this,' he said quickly. 'Did I get back on the bike and ride it to the nearest hospital?' He gave her a cocky grin and added parenthetically: 'I could have done, you know. Do you believe me?'

Isobel opened her mouth to speak.

'No,' he said. 'I did not.'

What he had done instead was to catch the bus to his local Sainsbury's. There, he had gone straight to the poultry produce aisle, extracted from its box a nice brown middle-sized *free-range* egg, and unobserved, dropped it on the floor. 'It broke,' he told us wide-eyed, as if this fact – the fragility of the egg, of eggs in general – surprised him even now. 'After that I thought I'd buy a few things.' He smiled reminiscently. 'So I got a basket and went round. The way you do.' He had picked up a nice cake, rum and butter; some Fetherlite condoms; and a packet of Ariel Ultra. ('I used to use Ecover but it costs more and it just doesn't fuck the environment up the same way.') Walking absent-mindedly down the poultry produce aisle again, he had slipped on the broken egg and fallen awkwardly into the shelves. 'I'm suing the fuckers,' he told us brightly. He held up his arm in its cast. 'Lucky it wasn't worse.' He shook his head. 'I was gob-smacked,' he said. 'They're supposed to take care of you in a place like that.'

He grinned at Isobel's expression.

'Fourteen hundred quid,' he said. 'That's what I'll get for a broken wrist. Brilliant. Eh? Don't you think?'

Isobel didn't know what to think.

'Anyway, come and look at this,' he said. He took her by the hand and pulled her across the pavement towards the motorcycle. It was that year's Honda CBR Fireblade, essentially a 900cc racing machine barely detuned for the road, with canted twin headlights the shape of a Japanese warrior's eyes, and the bright orange flames of some psychokinetic conflagration raging across its plastic skin. It was manga. It was *Akira*. It was ludicrous. Nobody knew that better than Choe. 'Isn't that fucking *over the top?*' he demanded.

Isobel, who could barely tell a motorcycle from a roller skate, made a disconcerted gesture with her whole body. She looked at me.

Help, said her eyes.

'I don't know what it is,' she said.

'You do,' Choe told her.

'I don't.'

'This,' he said, 'is the most phenomenal motorcycle ever made.'

He laughed up at her.

'*And now you're going to have a ride on it.*'

'China, no,' she appealed.

She tried to push Choe away from her.

'I'm not,' she said.

'You are.'

She started to laugh, stopped.

She said: 'No.'

She said: 'Can I have my hand back, please?'

Choe shrugged and let her go.

'I like it,' she said. 'But I won't go on it.' Suddenly she pointed to the Honda's exhaust. 'The back's hot,' she said. 'Is that bit supposed to be so hot?' She laughed. 'I don't even know what this is,' she said. 'It's a motorbike, isn't it?'

Choe stood back and appraised her performance. Then he looked over at me.

'I was right,' he said with satisfaction. 'Mick, she's a real—'

'Choe!' I warned him.

'Let's go in,' said Isobel, pulling herself away and running up the steps to the house.

'Let's eat.'

I had never seen her so confused.

'Fucking hell,' said Choe, towards the end of the meal. 'Marks and Sparks custard sauce.' He looked at Isobel, as if seeing her in a new light. 'My fucking favourite,' he said: '"Delicious hot or cold."'

'He's reciting that from memory,' I said.

'I don't doubt it,' Isobel said.

'From the *heart*,' Choe insisted. 'I'm reciting it from the heart.' He stared at Isobel. 'I'm not reading the fucking packet, you know.'

Despite herself, she had begun to smile.

'I know everything about custard,' he claimed: 'Me.'

She looked down at her plate.

'Eat it then, Choe,' she said carelessly.

She looked back up again.

'Eat the custard.'

Coming back from the kitchen with the coffee a few minutes later, we found him sprawled on the sofa. He had selected a CD remastering of some Champion Jack Dupree tracks from the 1940s, and was playing 'New Low Down Dog' quite loudly. The CD remote control dangled from his damaged right hand, while with his left he was holding to his eye – the way you would a lens – a bracelet of Isobel's. Celtic nouveau in cheap silver plate, the bracelet was thick and heavy, coppery at points of wear and a little weak at the clasp from over-use. Isobel had taken it off that morning and left it on the coffee table among half-read novels, scattered copies of *Scientific American* and *New Scientist*, and a slippery fan of catalogues from the genetic, medical and biological supply industry – glassware and electronics manufacturers, packing agencies, software firms.

'Here's your coffee, Choe,' Isobel said.

He didn't answer. He was reading – or pretending to read – through the bracelet. She put the mocha down on the table in front of him.

'Do you want this?' she said.

Choe looked up at her, the bracelet still to his eye.

'Through this ring I see the future.'

Isobel started to say something, but he had turned away and was staring up at the light fixture. 'The future,' he said in a resonant voice, 'is in Hanford-style sites. Trenches, cribs *in situ* vitrification.'

'Not in Britain,' I said.

We had had this argument before.

'What's Hanford?' asked Isobel.

'You don't want to know,' Choe said.

Isobel stared at him angrily.

'What's Hanford, China?'

'It's an open chemical toilet in Washington State,' I explained. 'Mainly radiotoxics. They lost control, overfilled the site, panicked. In the end the only way to stop it all draining into the Columbia River was to pump so much electricity into the ground everything turned to glass.'

Hanford Reserve: great feathery subsurface plumes of carbon tetrachloride, radioisotopes in solution, completely arbitrary combinations of wastes, even the organics like rubber and oil cooked into new substances. No records had been kept. Heat – radio heat, chemical heat – kept the cribs simmering. They cooked and cracked and leaked. Then everything turned to glass, like a fairy tale. The river was saved when everything turned to glass.

'They call it "uncertain chemistry",' I said. 'No one knows what's in there anymore.'

'China, how horrible.'

'China's real name is Mick,' said Choe, very quietly to himself.

He reached down slowly and, still staring into the light, tapped the front of the current *New Scientist*. ('Can We Grow

Younger?' asked its cover, across a picture of a nervous woman in a raincoat waiting for a train.) 'It will come,' he told me. 'It will be legalized and controlled, and people will make less money as a result.' He grinned to himself, as if that was all right with him; as if it was a challenge he badly needed. 'I see the future of anything,' he went on, 'but only when I look at it. Everything around it is a kind of rushing grey fog.' He turned away and hung over the arm of the sofa, making vomiting noises. 'It's nauseating, the unstructured future rushing past us like the wind.'

'Does he always behave like this?' asked Isobel.

I grinned.

'I've done something wrong, haven't I?' Choe appealed. 'The music's too loud, isn't it? Is that it? Oh God, I'm sorry, Mick.'

He spun Isobel's bracelet round his index finger until it became a silvery blur.

He shrugged.

He said to me: 'Maybe you're right.'

He listened for a moment to Champion Jack Dupree, then added:

'I can't understand why the educated classes make such a fucking fuss about Robert Johnson. You'd think he was the only fucker who ever played the blues.'

'He's the only fucker most of them have ever heard, Choe,' I said.

'Shall I leave you two boys to smoke your cigars?' Isobel asked.

She drank her coffee.

'Can I have my bracelet back?'

Choe looked at his watch and jumped to his feet.

'Fuck,' he said. 'I forgot.'

It was ten o'clock. He had to leave. He had promised to spend the evening with Christiana, his girlfriend. 'I'd better get back,' he said, standing up reluctantly. 'She's not feeling too well.' It wasn't so much he regretted leaving us, I thought, as that he regretted leaving any gathering, any occasion. 'Show me out,' he ordered. 'Or I'll never go.' At the door, he kissed Isobel, pressed the bracelet into her hand like a gift – closing her fingers round it gently with his own – and grinned fleetingly at me.

'Fucking hell mate,' he said.

Isobel snapped the bracelet closed on her wrist.

We stood in the hall together for a long time afterwards, listening to the Honda weave its way away through the night. Every time you thought it had gone out of earshot at last, you would hear its engine shriek up to the red line again – faint, distant, undeniable, eerie as an event on another planet – as Choe pulled out from under some dark railway arch in Bermondsey, wound it up tight, and went for the next roundabout with the front wheel off the ground and the fuel tank in his armpit at a hundred and ten miles an hour. Eventually, silence.

'Well, that was a bit tiring,' said Isobel.

'I thought he was on good form.'

'That's good form, is it?' she said. We were back upstairs, and she was walking vaguely round the dinner table, picking up the used dishes and putting them down again. 'What was all that business about the girlfriend?' she said. And then, before I could devise an answer: 'Do you think he really was supposed to be spending the evening with her?'

I thought it was very likely. I said:

'Who can tell?'

'For God's sake,' Isobel said suddenly. 'Come and help me here.' Then: 'What's she like?'

I heard myself sigh.

'She's the sort of woman who always thinks she's seen the waiter somewhere else.'

'China—'

'It's true.'

A girl on a bus, a boy at the zoo; they always remind Christiana Spede of someone you both used to know. 'Just have a look,' she urges you. 'It's X when she was younger.' You look but you can never see the resemblance. It hinges on some tiny factor around which all the others have realigned themselves in Christiana's mind – a turn of the head, a way of holding a knife, the first syllable of a laugh – seen or heard fifteen years ago.

'He's just a type,' you say of the waiter, and she looks brutally disappointed.

One of the first things I remember hearing her say was:

'I thought I saw a dead dog in the lavatory, but it was only an old coat.'

That was at the ICA, some time in the early eighties; some time, anyway, when we were both a bit younger – though Christiana was always a lot younger than me. She had intense blue eyes; a face like Claire Bloom, twenty years old, which she framed between a kind of orange post-punk haircut and a short black leather motorcycle jacket; and all the cultivated wrongness of that time. She shaved one eyebrow. She wrong-footed you with everything she said. Her body language was wrenched and odd. She was a performance which offended everyone she met until one day she smiled across some café table and they were seduced. She used the word 'transgressive' a lot.

She was never more than a friend of mine, though at that time I hardly liked anyone better.

I had walked down to the Mall from Piccadilly station one dark night in February to see an exhibition with her, knowing she would be late. It was one of those central London winter evenings with high winds, pissing-down rain, cold puddles. Commuters try to walk through you as if you aren't there, taxis will kill you on zebra crossings, the homeless are crushed up into the doorways to get their legs out the way. But on Regent Street, just before it met Pall Mall, among the Volvos and bottle-green Saabs like padded cells on wheels, someone had parked a little red Greenlight-modified M3: boxy lines, left-hand drive, yellow four-spoke alloy wheels and all, it was an amazing note of hope in a dull place. I stood near it for a moment, feeling a kind of psychic warmth come off the cold bonnet. I wanted to touch it but I was afraid of its alarm, and all too soon – a member for a day – I found myself in the ICA bar, grinning around like a feral dog at the hot pink décor and Rentokil condom machine or whatever it is they have there on the wall.

Christiana Spede wasn't in much better shape. She sat down next to me, wrenched at her red tartan micro-skirt until it covered the gusset of her tights and, after the comment about the lavatory, said:

'Every face I saw on Oxford Street I'd seen before.'

She offered me a drink from a bottle of Beck's, which I accepted.

'Cold out tonight,' she said.

She said: '*Institute of Cultural Anxiety*. I look round this place and I want to scream "Bollocks!" and walk out backwards, like a gunfighter in a film.'

She cocked her index finger and threatened some posters with it. I looked at her feet.

Steel-toecapped workboots.

I wasn't in advertising then; I wasn't in Soho. Neither of us had any money then. We could have made money, but not by doing the things we wanted to do. I learned about that, but Christiana never did. Some of those late seventies, early eighties people are easy with life. Others aren't. They manage to stay one step ahead of themselves on the high wire. They're always catching themselves just before they fall. It's a tiring performance. But I suppose it's better than the long drop.

'Tell me about it, Christiana,' I said. 'You could kick them to death,' I suggested.

Two years later we fell out over a Ken McMullen film, which, though it was interesting, just didn't make any really serious attempt to transgress gender boundaries, and I lost sight of her until she turned up with Choe at the other end of the decade.

During that time she had been a singer, a dyke, a dyke singer and a radical feminist dyke, before settling down as a wholesale wine salesperson travelling for Roederer champagne. By now her blue eyes seemed a little pale and watery. As she talked they would rest briefly and vaguely on other things: the cruet, a picture on the wall, the street outside whatever café you were in with her, sometimes on people coming and going in the room. It was unnerving to be the object of this attention, however briefly, because you felt you were drawing it away from its proper recipient. And it was always shocking to see her with Choe because although they were of an age he looked so much younger than her. Until she laughed – and she laughed less often than before – that peerless Claire Bloom face was lined and crumpled and sleepless-looking, wrinkled deeply at the corners of the eyes.

I couldn't decide why. Some private tension had worn her out. Or perhaps the decade itself had done for her, the way it did for so many: perhaps, I thought, she had simply never recovered from the attempt all her generation had made to politicize their inner lives, growing – without ever suspecting it – more and more exhausted by the attempt to resolve the appalling inconsistencies of their position in an age when even the Left had picked up Thatcherite rhetorics of self-reliance and economic necessity. I was close. If I had just said to myself that 'something inside' had aged Christiana, I would have been closer. But in the end I decided to believe that she had worn her face out by living in it, that the lines about her mouth and eyes were lifelines, the record of too much laughter and tears, eating, drinking, fucking.

About that I was completely wrong.

'I want to meet her,' Isobel said, and about a month after Choe had ridden his CBR out of Peckham and into the dark, she arranged for all four of us to have dinner. She chose the restaurant without asking anyone. It turned out to be at the wrong end of Frith Street, some staid survivor of the old Soho – brown walls, brown menus, dark brown food – a long way away from the new one. 'When in doubt,' I advised her, 'at least pick

L'Escargot.' Christiana and Choe arrived half an hour late. Choe was already drunk. Christiana was wearing a fur coat. 'I'm feeling better than I did a couple of hours ago,' she said, as if one of us had asked. She stared vaguely into the middle distance. 'I'm trying to remember when that was.'

'I thought you might choose us some wine,' Isobel suggested.

'Oh God, I'll drink any old muck.'

'She'll drink any old muck,' Choe said. He glanced uninterestedly at the menu. '"Sausage and mash with onion gravy." I've had that in hospital.'

'Shall I eat calamari?' Isobel asked herself.

Christiana shuddered.

'I don't like octopus. Well, they remind you of genitalia.' She thought for a moment. 'It's that great big bag of bits, isn't it?'

'She got that from Jean Genet,' Choe told us.

'Mind you,' he was forced to admit, 'she *has* seen them. On the fish counter at Tesco's.'

'Don't worry, love,' Christiana reassured Isobel. 'It's not me he hates, it's my alcoholism.'

Isobel picked up the wine list.

'Why don't we try this Mâcon Village?'

'Not at twenty quid a bottle.'

'Not at twenty quid a bottle,' mimicked Choe. 'Nothing good is good enough for her,' he informed me. 'Ever met people like that?'

'I just meant it was a bit expensive,' said Christiana.

She touched his hand and he moved it away.

'It's just a bit expensive for what it is, that's all.'

I could see it was a private game of theirs. He would pick a fight. When she tried to placate him, he would retreat into himself. The outcome would be much later and not in the restaurant at all. It wasn't a game for beginners: once or twice I caught him looking at her with real distaste, as if he was watching the behaviour of a stranger at some other table. In the end, Christiana seemed to give up. She started talking to Isobel instead. They drank house white. They put their heads together and laughed. I heard Christiana say, 'Mind you, what did that matter to me? I'd seen my first corpse at age fifteen, anyway.' And then a little later: 'I tried to be a beatnik when I was a kid but I got a rash from my pullover.' Choe curled his lip. He had won the game and lost his opponent. He sensed this.

'Let's go and have a piss,' he invited me, after the main course.

To get there, we had to pass the sweet trolley.

'Fucking hell,' said Choe. 'Look at that lot.'

In the loo he asked me suddenly: 'Have you ever wanted to piss on a wasp in the bath – ? I'm serious. I mean, seen a wasp settled on the bottom of the bath and wanted to piss on it there and then?'

He stared expectantly up at me over the partition between the urinals.

'I have,' he confided, when it became clear I wasn't going to say anything. 'More than once.'

After a moment he said mournfully:

'I don't think your tart likes me.'

I had spent all day feeling as if my eyes were focusing at different lengths. Every so often, things – especially print – swam in a way which suggested that for one eye the ideal distance was eighteen inches, while the other felt happier at twelve. Choe was the perfect object for this augmented kind of vision, swimming naturally in and out of view, one part of his personality clear and sharp, the rest vague and impressionistic. Any attempt to bring the whole of him into focus produced a constant sense of strain, as your brain fought to equalize the different focal lengths.

'Choe, her name's Isobel. She isn't my tart.'

'She fucking is, mate. Best I've seen.'

'Come on, Choe. Stop showing off.'

I got him to zip up and go back into the restaurant. On the way past the sweet trolley, he said, 'Want some strawberries with your tart?' When I didn't answer, he reached out and took a couple. 'Choe, you're an arsehole,' I said. He grinned. 'I won't be any more trouble, Mick,' he said. 'You'll let me stay, won't you?' At about half-past ten he looked around suddenly and said in a bright voice as if he was opening a conversation rather than interrupting one:

'So. Where are we, then?'

Isobel stared at him. After a moment, Christiana explained:

'We came in a cab. I don't think he looked out of the window once.'

'If I can find Oxford Street, I'll be all right,' Choe said. 'I can get home from there.'

'"We", darling,' Christiana reminded him. 'We can get home from there.'

She put her hand on his arm.

'Who's "we"?' said Choe, gently removing it.

Suddenly he said to her:

'Close your eyes and open your mouth.'

'Why?'

He winked at me.

'Just close them,' he said.

'I'm not very good at this sort of thing.'

'Go on,' he insisted.

While her eyes were closed, he produced one of the strawberries he had stolen on his way back from the lavatory.

'Open your mouth.'

'Is it something awful?'

'How will you know until you open your mouth?'

She tried, but her eyes popped open instead. Deftly, he hid the strawberry again.

'I can't do it,' she said.

Every time she lost her nerve, he hid the strawberry. She could close her eyes or open her mouth, but not both at the same time. A physical force seemed to drag her eyelids apart; a physical force closed her lips. Eventually she made herself do it. He popped the strawberry on to her tongue as deftly as he had

73

stolen it. Several expressions passed over her face: horror, puzzlement, then delight.

'You sod,' she said, when she had swallowed it. 'It tasted like rubber when it first went in.'

'You say that to all the boys.'

When we got home, Isobel said:

'He's just cruel, China.'

'Oh, come on, it was funny.'

'It was cruel.'

'Christiana loved it.'

'She loved the attention,' said Isobel.

'There's nothing wrong with that.'

'Yes, there is,' she insisted.

'Look,' she said: 'Even in low heels Christiana is an inch or two taller than him.'

'I can't say I noticed.'

'Exactly. He makes you feel . . .' A pause: 'I can't say it, I can't find a way to say it. It's sexual, I suppose; there's that extraordinary sexual attraction he has . . .' She laughed. 'No. That's not it, either. I don't know. He's demanding, but it's not you he wants. He's—'

'What?'

'He's constantly trying to make you feel awkward with yourself,' she tried to explain. 'The way you were at fifteen. If you're a woman, I mean.'

'It's very clever, what he does.'

And finally, with a helpless shrug: 'You want him to do it.'

'What?' I said. 'Do what?'

'For God's sake, China. Confuse you. Mystify the world, so he's your only safe place in it. You get on the back of the motorbike once: you have to trust him forever.'

She saw that I didn't understand.

'Forget it,' she said suddenly.

She looked round the bedroom.

74

'I love this house, China,' she said. 'Don't you love our house?'

By then, it seemed odd to be living in two or three rooms in Peckham.

'When you get tired of it, we can easily afford somewhere in west London,' I said.

Isobel shivered.

'I'll never get tired of it,' she said.

Certainly she never seemed to tire of the work it meant. 'Don't you hate fitted carpets?' she asked me the next morning. I wasn't really listening. It was still dark and I was still half asleep. I was late for a pick-up I had promised to make in Reading.

'I suppose I do,' I said.

That evening when I got home the whole house smelt of sawdust and varnish. She had hired a sander from Travis Perkins and stripped the floorboards to bare wood. She was delighted with herself.

'Take a photograph,' she said.

Isobel always wanted a photograph. I had photographed her in expensive restaurants and at other people's weddings. I had photographed her on the back of a camel during a two-week winter break in the Canaries; on mule-back in Yosemite National Park. At Refugio Beach, off Highway 101, I had photographed her sitting on the bonnet of a fat white rental Toyota; in Stratford, feeding a swan. We had albums of before and after shots of the Peckham flat, every step forward out of chaos, every room. 'Look. You won't believe the things they left behind,' Isobel would tell our friends. 'That's a postcard of Andrew and Fergie's wedding on the shelf. And look at the colour of the *radiator*.' Every time I bought a new suit or a new car, Isobel had to have a photograph. Isobel would photograph the dinner table if she thought she had made a special job of it.

'Go on,' she said.

And so I did; and in that shot, if you could find it, you would still be able to see her as I saw her then, standing in the middle of the living-room floor wearing industrial safety glasses, an

Ecuadorean cardigan over her best flowerprint frock and Doc Marten boots. Every crease and fold of her clothes was caked with fine sawdust. An Indian silk scarf was tied round her lower face to keep the worst of it out of her mouth. In her arms she cradled a Bosch Professional CPT.

'What do you think?' she demanded.

'I think you look like Arnold Swarzenegger. No, you look like Buddy Holly.'

'Thank you, China.'

I hugged her.

I said: 'Don't you ever get tired?'

'I love it,' she said. 'I love it all.'

She pushed her hair out of her eyes with the back of her hand.

'China, I want it to be *brilliant*.'

If Isobel's delight was invested in the flat, then mine was invested in Isobel. At the same time, in some way I find it hard to explain, Isobel *was* the flat. How can I put it? Like this:

Our back door opened on to a bitumen roof, about twelve feet square, sheltered from the wind by a low wall. Isobel called it 'the roof terrace'. One Saturday afternoon she painted the wall white and bought some terracotta pots into which she planted geraniums, morning-glory and miniature roses. 'Come here and look at your garden, China.' As early as the first weekend in March, I found, I could sit there and turn my face gratefully up to the sun, which cleared the upper storey of the house at one or two in the afternoon. The wall's shadow filled the rooftop like a pool, leaving a strip of sunlit about three feet wide which rapidly became too hot to sit in. My exposed skin tingled. I felt as if it was being gently stripped away, to reveal a fresher layer beneath.

'It probably is,' Isobel told me.

She had come to the door and was standing there in the well of shadows looking out at me with a smile possessive and ironic.

'What would you like to eat for lunch?'

By summer the heat was so strong that passing insects toppled out of the air paralysed; struggled for a moment on the soft bitumen of the roof where I lay reading Scott Fitzgerald; then blundered on.

Even in the winter, I used to stand out there in the rain and stare at the City of London in the distance and imagine the roof as the prow of a ship, pushing forward into time. The ship was my life, and the excitement of being on board it was so powerful as to be physically astonishing.

The last time anything strange or intense happened to me out there was one very hot August night. I got up for a piss at three o'clock, then staggered outside half asleep and half naked. Heat-lightning filled the sky. I stared up at it – pulse after pulse of weird silent green light reaching from the horizon to horizon – feeling drunk, elated, puzzled, lonely, all at once. I felt irradiated, but God knows what by. Something compelled me to dance about in my underpants, under the peculiar light, waving my arms in the warm air until I felt breathless and foolish. Then I went back to the bedroom and stared down at Isobel with an intensity of love I have never felt for anything since.

She, on the other hand, dreamed of some long, soaring, heartbreaking flight.

6 · NAGY SECZ

Business began to take up most of my time. Out of an instinctive caution, I dropped the word 'medical' from the company description and called myself simply Rose Services. I had someone design me a logo. We looked at several images, but the one which made most sense featured a rose and a reaching hand. Over the next eighteen months Rose Services became twenty quick vans, some low-cost, heavily fenced storage space off Ilderton Road in Bermondsey and a licence to carry the products of the nascent genetics industry to Eastern Europe. During that time I decided that, if I was to take advantage of the expanding markets there, I would need an office on the spot.

'Let's go to Budapest,' I suggested.

Isobel hugged my arm.

'Will there be ice on the Danube?' she said.

'There will.'

'Oh, China.'

When I put it to him, Choe liked the idea too.

'Fucking ace,' he said.

'Does that mean yes?'

'Ace to fucking base.'

'Bring Christiana,' I suggested.

'Do I have to?'

'Yes,' said Christiana. 'You bloody do.' She said: 'Thank you for inviting me, China.'

Choe looked at her, then out of the window at the passing traffic. We were in a café-bar called Gill Wing's just down from Highbury Corner, and Christiana had ordered us a bottle of Gamay de Touraine. 'I've never been to Budapest,' Choe said. 'That's in Hungary, isn't it? Is that in Hungary?' He turned away from the window, leant towards Christiana and ran his finger quickly down the back of her hand. 'Now tell me: Hungary. Is that left of Austria, or right?'

'Piss off, Choe.'

'I mean, as you look north?'

He tried the Gamay.

'Some days,' he concluded, 'you just can't get the taste of toothpaste out of your mouth from the word go.' Then he said to me: 'There's someone you ought to meet before we leave.'

'Arrange it then, Choe,' said Isobel.

Choe ignored her.

'His name's Ed,' he said.

'That's very informative,' Isobel said. She tipped back her chair so that her shoulders touched the wall. A long brown wool skirt from Comme des Garçons at Harvey Nichols fell into an attractive fold between her slightly parted legs. We had been at Gill Wing's for half an hour and it was the first time she had spoken. 'What does Ed do, do you think?' she asked me, as if Choe and Christiana weren't there: 'Insurance fraud?' She glanced down at her starter. 'We all look forward to meeting Ed,' she said, and then: '*Is* this fried Gruyère?'

Choe gazed levelly at me.

'Well, Mick, is it?'

'Choe,' said Christiana, 'are you going to drink that wine or am I?'

'Is it fried Gruyère, Mick? Don't be shy to tell us. Because to me, you know, it doesn't look like that at all. It looks just like—'

'Choe!' Christiana warned him.

'Drink that wine,' he mimicked.

He looked from Christiana to Isobel and back again. Then he grinned at me.

'Don't bloody whine,' he said. 'Eh, Mick?'

Ed, it turned out, was an American of Central European extraction. His surname was Cesniak: or so he said. 'Pronounce that with a "Ch".' During the late eighties he had made money out of the border between Poland and Belorussia and now he was looking for somewhere to invest it.

'Bring him to supper,' I suggested.

Choe seemed nervous.

'What can we lose?' I said.

I said: 'Set it up.'

At seven o'clock one cold night in January, an hour before they were due to arrive, Choe phoned to apologize: they would be late. 'OK,' I said. Fifteen minutes after that he rang again. Ed couldn't make it at all – the meet was off. 'Fair enough,' I said. Almost immediately it was back on again. But Ed only drank Valentines: could I go out and buy some? 'Of course,' I said – although I wasn't even sure I knew what Valentines was – and put on my coat. Predictably, this irritated Isobel.

'Couldn't you have taken him out somewhere?' she said, 'and all been boys together?'

When I got back from the off-licence in Camberwell it was eight o'clock. No one had arrived. Isbobel stared at me and then at the boeuf en croûte with chicken-liver pâté and fennel.

'How's it looking?'

'I might save it,' she said.

At nine a car pulled up outside. The phone rang. 'We're downstairs,' said Choe, when Isobel picked it up.

'He's calling from the *car*,' she told me in a voice of disbelief. She offered me the handset across the room. I shrugged and shook my head, no. 'Are you new to mobile phones?' she asked Choe loudly, and hung up. 'He's like a fucking seven-year-old.'

They were waiting for me when I got down, Choe grinning and turning over the junk mail on the hall table; the American swaying slightly, rubbing his hands together in the cold and wiping his feet compulsively on the thinning sisal doormat. Ed Cesniak was perhaps forty years old, an inch or so taller than Choe, and his front teeth had been comprehensively caried by amphetamine abuse. He was wearing a purple silk suit, five hundred dollar Rocket Buster cowboy boots in calf and kidskin, and a broad buff-coloured tie with port-wine skulls woven into it. A slender, mobile face, white from lack of sleep, made him look impermanent but determined. Ed would hang on, you sensed: he would endure. He would be there long after everyone else had left, or slept, or died. He had a Sony Sports Walkman in one hand – its headphones making a tinny noise like distant anger – and a cigarette in the other. He was shaking.

'Hi,' he said to me, putting two or three syllables into it. When he talked to you, he stared vaguely off over your left shoulder, as if he had seen something hallucinatory on the wall there. He gestured to his head. 'Robert Johnson,' he explained. '".38 Special". I have to hear it every day.'

'Well you do, don't you?' said Choe.

'Every day.'

'Ah,' I said, wondering what Isobel would make of that. 'Come up.'

In the end, she seemed rather charmed by him, perhaps because Ed was continually overcome by her cooking, groaning and murmuring in appreciation, then looking round to see if anyone had left anything he could finish. He switched the Walkman off but smoked Marlboros throughout the meal – holding them up close to his face, between the thumb and first two fingers, the remaining fingers loosely curled – and drank his Valentines in doubles, on the rocks. 'A while ago I thought I might be getting diabetes,' he confided, as he shovelled down the food.

'I'm surprised,' said Isobel.

'My grandpa developed it late. He was eighty.'

He looked uncertainly across the room.

'Is that a TV?' he asked. 'Do you all get CNN over here?'

'I think we only get the CIA,' said Choe.

Ed blinked.

'That's good, Choe,' he said.

He said: 'That's very good.'

81

We found him the Ceefax foreign news, an item of which immediately amused him; or seemed to.

RUSSIAN POLICE: SEVEN BODIES IN CAR.

Russian police found seven bodies in a Mercedes that was being towed through St Petersburg last night. All seven had been shot and wrapped in a tarpaulin. According to reports, the car towing the Mercedes was being driven by an unemployed man from Dushanbe in Tajikistan, who was armed with a pistol. The owner of the Mercedes, described as a company director, was later found dead at his home.

Ed grinned around.

'I heard this was on,' he told us with a chuckle. '"Company director." Isn't that fine?'

Isobel stared at him.

'I forgot,' he said. 'You guys didn't know Ive Kerensky, did you?'

Choe laughed.

'We'll never meet him now,' he said.

Ed stared at Choe, his smile fading. He took his cigarette out of his mouth.

'Some day you will,' he pointed out.

Choe looked away.

Isobel always worked hard to make her supper tables attractive. This one featured a centrepiece of stiff creamy-white lilies in a blue glass bowl which had originally belonged to her grandmother. From the start of the meal, Ed had been fascinated by the lilies, regarding them, as he became drunker and drunker, with expressions ranging from delight to puzzlement – as if he enjoyed seeing them there but couldn't work out what they were for. Now, suddenly, he reached out and with a movement almost too quick to follow, broke off one of the flowers and offered it to Choe.

'Hey, Choe,' he said: 'Want one of these?'

'No thanks, Ed,' said Choe. 'I've already had one.'

A complicated expression passed across Ed's features. Then he got up, switched off the TV and sat down on our Heal's sofa with the Valentines bottle and a fresh pack of cigarettes.

'So you guys move waste,' he said. 'Interesting trade.'

He stripped the cellophane off the Marlboros. 'Could you empty this ashtray, honey?' he called to Isobel. 'So where's the future for waste guys like you? Cribs? Trench dumping?'

'Not over here,' I said quickly.

I tried to explain: 'People won't accept that over here.'

'Well' – he pronounced it *warl* – 'no,' he said. 'Not right here in Great Britain. I was thinking of further east.'

He winked at Choe.

'I think the future lies further east for all of us, really,' said Choe.

'Here's your ashtray,' said Isobel. 'Do you want some ice cream?'

Ed saluted her.

'I was thinking of a long way further east,' he said, and lit another Marlboro from the stub of the last.

'Do you want some ice cream?'

Later he stopped shaking, but by then speech had become so difficult for him he had begun to lose his temper with it. He had finished a dish of Ben and Jerry's Chunky Monkey, stubbed out several Marlboros in the remains, then forgotten and tried to eat them with a spoon. Choe and I got him downstairs. It was two in the morning and, from Ed's ear-phones, Robert Johnson was still singing that he had a .32–20 and he guessed he'd burn in hell. Choe, who wasn't in much better condition than Ed, intended to drive him back to his hotel. 'I hope to God they get there,' I said.

'I hope to God they stay there,' Isobel said.

She came up and put her arms round my neck.

'Let's not do the washing-up,' she said.

She affected a corrupt drawl, wavering somewhere between

Kentucky and the Upper West Side: '"Could you empty this *ash-tray*, honey?"' She smiled. 'I really rather liked him.'

I smiled too, but I couldn't sleep.

'I'm not sure about Ed,' I admitted.

All evening his face – its powder whiteness, its curious dead-and-alive mobility, its air of being somehow both impish and ruined – had reminded me of someone. I couldn't think then who it was; although I was to remember quite soon.

Fourteen days later, Isobel and I descended into Hungary in a warm red light, the late sun blessing houses, woods and fields, the mist at the edge of the world. The approach was full of excitement; a great sudden swoop, then lots of manoeuvring. Servos whined, the control surfaces shifted, bronze light flickered suddenly along the wing. Banked hard over, the aircraft showed us long brown lanes, great tracts of birch and alder, roofs, smoke, a cemetery.

'I don't like it!' screamed a panicky toddler. 'I don't like it!'

'I love it,' whispered Isobel. 'I love it.'

She had never been out of Britain. Except in her dreams, she had never flown. She was as fascinated by the cramped seats and narrow aisle of the Tupolev as by the glimpse she got of its cockpit, finished a dull green and studded with obsolete little round dials; as delighted by the air-conditioning system and its bank of dirty plastic nipples as by the view out of her scratched and condensation-blurred plastic window. The interior design amazed her. She thought it was all part of flying. She craned her neck to stare at the other passengers – men with the soft brown eyes, dark moustaches and apologetic gazes of drunks, women whose heavy bodies and tired sensuous smiles would soon be shopping down by the Danube, wrapped in honey-coloured fur hats and coats.

'China, somebody has wallpapered the inside of this aeroplane.'

And then, in a fierce whisper:

'Are those *Hungarians*?'

'No,' I said.

I was enjoying it less than Isobel. Malev coffee had turned out to be instant, served with old-fashioned powdered milk which dissolved slowly and partially. I had flown before, in aircraft which did not have such obvious rivets.

I said: 'They're people who've just failed job interviews in Bolton.'

The toddler screamed. The Tupolev turned and swooped. Ferihegy airport rushed up to fill the windows. We filed down the boarding tunnel.

'Thank you and goodbye,' said the stewardess.

I had booked us into a hotel called the Palace, at the top end of Rakoczi Street on the Pest side of the river. That was a mistake. Like Budapest itself, the Palace had once been something: now it was a dump. Patches of render had fallen off its facade. Bare wires hung out of the light switches on the fourth-floor corridors. The wallpaper had charred in elegant spirals above the corners of each radiator. If the air was too hot, everything else – coffee, food, water from the cold tap – was lukewarm. But there we were at last, in the heart of Europe, where the hotel keys came attached not to a plastic tag but a strange hard black rubber ball, and clusters of opalescent lamps hung in the dining room like mystic grapes. There was a chambermaid, we discovered – a wispy, transparent old woman, who knocked very quietly at the door whenever we were in the room and made an incoherent attempt to speak German to us. And our room had french windows opening on to a balcony with wrought-iron railings, from which, bundled up against the freezing cold, Isobel could gaze at the other balconies, across a sort of high courtyard with one or two flakes of snow falling into it, each with its lovers, its yellow-lit window, its bottle of white wine left out to chill. That first evening, she loved it. She loved it all.

'China, isn't this romantic? Isn't it?'

'It is.'

'Well, put your arm round me then.'

'I wonder if Choe's here yet?'

'China!'

By the time we got downstairs it was late. Choe and Christiana had arrived, on a British Airways flight. We met them in the empty dining room, where the staff in their shabby striped waistcoats stood about quietly, adjusting a tablecloth or holding a knife up to the light. Next morning the same waiters would serve us eggs broken on to a layer of thin ham in the bottom of an oval glass dish, lukewarm and barely cooked. Christiana, asking for orange juice, would, after a twenty-minute wait, receive a glass of tepid orange squash. For now she stared around her, less startled by the frozen *Jugenstil* exuberance of the interior than by the way her cutlery had been presented, wrapped in half a carefully torn paper napkin. The first thing Choe said was:

'Mick, there's a fucking espresso machine over there with *three tits*.'

Then he said: 'Ed's in Szentendre.'

Isobel sighed.

'Look at this,' Christiana urged her. 'Have you ever seen anything like this?'

'He says he can't wait long,' Choe said.

'Good,' said Isobel.

Choe eyed her quietly for a moment.

He said: 'We should talk to him, Mick.'

Christiana put her hand on Choe's arm. She tried to show him the knife and fork. 'I can't believe this,' she said. 'Honestly, have you seen this?'

Without looking away from Isobel, he murmured:

'Will you just for now fucking shut up about the fucking cutlery?'

'Choe!'

Choe laughed.

'I mean, have a drink or something,' he said.

Budapest is a prime site for dreams: the East's exuberant vision of the West, the West's uneasy hallucination of the East. It is a dreamed-up city; a city almost completely faked; a city invented out of other cities, out of Paris by way of Vienna – the imitation, as Claudio Magris has it, of an imitation. Nineteen seventy-seven: representatives of fifteen countries gathered beside the Danube to ratify the Budapest Treaty, a dream of a document which, coming into force three years later, would govern the patenting of genetically engineered micro-organisms. Patentability means profit: commercial biotechnology dreamed its own dream here, and was brought forth in a welter of kitsch and whipped cream, one dream dropping – as slippery as a sac of amino acids – from another.

The dream I woke from on our first night at the Palace Hotel was one of rooms; opening out in front and closing behind. (They were layered and imbricated, like a handful of photographs. They were strange and familiar, large and small. I entered them and left them. They were rooms.) I had dreamed it once before, in Peckham, after Ed Cesniak came to supper. Now, as then, he featured largely: a curious, 1950s comic-book figure, icon of menace or fun according to which room he occupied, wearing a black and green chequered revolving bowtie. Tarot cards showered from the cuffs of his plum-coloured jacket. A point of bright light winked from the edge of his undependable, caried smile. Towards the end of the dream he bent over our bed. Isobel was enchanted. With a drowsy laugh she invited him, 'See if you can fuck me without waking me up.' And that certainly woke me, sweating and dry-mouthed beneath the peculiar fake-fur bedclothes they give you at the Palace. It was 3 a.m. The bathroom was even hotter than the bedroom. It smelt faintly of very old piss. When I turned the cold tap on to splash my face, nothing came out of it. I stood there swaying in the dark.

In Peckham the dream had left me unable to sleep. Instead I had gone into the kitchen and washed up the supper things, and then spent the rest of the night staring down at the cars parked along the street. At nine the next morning Choe Ashton phoned to ask:

'Well, what do you think of him?'

'I don't know what to think. He reminds me of the Joker. You know? Batman and the Joker?'

'Sometimes I wonder about you, Mick.'

In Budapest there was no washing-up to do, so I went back into the bedroom and touched Isobel's shoulder.

'Isobel?'

She was fast asleep. Her dreams, I assumed, were the same as always. We can't know other people's dreams. Her face was pressed into the pillow, her mouth a little open; she looked hot and irritated in her sleep, like a toddler with an infection. 'I don't like Ed,' I whispered, perhaps in the hope that she would hear me and sympathize. Lukewarm water gushed suddenly from the tap I had left turned on in the empty bathroom.

Next morning it was bright sunshine.

In Budapest in winter you can always find your way to the Danube. The temperature drops as you approach, the cold is like a force pushing you away; at the same time, the light seems to increase, the streets become livelier and more modern, the arcades fill with western goods. We left the hotel at nine and walked down Dohany Street past the 'Moorish-Byzantine' synagogue with its patterned brick and pale onion domes; then via St Stephen's and the Vaci utca pedestrian precinct to Belgrad Quay. As we went, Isobel raced out in front of us like an excited dog.

'China! The river!'

There it was, immense, placid, rafted with ice, full of reflections. Light lay on the pink-gold water, on the bridges and on the churches of the Buda shore, as shimmering, nacreous and delicate as a thirteenth-century blessing. The air itself seemed like light; substanceless, vibrant. For a minute we blinked across at the mirrored spires, unable to think of anything to say; then crossed by William and Adam Clark's bridge and made our way up on to Castle Hill. There the air seemed denser but still clear, the wintry trees and yellow walls of houses distinct and photogenic, the infamous *faux*-Romanesque battlements of Fisher Bastion a perfect Disney-white. (Reflected imperfectly in the windows of the Hilton Hotel, these arches and little mushroom-capped towers already seemed drunken, melting, pixillated as a *Snow White* dwarf, as if the whole thing were made of sugar and cream collapsing over a base of sponge: the architecture of torte.)

'Shit hot,' Choe said.

'All those bridges,' whispered Christiana. 'Look at them in the sun.' She had bought a new camera for the trip, quite an expensive Pentax with a motor-wind and zoom. 'I want you all in this one. Stand over there, Choe. No, *there*, you idiot.'

Before he left the Palace that morning, Choe had carefully pushed back the sleeves of his unstructured Paul Smith jacket. Underneath it he was wearing a black cotton T-shirt. The whole time we were in Budapest, I never saw him dress for the weather. Now he shivered, turned up his collar and whistled through his teeth. 'Shit hot,' he repeated, but I could see he was beginning to be bored. 'I'm just going to make a phone call.' Five minutes later he emerged grinning from the Hilton lobby.

'Tomorrow,' he told me. 'Lunch.'

'I suppose we ought to do some business,' I admitted. 'Now we're here.'

At this, snow began to fall, in flakes the size of five-forint pieces.

'China,' cried Isobel. 'See?'

She took my right hand in both of hers and tugged. 'Come here,' she said fiercely. 'This is the most wonderful river in

Europe, and now you are going to look at it.' She made me stand with her on the fan cobbles at the edge of the Bastion, where the snow eddied around us and down on to the bare trees and the broad elegant white stairs in the gardens below. Too close a look and you saw that the trees were full of plastic bags, the gardens trodden into bare frozen mud. Yet the tranquillity of the stone forced itself on this landscape of defeats; and on the other shore, Pest – a boom-town twice in one century – seemed to stretch away indefinitely into the east. 'China, I can see Dohany Street.' She hugged my arm. After a minute or two the snow thinned out, then stopped.

'Oh, damn. Oh, China, damn.'

Over the next three days Ed rang to cancel lunch at the Hilton, breakfast at the Hungaria coffee house and tea at the Gellert Hotel. Feeling more relief than agitation, I shopped for office space instead. Isobel came with me, and in the afternoons we toured the city. We photographed one another beneath the huge winged woman at the top of the Gellert Hill. We stared into hardware shop windows full of ordinary artefacts made bizarre by distance – tea-strainers, tins of shoe polish, Magyar brillo pads as outlandish as a political slogan. We translated the titles of the newsstand paperbacks.

'What does this mean, "*Nagy Secz*"?'

'You know very well what it means, Isobel.'

I looked at my watch.

I said: 'It's time to eat.'

'Oh no. Must we?'

Isobel hated Hungarian food.

'China,' she would complain, 'why has *everything* got *cream* on it?'

But she was enchanted by the street signs, 'TOTO LOTTO', 'TRAFIK' 'HIRLAP'. She loved the underground with its bookstalls, display cases and echoing, brightly lit expanses of tiled floor, slicked and patterned like lace with muddy water brought in on boots. The city's drunks delighted her, the way they swayed through the traffic like marine life, eyes focused on something inside themselves, a soft, childlike expression of interest on their faces. She was entranced by hats – 'China, don't you love the *hats!*' – honey-coloured fur hats, caps with earflaps, watch caps, ski caps, woollen caps with a bobble on a string, flat round leather caps with a peak, pork-pie or Tyrolean hats, chubby with fake fur. She loved the red and grey buses. She loved the children, racing down the broad grand steps of the Nemzeti Museum.

On Thursday morning she got out of bed and pulled up the blind.

'China,' she cried.

'What?'

'China.'

Half an inch of snow had fallen on the balcony. We stood there naked and looked out. Snow. Snow out of Russia, snow which had swung stealthily across Central Europe towards us in the night, to lodge as icing on the cake facades and ornate ledges, fill the bent elbows of plaster caryatids beside the grandiose doors of every hotel on Dohany, plug the holes in the bonnet of each abandoned Trabant, gather in the forks of trees and, at last, muffle the sound of the taxis, slowing them down for just an instant to the speed of traffic in a normal city.

'China. Snow.'

Now Isobel could embrace Budapest at last – take the whole of it deep inside her without further thought and let it advantage her there – a city, white, clean, redeemed, dreamy, finally picturesque.

7 · TRAFIK

In the Café Hungaria, where we had taken to breakfasting, we found Choe and Christiana. 'That waiter's actually rather nice,' Christiana was saying. She was already a bit drunk; or perhaps still drunk from the evening before. 'Well, he would be if they dressed him properly. He's got an unused look.' She kissed me hello and indicated her espresso. 'Why do you always get a glass of Andrews Liver Salts with this?'

'I've no idea, I'm afraid.'

'Oh, you're from *England*,' she said delightedly, as if we had never met before. 'For some reason I thought you were a local. It must be the haircut.'

I looked at Choe. He shrugged.

'Don't ask,' he said.

'It's snowing again,' Isobel announced. 'And I'm going to have two eggs.'

Although its Venetian chandeliers have long gone, the Hungaria, haunt of obsessive card-players and circus artists before the First World War, is still blowzy with arches, velvet curtains, little barley-sugar columns, mirrors and gilt ceilings, which every evening spray the light about above the heads of the diners in a kind of empty splendour. In the heyday of the Hungaria it was known as the 'New York', and the Danubian intelligentsia packed themselves in as tight as late arrivals on Ellis Island. They wrote polemic and edited journals. It was all laughter, politics and spilled ink. The playwright Ferenc Molnar threw the keys in the river, so that the waiters could never lock up.

Their caricatures remain, along with the marble floors and tabletops: but that morning the café was empty except for a few locals smelling of damp wool, clustered round a litter of espresso cups on a table near the door; and a tall middle-aged couple from Germany, who had come dressed as money. He wore fawn slacks and a cream cable-knit sweater. A black filofax the size of the Old Testament was placed squarely on the table in front of him. Her delicate bony frame supported a string of pearls and a blouse with high padded shoulders. A sleepy heat prevailed.

Isobel sat down next to Choe.

'Look, Choe: Germans. Tell us what they're saying.'

But before Choe could open his mouth, Christiana proposed: 'He's saying, "My friend, an Albanian, has recently taken up kendo, but finds it difficult to buy a sword."'

Choe gave her a withering glance.

'No he isn't,' he said.

'Then he's saying: "Our neighbour's hedge has been eaten by a cow."'

'He's not.'

Christiana's smile faded.

'What is he saying, then, Choe?'

'He's saying fuck off,' Choe told her. 'He's saying invent your own game.'

He winked cheerfully at Isobel and turned his attention back to the 'international' edition of the *Guardian*. '"Very cold air from Russia,"' he quoted. 'But that was yesterday. Hardly worth one hundred and fifty forints. What the fuck *is* a forint?'

Christiana had started to cry quietly.

'Choe, you're such a fucking bastard,' Isobel said.

He thought for a moment and then grinned.

'I such a fucking am,' he said. 'Aren't I?'

'I've been looking at the map,' I intervened. 'Why don't we go to the zoo this afternoon?' I gave Choe what I hoped was a warning look. 'After we've seen Ed,' I said. Choe didn't seem to be interested. He stared into the sediment at the bottom of his espresso cup.

'I can tell fortunes,' he revealed.

I said: 'You mean, "You will go to a place with many fissures . . .?"'

'"... And meet a man whose right ear is upside down." Yes.'

Christiana brightened up.

'I want to see,' she said.

'No.'

'Let me see.'

Between them they upset the cup.

'Look at that.' Choe pushed his seat back and stood up. 'The future's ruined, you stupid bitch,' he said.

'Choe!'

'You stupid drunken bitch.'

'For God's sake, Choe,' Isobel said.

He beamed at her suddenly.

'Only joking.'

He sat down again and stared away at the junction of Dohany and Lenin.

'There's no fucking future here anyway.'

By now, the dirt which always blows about Budapest – dirt from the Hungarian Plain, fall-out from the chemical plants up and down the Duna, domestic dust from courtyards – had turned the melting snow into a kind of fawn syrup, which was being pushed aimlessly about by teams of street sweepers with old-fashioned brooms, while pedestrians quickly churned to espresso anything that remained. Over the road a little knot of people, perhaps the staff, were trying to get into the Horizont cinema, which had the look of all empty cinemas at ten in the morning. It was showing *Cocoon*. After a bit they separated, shrugging, and went away in different directions. An old man slithered into view through the traffic on Lenin. He had a hat with fake-fur earflaps, and he was pushing a long two-wheeled handcart piled with flattened cardboard boxes, trotting patiently up into his load like a horse.

'Look at that,' Choe appealed. 'Handcarts are still big business here.' He laughed. 'I bet he got that hat at Asda. Don't you?' In an attempt to mollify her, he touched Christiana's arm. 'Don't you bet he got that hat at Asda?'

Christiana wiped her eyes and looked away from him.

If the cafés make you drowsy with comfort, the cold streets of Pest soon wake you up again. Choe and I left the Hungaria shortly before eleven and walked north-east along Dohany towards Varosliget. Choe kept his hands in his pockets and his coat collar turned up. Around us the city became progressively less international. The snow was thicker. Currency touting was less a way of life. Every block was hollow, the way people once imagined the earth to be, containing secrets – a garden, washing lines, sometimes a shabby arcade of shops, where you couldn't buy a Kodak film, a cream cake, or a single postcard of the Chain Bridge at night.

After about ten minutes we came to a courtyard off Damjanich, behind the China Museum. Access was by tiled archway, high and dark. The arch framed a well of grey light into which snow fell as slowly as the snow in a Tarkovsky film, every flake intensely visible, making the courtyard seem at once depthless and too deep, a lighted space the revelatory nature of which could only be experienced from outside.

'This is it,' Choe said.

Five floors of apartments surrounded the yard. At first they seemed abandoned. Dry render was flaking off the walls. The balconies, strung with winter-browned ivy and dead vines like rotten electrical cable, were falling to pieces. But after a moment a door slammed a long distance away and I heard children rushing about on what I thought was the second floor. Eventually a woman came out of her flat to the dustbins. A strong smell of vegetable peelings filled the courtyard. She looked down at us and called out cheerfully in Hungarian.

'What's she saying, Choe?'

Choe looked at me and shrugged.

'She's telling us to invent our own game.'

The stairs were cold, though the people who lived there had layered them with carpets – red, gold and black. Ed Cesniak was waiting for us on the fourth floor.

One room and a kitchen, that's how I remember it. Probably there were other rooms I didn't see. It was papered throughout in a water-streaked, pearlescent grey which had faded over twenty or thirty years from another colour. Most of the furniture had been pushed up against the walls, as if for some dull but desperately energetic dance, to reveal a black and white chequered floor-covering – less lino than a kind of compressed cardboard – buckled and worn into holes with sandy edges. The soft furnishings were burst or threadbare. From the kitchen issued a pervasive smell of wet gnocchi and paprika, steam from ancient boiled fish; beneath that the recent memory of a stopped-up toilet.

Ed's associates were lounging about in there like minicab drivers waiting for the pubs to close. To help pass the time they had set up three TVs, the largest of which, manufactured in East Germany, resembled a tank. They had it tuned to the local station, NAP – where someone who looked as if he used to run Butlins was interviewing someone who looked as if he used to run Bulgaria. The other two were Aiwas with flat screens, one downloading some sort of financial teletext from Tokyo via satellite link, while the other played a VTR tape loop – highlights from an old *Rem and Stimpy Show*, of which the cab drivers were clearly big fans. One of them grinned out at Choe as we came in. 'Play nice,' he warned, shaking his index finger.

Ed, who was sitting at a dining table in the main room, laughed loudly.

'Great guys,' he said. 'Great sense of fun.'

The table was covered in cigarette burns and overlapping ring-shaped stains. Veneers thin as a layer of varnish bubbled up at its edges to give a *mille-feuille* effect. In front of him on this corroded surface Ed had arranged a half-empty bottle of Absolut vodka, bought that morning on Vaci utca; a carton of two hundred Marlboros, as yet unwrapped; and his Sports Walkman, the batteries of which he was trying to replace. There was also a white ceramic bowl decorated with traditional designs like spidery drawings in dark blue ink. Ed would select a Duracell AA from the thirty or forty in the bowl: then, when it proved to be dud, throw it back in with the rest. The Sony headset was disconnected, but he was still wearing it. Every so often an exasperated expression would cross his features and he would work the earphones deeper into his ears, as if he wondered why he couldn't hear anything. His face was startlingly pale, filmed with moisture, the spots of high colour under the cheekbones exactly like those on the face of a ventriloquist's dummy.

'Could you get them to turn the noise down?' I asked him. I had to shout.

He shrugged. He could, though he seemed hurt to be asked. 'You should meet these guys,' he said. 'These guys used to steal cars with me.' He waved over at the men in the kitchen and they waved back. 'In the old days,' he said, 'we were moving a thousand units a week across the Polish border alone. We got them from all over – Mercs from Munich, Alfas from Amsterdam, BMWs from Birmingham.' He pronounced it *Birming Ham*. 'I once hid an 830 Csi under a ton of potatoes.' He chuckled. 'Adaptive gearbox and all. A ton of fucking potatoes!' He tried another battery. Nothing. 'Mind you, we never went much further than Minsk,' he said. 'Our part, we acquired the car, fitted it with papers and a driver, and took care of him maybe as far as the Beresina river.' He thought for a moment. 'Yeah. In some cases we would go that far. The Russians would take over from there. That was their part.' He lit another Marlboro, tried another battery. 'They were jealous about that,' he admitted. He blew smoke across the table. 'Still, everyone did business.'

'That's what counts, Ed,' Choe said.

'That's what counts, Choe,' Ed agreed pleasantly. 'I made money out of cars,' he told me. 'What I'm hoping to do now is move it over the hump.' He added: 'Crime to capitalism, tell me about it.'

'Hamlet Goes Business,' Choe said softly.

'Shut up, Choe,' I said.

Ed scooped a handful of batteries out of the Hungarian bowl and hurled them into the nearest corner, where they landed with a single compact thud, making a visible dent in the plaster.

'Fucking fuckers,' he said.

His associates chuckled amiably; you could see they had been waiting all morning for him to do something like that. On the TV, Rem and Stimpy began to break up. The story was that they had gone to another planet, lost their coherence and become no more than an ear, some wildly tapping fingers, a vapid ecstatic smile. 'Fucking fuckers,' Ed repeated, more quietly. He spread his hands out and examined them. He showed them to us. 'Still shakin' like a leaf,' he said. 'I want to move Russian know-how out. I want to move that other stuff in. The stuff we talked about.'

'Where's the profit?'

'Everywhere.'

Ed looked around him as if he was in a cartoon too, and I was in it with him, and the walls of the room were transparent. 'There's profit everywhere.' Then he laughed. 'OK. To you? Now? You corner the work from Brits who can't dump at home. You're cheaper than your competitors. More importantly, *you can handle stuff they can't.*'

He nodded vaguely eastwards.

'You can dump anything over there. Those people have been shitting in their own kitchen for sixty years.'

'What else?'

'You move product in the other direction,' he said. 'Secure containers, software.' He stubbed his cigarette out half-smoked on the table. 'That kind of thing.' Suddenly I noticed that his hands had stopped shaking. 'Nothing you don't already do.' He gave me a direct look and added: 'Except maybe live hosts.'

He said: 'Maybe the odd live host.'

'Animals?'

'Animals. People too. People need the work.'

I felt suddenly depressed and hopeless; I didn't know why. Perhaps it was the smell from the kitchen. The painted white chairs and torn lino looked like a set from *Stalker*. They looked like furniture from a bed and breakfast in Barnsley in 1948. I got up and went to the door.

'I won't do that,' I said.

'For Christ's sake, Mick,' said Choe. He seemed genuinely worried, and I was glad. He pushed back his chair, which made a shrieking sound loud enough to hear above the TVs in the other room. One of the men in there wandered over and leant against the kitchen doorway. Unlike the others – who wore longish black leather jackets belted at the waist, or acrylic pullovers with simple black and white designs – he had on a suit. He was short, five foot three or four, with curly hair, a dirty blond colour, surrounding his hard triangular little face. The suit was a kind of forest-green corduroy. Its jacket was cut too tight across his shoulders and too loose at the waist. Its crumpled trousers gathered above his shoes. The effect of this should have been laughable: instead it seemed deliberate, a costume chosen to be raw and to offend.

He studied me, then grinned. 'Hey, Steempy,' he said. 'What's it all about?' He made a ring with the thumb and index finger of his right hand and moved it up and down rapidly in front of him.

'Get this fucker off me,' I said to Ed.

'He's advising you not to be a wanker all your life,' Choe said.

'Fuck you, Choe.'

'It's a universal sign, Mick.'

'Get him out of my way,' I said.

Choe made a tired, rejecting gesture of his own, then turned his back on me.

'For Christ's sake, Ed,' he apologized.

Ed Cesniak shrugged.

'If he won't deal, Choe,' he said, 'he won't deal.' He looked at me. 'Maybe another time,' he said. He coughed. Then he selected two batteries from the bowl and slipped them deftly into the Sony. He plugged the headset in and switched on 'All the doctors in Wisconsin', Robert Johnson boasted tinnily out of the headset, 'sure couldn't help her none.' To leave we had to push out past the man in the suit. His bright blue eyes were full of broken veins, the taut skin over his cheekbones reddened and pitted. 'Steenky,' he said to me. 'Eh? Steeeenky.' He burst out laughing. He watched us go down the stairs and out into the snow.

Outside, Choe said:

'I'm just fucking puzzled, that's all, Mick. I'm just fucking puzzled as to why you aren't interested in making some fucking money.'

'Live hosts, Choe? Women with patents *in utero*?'

'Oh come on, Mick. You've done worse, only you just don't know it.'

I stopped and pushed him against the wall.

'I'd better not have, Choe,' I warned him. 'I'd better not have.' I felt very tired. 'He had a gun under his coat,' I said. 'I felt it there. The little bastard had a gun.'

In the parks, where it had been allowed to lie, the snow was two or three inches thick. The four of us walked across the north-eastern tip of the Town Park, Varosliget, from Heroes' Square. It was our last day in Budapest. Bored soldiers hung about on the steps of the Museum of Fine Arts in fatigue trousers and earflap hats. In the distance strings of children skated to music on the ornamental lake. Attracted by the hot-food kiosks, then the shabby frontage of the circus featuring a giant poster of performing bears, we zigzagged towards the zoo: to find that the weather had rendered it miraculous, a little piece of some endless, entangled imaginary Middle European wood. The city sounds were absorbed by the snow before they penetrated to these softened trees, padded hummocks and blurred little pathways. Few animals were about. Isobel found a pair of white owls staring interestedly from their hutch at the weather; but even they had ceded their ambition to the crows. The crows pecked about half-heartedly, sometimes working themselves up into a ludicrous, floundering run.

It got dark. From the zoo we took a taxi across town to have tea. By now the snow was falling thickly again, huge flakes slanting through the street lights and on to the expensive German cars parked in front of the Gellert Hotel. Visibility was down to four or five hundred yards. A tram crept past in the direction of Lagymanyos. The river had vanished. We sat in the steamy heat and bright light, the smells of the coffee house – marzipan, ground hazelnuts, hot milk – and drank mocha-and-chocolate.

'It's like Christmas,' said Christiana.

She sniffed at the sleeve of her coat, then wiped at it ineffectually for the fourth or fifth time with a handful of paper napkins. She had already tried washing it at the sink in the women's room.

'Oh dear,' she said. 'I still smell.'

The big cats of Budapest zoo are kept in an art nouveau building which conceals a line of old-fashioned cages each fifteen feet by ten. The air in there is dark with ammonia and pheromones and the great coughing grunts of the trapped cats. Edging down the narrow viewing aisle that afternoon, we had come upon the biggest leopard I have ever seen, working itself into an extraordinary temper – pacing to and fro, turning suddenly on its haunches, slamming into the bars. Quick as lightning (as Christiana put it), the animal had presented her with its arse; quick as lightning, she had shrieked and jumped back. Too late.

Now she said:

'Animals are always doing that to me. A sea lion soaked me when I was eight.'

I was impressed.

'You've been pissed on by a sea lion?'

'No. It jumped into the water near me, and I was soaked. Later a pelican ate my best doll.'

She dabbed at her sleeve again.

'I never forgave it for that.'

'Not many people can say they've been pissed on by a leopard,' I pointed out.

Isobel said: 'It's probably lucky.'

'It fucking isn't,' said Choe. 'Nobody with any brains gets pissed on.'

By five o'clock the pavement outside the Gellert was white, the road a dark, chocolaty brown, the central reservation fawn, the far pavement white again. 'Oh no,' said Isobel. 'Layer cake. I'm going home.' For some reason we decided to walk back to the Palace. It was the rush hour. Ladas and Dacias huddled together on the bridges, slow and hesitant in the growing dark and flying snow. Electricity flared from the tram wires overhead in showers of blue-green sparks. The Margaret Bridge was packed with commuters spilling out of Pest, hunched and huddled in fur hats and coats, clutching their briefcases, shuffling through the slush. Isobel led the way. She still tended to walk ahead of us wherever we went; but now her hands were deep in the pockets of her dark blue rever jacket, and her stride had become the determined trudge of a child who has taken on too much but won't admit it. Halfway across the Danube she dropped back until she could put her arm through mine. She looked up at me; I smiled down in surprise. 'Pull me along, China. I'm cold and I'm tired.' For a moment we walked together like that. Then she murmured:

'China, will you do me a favour?'

'You know I will.'

'Will you talk to Choe about Christiana?'

I looked back. Choe and Christiana were dawdling some yards

behind. I didn't know whether they had made it up yet, but they too were arm in arm. A foreign city will do that for you.

'Choe's not talking to me just now,' I said ruefully.

That evening Isobel and I ate alone at the Senora, a Korean restaurant which advertised, 'Grill yourself at the table without any smell'; then, planning to go to bed early, we went back to our room at the Palace. There we found that the chambermaid, tipped a few forints, had left us a new roll of lavatory paper – pink, but still with the texture of the stuff they give you to wipe your hands with at a motorway petrol pump – and a very small cake of scented soap (roses). Isobel was pleased.

'Oh good. Now I can have a wash.'

While we were undressing, I said: 'I've no idea what's got into Choe.'

'Oh, come on. It's so fucking obvious.'

'I'm sorry?'

'You're such a child. He's finally found someone he can be impressed by.' As if he was in the room with us, she congratulated him. 'Good choice, Choe: a fucking gangster.'

She looked at me in the mirror and smiled.

'The fact is, Choe's in love. Isn't that sweet?'

Budapest is rarely quiet, even late at night. The traffic, death oriented and wild like the ride of the Erl King, never stops. Ambulances and police cars warble musically past on their way to the carnage. Drunks scream suddenly or make noises like animals. From the start, these noises had worked themselves into our sleep: but all I dreamed of that night was the steward of the outgoing flight, Malev MAO116, with his sad eyes and soft black moustache. All night he pushed a trolley up and down the aeroplane aisle of my dreams, pronouncing the word 'dollars' as 'dollas' or even 'do las' . . .

'You like to buy something, please? Scarf for the lady? Tie for you? You like to buy something? It is very nice, this Chanel Number Five. You like to buy this tie?'

'WELCOME,' said the advert on the side of the trolley, 'TO THE CHEAPEST DUTY FREE IN CENTRAL EUROPE.' Discovering that the tie cost forty do las and realizing with terror that I was going to make him an offer, I woke up to find a little grey light leaking through the metal shutters of the room. The heat was like magma in the central-heating pipes. The radiators were vibrating against the wall. I worked my tongue against the roof of my mouth. I sat up, swung my legs out of the bed and went over to look through the shutters. Isobel groaned and pulled the blanket over her.

She said reasonably:

'It's a system fault.'

After a moment she said, 'Oh no. Oh no,' in such a quiet and sad voice that I went back to the bed and touched her gently.

'Isobel. Wake up.'

She began to whimper and throw herself about.

'The system's down,' she tried to explain to someone.

'Isobel. Isobel.'

'The system.'

'Isobel.'

She woke up and clutched at me. She pushed her face blindly into my chest. She trembled.

'China.'

It was midnight, February, perhaps two years after we had met. I didn't know it, but things were already going wrong for her. Her dreams had begun to waste her from the inside.

She said indistinctly: 'I want to go back home.'

'Isobel, it was only a dream.'

'I couldn't fly,' she said.

She stared up at me in astonishment.

'China, I couldn't *fly*.'

She was inconsolable. In the end I made her get up and dress.

'Come on,' I said. 'It's not so late.'

'China, why?'

'We're going to find you a bridge.'

On the way we drank bitter espresso in an Italian restaurant at the corner of Regi Posta and Apaczai Csere Janos. The waiters were sleepy, but amused. They offered us torte and whipped cream, and a bottle of Chianti in a raffia basket. Behind the till was a notice which said in English: 'NOBODY IS UGLY ... AFTER 2 A.M.' Isobel looked at the waiters and then pointedly at her watch. The waiters laughed. Outside in the street again, she hugged my arm. Her breath surrounded us, warm and comforting in the bitter night.

'Trust us to find the worst restaurant in Budapest,' she said.

'I don't think I've seen Chianti bottles in raffia baskets since nineteen sixty-three. And that was in Coventry.'

'I wasn't born in nineteen sixty-three.'

'I know you weren't.'

She pulled me towards the river, a vast black sweep outlined in light, draped in light, to the Erzebet Bridge.

'I love it, anyway,' she said. 'China, I just love being here.'

She said:

'Look. China, it's fucking huge. Isn't it fucking huge?'

I said: 'Look at the speed of it.'

We stood in the exact centre of the bridge, gazing north. Szentendre and Danube Bend were out there somewhere, locked in a Middle European night stretching all the way to Czechoslovakia. Ice floes like huge lily pads raced towards us in the dark. You could hear them turning and dipping under one another, piling up briefly round the huge piers, jostling across the whole vast breadth of the river as they rushed south. No river is ugly after 2 a.m. But the Danube doesn't care for anyone: without warning the medieval cold came up off the water and reached on to the bridge for us. It was as if we had seen something move. We stepped back, straight into the traffic which grinds all night across the bridge from Buda into Pest.

'China.'

'Be careful.'

You have to imagine this:

Two naive and happy middle-class people embracing on a bridge. Caught between the river and the road, they grin and shiver at one another, unable to distinguish between identity and geography, love and the need to keep warm.

'Look at the *speed* of it.'

'Oh China, the Danube.'

Suddenly she turned away.

She said: 'I'm cold now.'

She thought for a moment.

'I don't want to go on the aeroplane,' she said. 'They're not the real thing after all.'

I took her hands between mine.

'It will be OK when you get home,' I promised.

Everywhere in Budapest that night, mysterious and crude road repairs were being done. At one junction we found a shallow floodlit crater. A line of men holding strange, long-handled spades blinked benignly into the glare, while three engineers stared at the great mass of thin fibrous wires that had escaped from a broken telephone trunk line. Their hands were full of wire. Clearly they would never understand it. Just before dawn they would scratch their heads, stuff it all back into the conduit and go home, leaving the patient men with spades to fill in the hole.

One of the last things we saw, as the taxi conveyed us like parcels to the airport the next morning, was the graveyard of a little Serbian church, all its gravestones wrapped in sacking to insulate them against the frost, and its walls decorated low down with neat, careful reproductions of Western brand names – Adidas, Nike, Levi. They were less graffiti than cave-paintings, pictures of the prey. After that it was foggy leafless woods and lines of colour-washed houses – ochre, green, dark pink, pale blue – then motorways, diagrammatic beyond sense, slabs of cement raised on lines of tubular greyish-brown piers, all the way to Ferihegy.

The cab stopped suddenly.

'What is it?' I asked the cab driver.

He turned down the radio and said something in Hungarian.

'Can you make any sense of that, Choe?'

'I can't make any sense of anything mate. Not since yesterday morning.'

'Thanks a lot, Choe.'

'What's going on?' asked Isobel, who had been dozing on my shoulder.

As she spoke, someone opened the door nearest me and raw wet air filled the cab. A boy of about twenty extended his big pale hand in front of us. There was a machine gun slung over his shoulder on a black leather strap. The sleeve of his combat jacket had a damp, somehow reassuring smell, like the clothes displayed outside the Army and Navy store on Camberwell Road. An empty landscape opened up behind him: a few trees; a wire fence; some fields, flat and snowy; and in the middle ground, three or four other men in uniform going through the boot of the car in front of us. You couldn't see the airport. You couldn't see the city. For a moment, in a place like that, nothing has any personal identity. The snow comes down. Water vapour billows up to meet it from the car exhausts. You sit and wait in your good-quality clothes, feeling like people trying to step carefully from one window ledge to the next, three floors above an empty street.

'Choe, have you and Ed done something?'

'*Done* something?' he said. 'It's passports, Mick. It's a passport check.'

'Passport and tickets,' agreed the boy with the gun. His eyes searched mine, flickered with a brief interest, only to retreat immediately into an apathy not so much personal as national. He had a cursory glance at our Malev boarding vouchers, then with an abrupt laugh motioned us on.

Choe grinned out of the window. 'Done something,' he mouthed silently.

'Fuck off,' I said.

'Don't be a wanker all your life, Mick.'

They were still searching the car in front of us. As the taxi moved slowly forward and around it, I thought I saw a civilian, a short blond-haired man wearing only a badly tailored corduroy suit and slip-on shoes despite the weather, pulling suitcases out of its boot. The soldiers had dropped back to let him get on with his work. He was opening the suitcases and dumping people's things in the snow in front of them, making no effort to hide his pleasure in the act. I was sure that if he saw us we would be stopped again. He would have us out of the car and into the snow; push his raw triangular face up close to Isobel's as he searched her; then empty her jeans and clean underwear on to the road. Finally, opening his coat to give her a glimpse of the 9mm pistol in its thick brown leather holster underneath, he would mimic the last thing he had heard me say, in the courtyard off Damjanich Street;

'"The bastar'. The little bastar' have a gun."'

8 · WHAT COULD HAPPEN

'It will be all right when we get home,' I had promised Isobel on the Erzebet bridge. But London didn't seem to help. For weeks I woke in the night to find she was awake too, staring emptily up at the ceiling in the darkness. Unable to comprehend her despair, I would consult my watch and ask her, 'Do you want anything?' She would shake her head and advise patiently, 'Go to sleep now, love,' as if she was being kept awake by a bad period. In the day it was different. Suddenly, the flat she had so loved seemed small, unsuitable, full of naive objects. As her dream of flight failed her she began to do pointless, increasingly spoiled things to herself. She caught the tube to Camden Lock and had her hair cut into the shape of a pigeon's wing. She had her ankles tattooed with feathers. She starved herself, as if her own body were holding her down. She was going to revenge herself on it. She lost twenty pounds in a month. Out went everything she owned, to be replaced by size nine jeans; little black lycra skirts; expensively tailored jackets, which hung from their own ludicrous shoulder pads like washing.

'You don't look like you any more,' I said.

'Good. I always hated myself anyway.'

'I loved your bottom the way it was,' I said.

She laughed.

'You'll look haggard if you lose any more,' I said.

'Piss off, China. I won't be a cow just so you can fuck a fat bottom.'

I was hurt by that, so I said:

'You'll look old. Anyway, I didn't think we fucked. I thought we made love.' Something caused me to add, 'I'm losing you.' And then, even less reasonably: 'Or you're losing me.'

'China, don't be such a baby.'

We weren't always at one another's throats. I bought the house in Stepney at about that time. It was in a prettily renovated terrace with reproduction Victorian street lamps. There were wrought-iron security grids over every other front door, and someone had planted the extensive shared gardens at the back with ilex, ornamental rowan, even a fig. Isobel loved it. She decorated the rooms herself, then filled them with the sound of her favourite music: The Blue Aeroplanes, 'Your Own World'; Tom Petty, 'Learning to Fly'. For our bedroom she bought two big blanket chests and polished them to a deep buttery colour. 'Come and look, China. Aren't they beautiful?' Inside, they smelt of new wood. The whole house smelt of new wood for days after we moved in: beeswax, new wood, dried roses.

I said: 'I want it to be yours.'

It had to be in her name anyway, I admitted: for accounting purposes.

'But also in case anything happens.'

She laughed.

'China, what could happen?'

What happened was that Choe threw a tantrum.

Budapest had left him depressed and lethargic, a condition characterized in Choe by the short periods of ferocious, undirected enthusiasm which interrupted it. He went to the cinema every afternoon, but seemed confused when you asked him what he had seen. Later you found out he had been watching, over and over again, the opening twenty minutes of a film called *Stargate*. Such preoccupations caused him to lose interest in Rose Services. He was often late with deliveries; sometimes he failed to turn up at all. If he visited the office it was only to spend an hour reading out loud from the trade catalogues, an incongruous and over-produced literature that pitched its wares in the language of restriction enzyme and biocompatible liquid chromatograph:

'At last!' GenEx Plc International of Coventry were pleased to announce. 'We can offer Fractimaster, an attractively priced yet competitively specified low system for Gradient Elution Applications!' And they followed with the stark but chatty: 'Work Safe with Radiochemicals!'

'Listen to this, then, Mick.'

'Choe, I'm trying to work.'

'No, honestly, you'll kill yourself if you miss this one. Listen.'

'Choe.'

'But just listen to this.'

'What?'

'"Samples from the Dissolution Bath."'

'It's good,' I had to admit. 'But not as good as "Large volumes of mobile phase".'

There were no limits to biosupply, an industry so new and expansive it couldn't keep up with its own jargon, or indeed invent new jargons fast enough: there was no end to the money that could be made. We were taking on a lot of contract work the medium-sized companies like Abney no longer had time to handle. But there were bigger and more interesting fish floating around down there in the standing pool. It would have been useful to have help netting them. When he put himself out, Choe could be impressive. The biologists – overweight boys who, barely out of university, had already taken up golf and a once-a-week facial sauna – were charmed despite themselves by his stories of solo rock-climbing and fast motorcycles. He got them tickets for ENO, and they loved that too. But now, when I asked him to be at a meeting, he would only shrug and say vaguely, 'Nothing real is ever worthwhile.' And then: 'Nothing worthwhile is ever real.' Or he would arrive at the offices of HDC Biotech, D'Courtney Cabe or FUGA-OrthoGen and refuse to come in. We would have an argument in the lobby or a corridor, which he would terminate by shouting:

'Why should I take any notice of a bunch of fucking twenty-five-year-old wankers in *chinos*?'

'Because they're our bread and butter.'

'Off to fucking conferences in fucking Marks and Spencer shirts—'

'Choe, they can hear you.'

'Who gives a shit? You know what, China? You know what?'

'What?'

He lowered his voice.

'Every one of them is already infected.'

'What?'

'*E.Coli*, mate. Mutated *E.Coli*. Class five organism. Dormant now, but in ten years' time—'

'Oh, for God's sake, Choe.'

'Know what it'll do then, Choe? Eh? Go on: ask me. Ask me what it'll do in ten years' time.' And then, on an ascending triumphant note when I refused to join in: 'Melt the fucking fat off their bones. Melt it off like wax off a fucking scented candle.' He grinned. 'They'll *shit* it off, Mick. To the accompaniment – no, listen, *to the accompaniment, mate*, of sensations so pleasant as to amount to ecstasy.'

The business bored him. It was too successful. It was too ordinary. He wanted a share of Ed Cesniak's world. He wanted to be a gangster. He drew into himself and became elusive in a way no one – not me, and certainly not Christiana Spede, it turned out – could engage.

Two or three weeks after we came back, he sent me an expensive old edition of Turgenev's *Sketches from a Hunter's Notebook*, on the front endpapers of which he had written in his careful designer hand:

Turgenev records how women posted flowers – often pressed marguerites and immortelles – to the child-murderer Tropmann in the days before his execution. It was as if Tropmann were going to be 'sent on before'. Each small bouquet or floret was a confused memory of the pre-Christian plea 'Intercede for us', which accompanied the sacrifice of the king or his substitute. But more, it was a special plea: 'Intercede for me'. These notes, with their careful, complex folds, arrived from the suicide provinces – bare, empty coastal towns, agricultural plains, the suburbs of industrial cities. They had been loaded carefully into their envelopes by white hands whose patience was running out between their own fingers like water.

I phoned him up.

'Choe, what a weird quote. Where did you come across it?'

'I'm not stupid, you know,' he said, and put the phone down. He had written it himself. For two weeks he refused to speak to me, and in the end I won him round only by promising him I would go to the Tate and spend a whole afternoon with the Turners. He shivered his way down to the Embankment from Pimlico tube station to meet me. The sleeves of his jacket were pushed up to his elbows, to show off slim but powerful forearms tattooed with brilliantly coloured peacock feathers which fanned down the muscle to gently clasp his thin wrists.

'Like them? They're new.'

'Like what, Choe?'

He laughed. I was learning. Inside the gallery, the Turners deliquesced into light: *Procession of Boats With Distant Smoke*, circa 1845; *The Sun of Venice Going Down to Sea*, 1843. He stood reverentially in front of them for a moment or two. Then the tattooed arms flashed, and he dragged me over to *Pilate Washing His Hands*.

'This fucker though. It can't have been painted by the same man.'

He looked at me almost plaintively.

'Can it?'

Formless, decaying faces. Light somehow dripping itself apart to reveal its own opposite.

'It looks like an Ensor.'

'It looks like a fucking Emil Nolde. Let's go to the zoo.'

'What?'

He consulted his watch. 'There's still plenty of daylight left,' he said. 'Let's go to the zoo.' On the way out he pulled me over to John Singer Sargent's *Carnation, Lily, Lily, Rose*. 'Isn't that fucking brilliant?' And, as I turned my head up to the painting, 'No, not that, you fucking dickhead, the *title*. Isn't that the most brilliant title in the world? I always come here to read it.'

Regent's Park. A cold April. Trees like fan coral. Squirrel monkeys with fur a distinct shade of green, scatter and run for their houses, squeaking with one high-pitched voice. A strange, far-off, ululating call – lyrical but animalistic – goes out from the zoo as if something is signalling. Choe took me straight to its source: lar gibbons. 'My favourite fucking animal.' These sad, creamy-coloured little things, with their dark eyes and curved arthritic hands, live in a tall cage shaped like a sailing vessel. Inside, concrete blocks and hutches give the effect of deck and bridge fittings. The tallest of these is at the prow, where you can often see one gibbon on its own, crouched staring into the distance past the rhino house.

'Just look at them,' Choe said.

He showed me how they fold up when not in use, the curve of their hands and arms fitting exactly into the curve of their thigh. Knees under their chins, they sit hunched in the last bit of afternoon sun picking over a pile of lettuce leaves; or swing through the rigging of their vessel with a kind of absent-minded agility. They send out their call, aching and musical. It is raw speech, the speech of desires that can never be fulfilled, only suffered.

'Aren't they perfect?'

We watched them companionably for a few minutes.

'See the way they move?' Choe said suddenly. Then: 'When someone loves you, you feel this whole marvellous confidence in yourself. In your body, I mean.'

I said nothing. I couldn't think how the two ideas were linked. He had turned his back on the cage and was staring angrily away into the park where, in the distance, some children were running and shouting happily. He was inviting me to laugh at him. When I didn't, he relaxed.

'You feel good in it,' he said. 'For once it isn't just some bag of shit that carries you around. I—'

'Is that why you're trying to kill yourself?'

He stared at me.

'For fuck's sake,' he said wearily.

Behind us the lar gibbons steered their long strange ship into the wind with an enormous effort of will. A small plaque mounted on the wire netting of the cage explained: 'The very loud call is used to tell other gibbons the limit of its territory, especially in the mornings.'

I thought that was a pity.

'This is a bit different from the last zoo we were in,' I said; but Choe didn't answer.

'China, what could happen?'

What happened was that a couple of months later, in early June, I had a phone call from Christiana.

'Is Choe with you?' she said hesitantly.

She hadn't seen him for a week.

'Neither have I,' I said. 'I shouldn't worry, Christiana.'

'You're as bad as he is.'

She rang off.

The next day she came into my Bermondsey office with Isobel. Outside in Ilderton Road they had a black cab with its meter still running, and they were struggling with two or three large pieces of Louis Vuitton luggage. Christiana kept her head turned away and wouldn't look at me. She was crying openly, sniffing and wiping her nose with the back of her hand. She had smeared lipstick across her cheeks, and her eye make-up had run down to join it. She looked tired and defeated. But Isobel was furious enough for both of them.

'What's going on?' I said.

Isobel gazed at me as if she wasn't sure what species I belonged to.

'Your friend walked out on her,' she said. 'I don't suppose you know where he is?' It was less a query than a sneer; and she wouldn't say anything more until she had got Christiana back into the cab, which pulled away north towards Rotherhithe and the tunnel. Isobel watched it go, then came and sat down wearily on the end of my desk. 'Sometimes I wish I smoked,' she said. When I tried to hug her, she moved away. She indicated the luggage.

'Christiana wanted to do this by herself. I told her his stuff was too heavy.'

'What's happened?'

At first she wouldn't answer. Then she said:

'I never liked that little bugger.'

'I know, Isobel—'

'When you do see him, give him these' – she kicked one of the suitcases – 'and ask him what he said to her to finish it.'

'Isobel—'

'Just ask him.'

I shrugged. I knew she would tell me when she calmed down.

'Whatever you think,' I said, 'I honestly don't know anything about this.'

'You'd better not, China.'

It was a few days before Choe phoned me.

'Ay up, Mick.'

'That's not going to get you anywhere, Choe.'

'I know, Mick. I know it isn't.'

There was a pause. Then he laughed.

'I suppose I just can't stop doing it,' he said, as if he was talking about someone else – someone whose Martian levels of dissociation and unreliability impressed even him.

'I suppose she hates me,' he said: 'Christiana.'

'For God's sake, Choe.'

He said: 'I could do with a beer.'

We met that afternoon. It was London summer: dogs barking; air baked yet humid; the continual unresolved murmur of conversations in the street. We sat on the Victoria Embankment, on a bench in the shade of a plane tree, and, surrounded by the continual groan and thud of the traffic, had a look across the river. The tide was down as far as the first pier of Waterloo Bridge, beneath which roiled water the colour of milk chocolate. Seagulls busied themselves on the shingle, planing out of the Embankment shadow and into the sunlight, then back again. The receding water had sorted the stones into neat lines and strands. Pleasure boats patrolled up and down, stubby and peeling. That afternoon the whole of the Strand – street after street spread out in the strong sunlight – had smelt of roasting coffee.

'Did you have to tell her she was old?' I asked him.

Instead of answering directly, he said:

'For weeks I thought I could hear a dog howling two or three houses down the street. But when I went out there was nothing there. No noise, no dog. Then, as soon as I was back inside again . . .'

He looked suddenly restless, got up, said, 'Let's have a look at Cleopatra's Needle,' and as we walked went on: 'It was a delusion, Mick. There was no dog. Have you ever had anything like that?'

I didn't know how to answer.

He stopped and stood in front of me so that I had to stop too.

'I'm really serious, Mick. Some buried part of me had cracked. It was giving out this signal.' He began to laugh. 'Mick, that howl was a sign of *deep inner mourning*.'

'Oh, grow up, Choe.'

'I got you, though, didn't I? You believed me.'

'Just grow up.'

When we arrived at the Needle it was surrounded by tourists: Germans amused by the Victorian lamp standards with their bizarre design of intertwined fish; Japanese photographing barges in midstream – THAMES & GENERAL LIGHTERAGE COMPANY. A woman on her own stared at us, then thoughtfully down the waterstair.

'We never fucked, anyway,' said Choe. 'Christiana and me.'

Then he said:

'It was making *me* feel old.'

A light breeze brought us the smell of the Thames mud, causing the tourists to laugh uneasily and move away.

'You're a bastard, Choe.'

'I know, I know.'

He grinned.

'It's better than being a wanker though. Don't you find that?'

'China, what could happen?'

What happened was that I asked Isobel to make a delivery for me. The way it happened was this: Choe had been filling in. Without him, I had to reshuffle to cover my national commitments. As a result I was temporarily down on local help.

I told Isobel: 'It's not far. Just across to Hammersmith. Some clinic.'

I passed her the details.

'A Dr Alexander. You could make it in an hour, there and back.'

She stared at me.

'*You* could make it in an hour,' she said.

She read the job sheet.

'What do they do there?' she asked.

I said irritably: 'How would I know? Cosmetic medicine. Fantasy factory stuff. Does it matter?'

She put her arms round me.

'China, I was only trying to be interested.'

'Never ask them what they use the stuff for,' I warned her. 'Will you do it?'

She said: 'If you kiss me properly.'

'How was it?' I asked, when she got back.

She laughed.

'At first they thought I was a client.'

Running upstairs to change, she called down:

'I quite like West London.'

'China, what could happen?'

What happened was that, in the end, nothing helped.

When I think about that time now, I see us like this:

We are in the nice new kitchen area in Stepney, with its Whirlpool hob and pale oak floor. We are pursuing a dull argument about ourselves, or about Choe Ashton. Isobel, who has a summer cold, is trying to ease her sinuses according to some prescription of Margaret Avens' involving an infra-red lamp which she has arranged on the stainless-steel work-top. The lamp surrounds her head with a violent corona, throws pale green shadows on the white walls. She leans forward and stares intently into it with closed eyes. Sitting the other side of the beechwood table on a rattan chair from Heal's, I hold the *Daily Telegraph* up to the side of my face to keep from being dazzled.

I see this as a photograph, oblique and odd, without any aids to interpretation. Who are these two people, in their little open-plan house which runs the kitchen seamlessly into a quasi-minimalist living room relieved by one or two framed Leendert Blok autochromes of tulips? How do they relate to one another? The photographer is not telling us. We see the books on the shelves, the litter on the table, the infra-red reflected like a tiny star from the flat black screen of the television. A telephone with answer-, fax- and call-splitting facilities. On a side table, two pieces of chalk like lumps of eroded bone. These things are not in any sense aids to navigation. We are left with a feeling that everything in the room is alienated from everything else. A photograph you might put down with a shiver, a film from which you might walk out because it is too modern to understand.

In late June or early July we had a short holiday in Tenerife. Neither of us wanted it. 'I suppose I can just lie on the beach for a week,' Isobel said. In the event she rarely got that far, but sprawled face-down on a recliner on the tiled surround of the San Marino Apartments pool, while I drove a rental SEAT to Las Cañadas and the El Teide parador; or toiled upwards in the heat under the blistered walls of the Barranco del Infierno. Caught in the slanting light of early morning, the distant pantile roofs and campaniles of the partly finished Los Cristianos hotels and bars took on a translucent quality, as if they were made of porcelain. But in the afternoons the sunlight was like a fierce violet transparency laid across the burnt beachfronts, rubbish, stray cats and dogs, old people who stared into space, the English girl in the wheelchair pushed by the fat boy with the butterfly tattoo. (They had hoped for so much, they told me, before she contracted muscular dystrophy. They were going to have this holiday anyway, 'Whatever happens.') And there! Lizards! A flicker of bitter light off a broken terracotta tile. Balconies replicated giddily in the sun; and the squared-off helices of the exterior staircases, with their hanging mats of pink and purple flowers, ascended diagrammatically towards the air where all buildings finish and can never go.

I thought: It's the perfect place for people like us.

Isobel, photographed sunbathing at Médano:

She lies on her stomach, the upper part of her body raised on her elbows, her skin shiny with Clarins sun lotion. She has a drink, a towel, an unopened book. I hardly recognize her. Heavy-framed Raybans make her seem oracular, equivocal: half skin-diver, half sphinx. Half pilot. Is it her – can three halves be anything at all? – or quite some other woman? The beach curves away in the background to something that might be rocks or, equally, a laurel forest.

*

'China, what could happen?'

What happened was this:

One afternoon, a week after we got back, she came downstairs to the living room, where I was trying to read a book called *The Language of the Genes*. We hadn't been speaking. Since Tenerife she had spent her mornings on the phone, then taken herself off to shop in a preoccupied way at Waitrose, where she bought oranges, olives, anything that reminded her of the sun. She came and stood by the arm of the sofa. I took my reading glasses off and looked up at her.

'Hi.'

'Hi.'

She looked at me uncertainly.

'China, I want to talk to you.'

I knew exactly what she was going to say.

'China, I . . .'

There was a kind of soft thud inside me. It was something broken. It was something not there any more. I felt it. It was a door closing, and I wanted to be safely on the other side of it before she spoke.

'What?' I said.

'It's . . .'

'What?'

'China, I haven't been happy. Not for some time. You must have realized. I've got a chance at an affair with someone and I want to take it.'

I stared at her.

'Christ,' I said. 'Who?'

'Just someone I know.'

'Who?' I said. And then, bitterly: 'Who do you know, Isobel?' I meant: Who do you know that isn't me?

'It's only an affair,' she said. And:

'You must have realized I wasn't happy.'

I said dully: 'Who is this fucker?'

'It's Brian Alexander.'

'*Who?*'

'Brian Alexander.'

I had no idea who she was talking about. Then I remembered. 'Christ,' I said. 'He's just some fucking *customer*.'

She went out. I heard the bedroom door slam. I stared at the books on the bookshelves, the pictures on the walls, the bar of dusty gold afternoon light. I couldn't understand why it was all still there. I couldn't understand anything. Twenty minutes later, when Isobel came back in again carrying a soft leather overnight bag, I was standing in the same place, in the middle of the floor. She said:

'Do you know what your trouble is, China?'

'What?' I said.

'People are always just some fucking this or that to you.'

'Don't go.'

Two days later, when it was clear she wouldn't come back, I left the house and moved in with Choe Ashton, who had bought the upper maisonette of two in a large, shabby Edwardian house just off Green Lanes, midway between Turnpike Lane and Manor House. Like much he owned it was expensive but disused-looking, as if he had loved it once and then walked away. There were French film posters on the walls and piles of fading adventure-sport magazines subsiding day by day into dusty moraines on the living-room carpet. I found its shabbiness intensely comforting. Not that I had much comfort at that time.

9 · FUCK EVERYTHING AND RUN

Afternoons were the worst.

So were evenings.

Nights were the worst.

I kept imagining her at orgasm. It made me masturbate helplessly. I had her mixed up with the Sophia of Valentinus. I had her mixed up with my own anima. I had her mixed up with Kate Bush, singing 'The Hounds Of Love'. You can't get much more mixed up than that. Staring up at the ceiling of my room, hearing the restless creak of the cheap wicker rocking chair downstairs in Choe Ashton's lounge as Choe watched *Nigel Mansell's Indycars* late into the night, I would begin to miss her for no reason, only to realize after a moment what the noise reminded me of: the slow, delighted rhythm of sex in some hotel- or boarding-house bed when we were still new to one another.

Mornings were the worst.

Listen. I'm not here now. I'm free now. Nothing has ever happened between me and Isobel Avens. All I'm doing now is driving slowly through the wet city streets in my favourite car. Make? I've had them all. Model? You choose. The interior has that unmistakable smell, acrid and comforting at the same time, of new plastic trim. The sound system – let's say it's a 120-watt Alpine RDS CD tuner with a six-disc changer in the boot – is playing Patti Scialfa, 'Rumble Doll' from the album of the same name, so quietly I can almost hear it, while the lights of approaching vehicles star out in the droplets of water on the unswept part of the windscreen. Brake lights flare ahead. Traffic lights change from orange to red. Intersections appear slowly and slowly move away, to the right or the left and always to the rear. Brightly lit shop windows drift by, full of comforting goods. I'm not driving quickly. Do you understand? I am making only the required decisions. While I drive with care and keep the music low, nothing that can happen to me here is significant. I may reach absently into the glove compartment, looking for something I have forgotten even as my hand touches it. A paper tube of sweets. A book of matches (Ruby in the Dust, Camden Town, her favourite restaurant for a week). A packet which contains one cigarette. I may even light the cigarette, although I have not smoked for twenty years. But I will never leave the city however far I drive. Johnny Rockets Original Hamburger will precede Hip Bagels. Each pizza house will be succeeded by a Thai palace recommended – as Thai palaces inevitably are – by *Time Out*. Patti Scialfa will pass on to 'Spanish Dancer', just loud enough to hear, but never loud enough to centre herself in my awareness.

I can do that because I'm free now.

To start with, I was unwilling to drive. Everything was raw. Everything stuck out at the wrong angle. Everything was amputated, or needed amputating. Do you know what I mean? Everything smelt too strong in the mornings. All I had was panic and the sudden sickening calm that follows it, as if you have been given a painkilling drug you don't want. I felt like an invalid. If I drove my car, I told myself, I would only make some appalling error of judgement. Lose interest suddenly and run over a pedestrian. Coast to a halt on the South Circular somewhere near Catford, having forgotten who or what I was, while the early-morning traffic piled up behind me, at first confused and then enraged.

I couldn't drive so I walked. I walked the first week away. I got up early every day and, in Caterpillar boots and a leather coat, walked to Turnpike Lane tube station. Then I walked back. It was always raining, and I took care at kerbs. I knew I wasn't fit to be allowed out. But what else was I to do? As long as I was moving I could eat, even at seven a.m., when eating is hardest for the recently bereaved, the recently divorced, those who have lost their children or their houses or their jobs or all of those things. The recently dead, as Choe Ashton was later to put it. First I could eat a hot bacon sandwich. Then I could remember which café to order it from. Then I could begin to wonder why every morning as early as half-past seven there was an old woman reading Lawrence Durrell in the Green Lanes all-night launderette. It's true. She had grey, thinning hair, spectacles with violet frames, a pink crocheted top over pale blue cotton trousers, Dr Scholl sandals. Her skin was stretched and full of broken veins, her ear-lobes swollen, her upper chest reddened, grainy and mottled, as if she had recently spent time in the sun. She wore an old-fashioned man's watch with an expanding metal bracelet. By her feet was a green cloth shopping basket. She would read a paragraph of *Mountolive*, look up with a vague, digestive expression. There was her washing, going round in the machine.

Then one morning I put an old pair of Adidas squash shoes on and went out to look at my car. It was still parked half up on the disintegrating pavement a few yards down from Choe's house, where I had left it with the driver door hanging open the evening I arrived. Choe had locked it up, but he hadn't taken care of it. Scraps of waste paper were plastered to its windscreen. There were streaks of road mastic running down from the old wiper marks at the rear. In the dirt, someone had written with a finger: 'LORA IS A SPOLT BITCH.' It looked abandoned already. But when I disarmed the security system, and got in, and turned the key in the ignition, it started immediately. Welcome home, I thought. I released the handbrake. I selected first gear, let the clutch come up, and faces appeared at windows all along the street. One and a half hours later I was drinking pale grey coffee from a styrofoam cup in a petrol station on the outskirts of Stratford-upon-Avon. I rang Choe.

'Jesus, Choe,' I said. 'Where am I?'

Choe said: 'Fucked-up Street.' He laughed. 'How would I know, dickhead? Can you see any road signs from there?'

'I can't see any fucking thing.'

We both laughed. I could hear music in the background. If I turned up the gain on the Vodafone and listened carefully I could hear Lou Reed singing 'What's Good' from *Magic and Loss*. *Magic and Loss* was Choe's favourite album that month, just as *Rumble Doll* was mine; and 'What's Good' was his favourite track.

'I bet you can't get back here before half-past eleven,' he said.

I looked at my watch.

'What's good, Choe?' I asked him.

He said: 'Not much at all. I bet you can't do it.'

He was right. But I got a hundred and thirty up on the clock somewhere south of Oxford, in broad daylight, with all my lights on.

'I'm back, Choe.'

'That's what you think today, sucker.'

After that, from being my worst, mornings became my best time. I drove to Dunwich in Suffolk and walked along the beach; I drove to Cambridge. I drove to Reading.

I often went back to Stratford, where I sat in the cool early-morning air on Waterside, watching the river go past and whispering, 'You fucking bitch, Isobel. You fucking spolt bitch.' And once I drove to the car-park of the Woodcotes Country Hotel, and tried there to remember our first night together. All that came back was our first fuck. All that came back was saddle of lamb with rosemary, the fat Colin with his safe pair of hands and Isobel saying, 'Colin and Jenny deserve to have the best time they can. You mustn't feel superior to them.' I couldn't for the life of me now see why. It was lunchtime, but nobody was in the place. Beyond the deserted car-park, through a dark fringe of hedge, I could see a field. There was a single magpie hopping about in it. One for sorrow, I thought, and then rejecting that instantly: fuck off. Wherever I went after that, it was *one for sorrow, fuck off*. Wherever I went I rang Choe from the Vodafone and asked him where I was.

Choe hated it. 'You moron, I was asleep.' By the time I got home he had managed to make himself a cup of tea and, in a black singlet and a pair of those very loose, pleated black trousers Asian boys wear, was sprawled in the rocking chair watching television. The dusty, buff-coloured curtains were still drawn. His tattoos seemed to fluoresce in the stale light. Whenever he was at home he watched TV all day. He liked cartoons. He liked *Biker Mice From Mars, Talespin, Rude Dog and the Dweebs*. (Rude Dog, the cool California bull terrier, had an outline so radical it made him look like a diagram of a dog, a fashion sketch of a dog done with one economic line.) But much of the time he sprawled on the sofa and watched with the sound turned down.

'I'll fucking kill you if you do that,' he said, the first time I walked into the front room and tried to turn it up.

'Choe, it's the news.'

'Who gives a fuck? This is *prophecy*.' He grinned. 'Prophecy's more important.'

I stared at him wearily.

'Choe—'

'Look, I'll show you how to do it.'

He made me sit down. He gave me the TV control.

'Change the channels,' he said.

He said: 'Watch.'

He said: 'What do you see?'

On all four channels people were opening doors. The news they got was good, bad, good, good.

'See?' said Choe. 'A good chance of success in any project you might be pursuing.'

'Choe—'

'That's a very pure example, of course. It makes the method easy to understand: good news outweighs bad.'

127

He took the control from me.

'But what if you turn on the set to find one man looking out of a caravan window, while another one seems to be straining his head in through the same opening to look out of the set and talk to you?' Surfing absently into cable – I saw Hitler, I saw Stalin, I saw a snowboarder wipe out on some almost vertical slope, I saw a fraction of a scene from *Basic Instinct*, fat Michael Douglas, every woman's dream – he said: 'What if they both look dead? I suppose you can switch to another channel for confirmation: any direct mailing ad, especially one for stain-remover – stay at home that day; *Gardeners' Question Time* – perhaps not so bad, but avoid dogs.'

Suddenly, he switched the set on to standby and swivelled round on the sofa to stare as closely into my face as Isobel had ever done.

'Whatever you do,' he said, 'when using this method, *never turn up the sound.*'

He got up and stretched.

'What's for lunch?' he said.

I hated to eat with him.

'Know what my favourite food is?' he had said one day. 'I bet you can't guess. Go on. Try.'

'I don't know, Choe.'

'Told you. Well, it's this: get fish and chips from down the Green Lanes chippie, melt half a pound of St Agur cheese over it in the fucking microwave.'

He licked his lips.

'Brilliant,' he said. Then:

'You don't think I mean it, do you?'

How could anyone tell what Choe meant? He was working on the rigs again, two weeks on, two weeks off. He had more money than ever. He was more restless than ever. He was more unassuaged. Enthusiasms passed through him in a week, left him shaking but complacent. His life was full of objects but drained of anything else. He seemed to relish that. He would not talk about Christiana. He gave up kick boxing and took up cave diving, 'The most dangerous fucking sport in the world.' He bought two or three compact discs a day. His tastes were fluid: Lou Reed, Joe Satriani, a brilliant Brazilian jazz guitarist called José Neto he had heard one night at Ronnie Scott's. 'Listen to this. It's fucking amazing,' he would insist, play it the once, and stop listening halfway through, his expression sliding into vagueness. He took up mountain biking, and bought a machine the composite *frame* of which cost fifteen hundred pounds. 'Just look at that,' he would whisper in awe. 'Isn't that fucking obscene?' It hung on the wall of the lounge, its exotic alloys glowing with interference patterns, like a huge insect: within a week it was gathering dust. A week after that he had given up his job.

'I'm going to take the CBR round Europe,' he said in explanation. 'You need the dosh to pay the speeding tickets.'

He thought for a moment. 'I like Europe.'

And then, as if trying to sum up an entire continent:

'I once jumped over a dog in Switzerland. It was just lying in the middle of the road asleep. I was doing a hundred and ten. Bloke behind me saw it too late and ran it over.'

'Have a good time, Choe.'

He was away for two weeks. The day he came back it was the last good weather of summer.

'Ay up, kid,' he said.

He was wearing Levi 620s, brand new sixteen-hole DMs, a black sleeveless T-shirt, which had faded to a perfect fusty green, and a single gold ear-ring. We had a drink, then drove over to Camden and walked up between the market stalls to Camden Lock, where we sat in the sunshine blinking at the old curved bridge which lifts the towpath over the canal. Choe's arms had been baked brown in Provence and Chamonix, but the peacock feathers still rioted down them, purple, green and electric blue, a surf of eyes; and on his upper left arm one tiny perfect rose had appeared, flushed and pink.

'How was Europe?' I asked him.

'Fucking brilliant,' he said absently. He seemed nervous. 'It was great.'

'Get many tickets?'

'Too fucking right.'

'I like the new tattoo.'

'It's good.'

We were silent for a bit. Then he said:

'I want to show you something.'

'What?'

'It would mean driving up north.'

I said: 'I've got nothing else to do.'

'Are you sure you want to know this?'

I wasn't sure. But I said yes anyway.

He wheedled me into letting him drive. A blip in the weather brought strong south-west winds which butted and banged at the Ford as he stroked it up the motorway at a steady hundred and twenty. Plumes of spray drifted across the carriageways, so that even the heaviest vehicle, glimpsed briefly through a streaming windscreen, seemed to be moving sideways as well as forwards, caught in some long dreamlike fatal skid. Beyond Nottingham, though, where the road petered out into roadworks, blocked exits and confusing temporary signboards, the cloud thinned suddenly.

'Blue sky,' said Choe, braking heavily to avoid the back of a fleet Cavalier, then dipping briefly into the middle lane to overtake it. Hunched forward over the steering wheel until his face was pressed against the windscreen, he squinted upwards.

'I can see sunshine.'

'Will you watch where you're fucking going?'

He abandoned the motorway and urged the car into the curving back roads of the White Peak, redlining the rev counter between gear changes, braking only when the bend filled the windscreen with black and white chevrons, pirouetting out along some undrawn line between will and physics.

'Bloody hell, Choe.'

'Don't talk.'

After about twenty minutes he stopped the car and switched the engine off.

'This is near enough for now.'

We were in a long bleak lay-by somewhere on the A6. The road fell away from us in a gentle curve until it reached the flatter country west and north. Down there I could see a town – houses for quarry workers, a junction with traffic lights, a tall steel chimney designed to pump hot gases up through the chronic inversion layers of spring and autumn.

'When I was a kid,' Choe said, 'I lived a few miles outside that place.' He undid his seatbelt and turned to face me. 'What you've got to understand is that it's a fucking dump. It's got that fucking big chimney, and a Sainsbury's and a Woolworth's, and a fucking bus station.' He adjusted the driving mirror so that he could see his own face in it. 'I hated that fucking bus station. You know why? Because it was the only way in and out. I went in and out on one of those fucking buses every day for ten years, to take exams, look for jobs, go round the record shop on a wet Saturday afternoon.' He pushed the mirror back into its proper place. 'Ever spend any time in bus stations?'

'Never.'

'I didn't think you had. Let me tell you, they're death on a stick. Only people who are recently dead use a bus station.'

Everything warm, he said, went on at a distance from people like that. Their lives were at an ebb. At a loss. They had to watch the clean, the happy, the successfully employed, stepping out of new cars and into the lobbies of warm hotels. If the dead had ever been able to do that, they would never be able to do it again. They would never be able to dress out of choice or eat what they would like. Nothing they had been or wanted to be would ever come to anything.

'They're old, or they're bankrupt, or they've just come out of a long-stay mental ward. They're fucked.'

All over the north of England they stood around at ten in the evening waiting for the last bus to places called Chinley Cross, or Farfield, or Penistone. By day it was worse.

'Because you can see every fucking back-end village you're going through. The bus is fucked, and it never gets up any speed.' He appealed to me: 'It stinks of diesel and old woollen coats. *And the fuckers who get on are carrying sandwich boxes.*'

I laughed.

'There's nothing intrinsically wrong with a sandwich box,' I said.

'Do you want to hear this or not?'

'Sorry Choe.'

'I hated those fucking buses except for one thing:'

He was seventeen or eighteen years old. It was his last summer in the town. By September he would be at Sussex, doing his degree. He would be free. This only seemed to make him more impatient. Women were everywhere, walking ahead of him on every pavement, packed into the vegetarian coffee shop at lunchtime, laughing all afternoon on the benches in the new shopping plaza. Plump brown arms, the napes of necks: he could feel their limbs moving beneath the white summer dresses. He didn't want them. At night he fell out with his parents and then went upstairs to masturbate savagely over images of red-haired Pre-Raphaelite women he had cut from a book of prints. He hardly understood himself. One afternoon a girl of his own age got on the bus at Stand 18. She was perfectly plain – a bit short and fat, wearing a cardigan of a colour he described as 'a sort of Huddersfield pink' – until she turned round and he saw that she had the most extraordinary green eyes. 'Every different green was in them.' They were the green of grass, of laurel leaves, the pale green of a bird's egg. They were the deep blue-green of every sea-cliché he had ever read. 'And all at the same time. Not in different lights or on different days. All at the same time.' Eyes intelligent, reflective of the light, not human: the eyes of a bird or an animal. They seemed independent of her, as if they saw things on behalf of someone else: as if whatever intelligence inhabited them was quite different to her own. They examined him briefly. In that glance, he believed, 'She'd seen everything about me. There was nothing left to know.' He was transfixed. If you had ridden that bus as an adult, he said, and seen those eyes, you might have thought that angels travel route X39 to Sheffield in disguise.

'But they don't. They fucking don't.'

After that first afternoon she often travelled from Stand 18. He was so astonished by her that when she got off the bus one day at a place called Jumble Wood, he got off too and followed her. A nice middle-class road wound up between bungalows in the sunshine. Above them, on the lip of a short steep gritstone scarp, hung the trees: green and tangled, rather impenetrable. She walked past the houses and he lost sight of her: so he went up to the wood itself. Inside it was smaller than he had expected, full of a kind of hot stillness. He sat down for a minute or two, tranquillized by the greenish-gold light filtering down into the gloom between the oaks; then walked on, to find himself suddenly on the edge of a dry limestone valley. There was a white cliff, fringed with yew and whitebeam. There were grassy banks scattered with ferns and sycamore saplings. At his feet purple vetches twined their tendrils like nylon monofilament round the stems of the moon daisies. He was astonished by the wood avens, pure art nouveau with their complaisantly bowed yellow-brown flowerheads and strange spiky seed cases. He had never seen them before: or the heath-spotted orchids, tiny delicate patterns like intaglio on each pale violet petal.

When he looked up again, sunshine was pouring into the narrow valley from its south-western end, spilling through the translucent leaves of young ash trees, transfiguring the stones and illuminating the grassy slopes *as if from inside* – as if the whole landscape might suddenly split open and pour its own mysterious devouring light back into the world.

'So what did happen, Choe?'

Instead of answering he stared away from me through the windscreen, started the car up and let it roll gently down the hill until, on the right, I saw the turning and the sign:

'JUMBLE WOOD.'

'You decide,' he said. 'We'll walk up.'

I don't know what he wanted me to see, except what he had seen all those years ago. I found what he had already described – the wood, smaller than you might expect, full of dust motes suspended in sunshine – and beyond that, on the knife-edge of the geological interface, the curious little limestone valley with its presiding crag like a white church.

'You're going to have to give me a bit more help,' I said.

He knelt down.

'See this? Wood avens. I had to look it up in a book.'

He picked one and offered it to me.

'It's pretty. Choe, what happened here?'

'Would you believe me if I told you the world really did split open?'

He gazed miserably away from me.

'What?' I said.

'Somehow the light peeled itself open and showed me what was inside. It was here. She walked out of it, with those eyes every green in the world.' He laughed. 'Would you believe me if I said she was naked, and she stank of sex, and she let me push her down there and then and fuck her in the sunshine? And then somehow she went back into the world and it sealed itself up behind her and I never saw her again?'

'Choe—'

'I was eighteen years old,' he said. 'It was my first fuck.'

He turned away suddenly.

'It was my only fuck,' he said. 'I've never done it since.

134

Whatever lives here loves us. I know it does. But it only loves us once.'

He drove back to London in silence, parked the Ford on Green Lanes and walked off towards Manor House tube station.

'Choe,' I called.

No answer.

10 · FLYING BLIND

Never any answer.

After he had gone I kept to the flat, playing *Rude Dog* reruns in the gloom until half-past seven or eight in the evening, when I could switch over to *EastEnders* with its obscurely comforting theme music. Dust continued to gather on the piles of books and magazines. Choe was gone three weeks, then four. The phone didn't ring. Waste paper rustled and scraped along the pavement outside, children howled and shrieked motivelessly along the road, their voices echoing away between the houses; I barely heard any of it. I was trying to reconstruct my life with Isobel.

She was easy to see, even at that distance. I remembered her asleep on an Intercity express to King's Cross, just after we had met, curled up so tight she hardly took up the space of one seat. I saw her perched not much later on a bar stool at the Criterion brasserie, drinking Kronenburg from a bottle. I saw her in grey jeans and black DMs. I watched her frowning amusedly at herself over a new frock in a long mirror at Monsoon in Covent Garden. I saw her in a camisole top the colour of ivory and nothing else at all. It was easy to remember the pattern of frost on a south London window, the confused song of a bird in the middle of the night, a photograph of a pair of her shoes nesting in a spill of satin things she had just taken off. It was easy to see Isobel. What was hard was to make anything of her. With each new item of clothing, each new image of herself, she had changed completely and yet somehow become more completely the person I already knew. Almost as soon as we met, she had been warning me:

'Don't be a baby, China. Nothing stands still.'

Isobel had always been easy to see and impossible to see past.

Somehow she had taken cover behind her own image, long before she forgot how to fly, or met Brian Alexander. Washed up on Green Lanes among Choe Ashton's abandoned toys, I understood suddenly how I had begun to mourn her *before* she left, hardly daring to revisit my memories of Stratford or our first few months in Peckham, because by then the colour of sunlight in the morning, the angle of a shadow across the bedroom carpet, was never quite enough to bring it all back.

I wrote these things down every night, in letters which I did not post to her. The word I used most often was 'remember'. 'Do you remember this?' I asked her: 'Don't you remember that?'

Remember how couples in restaurants in Chelsea and Blooms-bury and Covent Garden came over to our table to tell us how special we looked together, as if that might give them good luck in their own faltering and fucked-up affairs? Remember how the traffic hushed, slowed, held back, *parted* for us on Shaftesbury Avenue at eight o'clock on a summer evening? How we were Oberon and Titania, and not just to each other, but also to the waitresses at Peppermint Park, whose hair was peroxided a violent white-blond to go with their spotless white aprons and little black bowties, a uniformity which made them look more rather than less human?

'Remember,' I wrote, 'how all of that happened, and isn't just the false memory of hallucination of someone who used to be in love?

'Look, don't you even remember St Helier?'

Two weeks in a fifth-floor suite directly under the sign at the Hotel de France. We lay awake every night listening to the neon tubes creak as the wind streamed through them. 'Or I did, anyway. Now I begin to wonder if you didn't just go to sleep.' The wind in the neon. You could see that sign from all over the town. We had always known where our room was – there, a little left of centre, under the 'el' of 'Hotel'.

'Don't you remember?'

If Isobel remembered, she was saying nothing. She had begun

to abandon me again, every morning at about five o'clock, in dreams. She was openly and aggressively unfaithful, yet we lived on in the same house. I couldn't make her help me, I couldn't make her leave: I couldn't make myself leave. I was financially dependent, afraid of heights and stairs, of falling. I cried easily in the afternoon. Each dream was different; they were all the same. I was in a mess. I woke up shocked and cold, or full of a pure, convulsive aggression. I woke up with my mouth thick and dry and a throat full of something which felt like hot cotton wool.

But the worst dream seemed to have nothing to do with us at all. In it, I was someone else. I was someone else, dreaming every night of trying to find out what had happened to the woman I loved. Isobel was someone else too – a pianist and a writer with her blond hair in a complex braid. We had met in New York when she played a concert of American and British music. She had reminded me how I was once able to dance. Now, some time later, she had come to Britain to find me. But she could no longer speak, only weep. How had she travelled here? Where did she live? What was she trying to say? It was a dream heavy with sadness and urgency. All avenues of inquiry were blocked. There were people who might know about her, but always some reason why they could not be asked, or would not tell. I walked up and down the streets, examining the goods on the market stalls, my only clue the reissue date of a once-banned medicine. She was close. She was *that far* from me, I knew I wouldn't find her.

I woke up shaking. I wrote:

'I know you hate me for needing you, I know you hate me for only having one argument – *Don't leave me, I love you.*'

Of all the letters, I sent that one.

Isobel replied by return of post on expensive paper, thick, lavender-coloured, heavily recycled to have the writing surface of raw chipboard. She was happy, she said, though she missed me. Things were hard for her too. 'I don't hate you, China,' she wrote. 'Why should I hate you?' She asked me if I would like to meet her one day: perhaps for early-evening drinks.

I crumpled up the letter and threw it across Choe's front room.

'For Christ's sake, Isobel,' I told her quietly. *'Early-evening drinks?* Where do you get this stuff from?'

Two days later I was waiting for her in a pub near the south end of Hammersmith Bridge, already wondering where she would go on to, and who with; and why the wound was still so raw.

The bar of the New Buccaneer was a bleak and windswept runway dedicated to someone's scrubby, vanished myth of flight. Perhaps that was why Isobel had chosen it. A wooden propeller hung on one wall, and, above the spirit optics, two whitening colour photographs of old-fashioned naval jets climbing steeply away from an aircraft carrier on a storm-tossed but somehow gelid sea. Scattered here and there were equally faded prints of Canadian Pacific short-haulers of the 1940s, fitted for desperate landings above the Arctic Circle.

Six o'clock. The weather was bad, and nothing much was flying in or out. Four middle-aged women had stalled on the runway. As a group they were bright, noisy, attentive to one another; left alone for a moment, they slumped and studied the bar furniture with an interest bordering on anxiety.

'Well, anyway, psoriasis,' one of them said suddenly.

'I'll have a Beck's,' I told the barman.

'Will you want a glass with that, sir?'

'No, I won't.'

'Is that all then, sir?'

'No it isn't.'

I stared past him at the optics.

'I'll have a Captain Morgan, too.'

'That will be five pounds altogether, sir.'

'Christ.'

I sat down in a corner. Every time the street door opened I looked up, though I had promised myself I wouldn't. The wash of neon in the open doorway was the exact colour of early daylight, as if the women, the barman and I had already drunk ourselves into the next morning. I got up again and wandered around. I looked at the pictures. I looked into the deserted restaurant section, where girls were laying tables for dinner. They reminded me of Isobel as I'd first met her. What would happen when I saw her now? I would be able to smile: I was sure of that. But she would be smiling too. She would come in with that swinging, sexy walk, stooping slightly as if she was a taller woman. She would be smiling, but it wouldn't be the smile I remembered – unarmed, candid, whole. She would be smiling as if I was an appointment. She would be someone who said 'early-evening drinks', and 'six for six-thirty'; someone who said 'K' when they meant 'thousand'. Someone who had gone so far away I would never be able to interpret her smile again.

By six-fifteen, when I next looked round, one or two regulars had come in to erratic crosswind touchdowns, oil-pressure at zero and instruments undependable. An old man with an artificial hand sat trembling at the table underneath the 'Toilets' sign. Just down the bar from him, a Jack Russell terrier dashed repeatedly at its owner's foot, barking, while he laughed and fended it off with mock growls. (If he looked round for applause, it was all for the dog.) A tall wasted boy in ripped jeans and leather jacket dragged himself from table to table as if he could forget the pain of his last crash-landing only so long as he was on the move. Leaning tiredly over the juke box, he twice selected the old Roxy Music hit 'Virginia Plain'. Finally he sat down between the man with the dog and the man under the 'Toilets' sign and, without giving any indication that they knew one another, all three began to talk at once. It had been an early Jack Higgins' novel for them – a long haul through thick air and electrical storms – and I thought I heard one of them say:

'She can't bear to touch the chickens.'

This sentence brought me a clear vision of my future without Isobel. I would live in a two-star hotel in the Mumbles. I would buy an Austin Allegro. Every night I would drive it to some pub like the New Buccaneer and – after a period of aimless walking up and down – join the other cripples at the bar. 'Supports *cats*, does she?' I would hear myself say. 'Bloody waste of money, that.' One night there would be a smell hanging on the stairs next to the men's lavatory; it would be the exact smell of a fat-rendering factory in Preston. I would try not to smell it – too late – and it would lodge inside me, recurring unpredictably, always at one crucial juncture, souring my joy, undermining my confidence, marring my life forever.

I sat down again. Let Isobel come to China, by the Hammersmith Bridge. I would see her in the mirror behind the optics, underneath the picture of the climbing Buccaneers, long before she saw me.

Six-thirty. Nothing.

I thought: The traffic will have made her late. She will be parking her car. Why did she suggest this? Why did I agree? I heard one of the cripples say to the other two:

'If you killed yourself I'd never speak to you again. I just wouldn't respect you.'

At this, the Jack Russell yapped, the barman smiled as if he understood some joke no one else had caught, the women looked up briefly then went back to their drinks. One of them said:

'Now you *are* in on Monday aren't you, dear?'

'Yes, yes I am.'

'And – ' turning to someone else ' – you are too, dear, because I've just arranged a whole new pricing structure.'

The door opened. Isobel Avens was caught in the wash of neon, thin, hesitant, angular, oddly posed with one hand still raised to the door as if she was leaning against a wall in some alley. For a moment she looked confused and terrified. She looked ill. I had a clear memory of her saying: 'China, I couldn't *fly*.' Behind her I glimpsed an endless stream of cars going to and fro across the Thames, and Budapest went across me like a pain in the heart, a crack across the mirror, and we were on the

Erzebet Bridge at midnight watching the ice floes race towards us through the Middle European night, and Isobel was in my arms and whispering:

'I thought I'd never hear from you again.'

Everything inside me suddenly went very still.

'I—'

'Would you—?'

'No, let me—'

'I—'

'Let me.'

'You look nice.'

We stepped back as suddenly as we had embraced. Isobel took out her purse.

'You look so nice.'

'I'll get these.'

'Is it raining?'

'I got a taxi.'

'Are you . . .?'

'I came over from Putney.'

She had dressed for dinner, in a long, clinging black frock.

'It's a John Rocha. Do you like it?'

'Turn,' I said.

'I love it,' I said.

She laughed and turned again.

'John Rocha,' I said.

I said: '*Very* upmarket.'

She had been shopping all afternoon. She had visited some friends. 'I wasn't even sure you would be here,' she said. She had come in a taxi, straight to me from Putney, wearing a John Rocha frock. Only Isobel could have chosen something so inappropriate.

'Let's have a drink, then go on somewhere else to eat,' she said.

She thought for a moment.

'Let's go to dell 'Ugo's.'

Instead of 'dell 'Ugo's? In a John Rocha frock?' I said:

'Brilliant.'

I would have gone anywhere for another hour with her. I would have gone anywhere for another ten minutes.

'Brilliant,' I said.

'Oh China, I have missed you.'

She looked around the bar, smiling vaguely. The barman smiled back; while the women, ashamed for her without entirely knowing why, avoided her eyes.

'I'll fetch the car,' I said, a little later. 'It's a couple of streets away.'

'Don't be silly, China. I'll walk.'

'If you're sure.'

It had stopped raining, and a feeble quarter of moon was hauling itself up over Arundel Terrace. A Claude Montana raincoat slung across her shoulders, arms folded beneath her breasts for comfort, Isobel walked with her upper arm brushing mine. Unsure, perhaps, how close she should get to me, how far into her new self she could safely admit me, she spoke only to admire the red-brick apartment houses or complain about the cold wind from the river. 'You don't have to be so careful,' I wanted to reassure her. I wanted to say: You were never so wary before. But how could I know that? Some people, I thought, always withhold themselves: some people give themselves to you without ever giving you anything at all – an accusation which hung there between us on the edge of being spoken, where it only added to Isobel's uncertainty.

I had parked my Greenlight Cosworth at the end of the road, next to the weed-infested concrete expanse of the Harrods' Repository yard. She stood expectantly by the passenger door.

She said: 'The old Sierra.' She said: 'China, I'm so glad you kept it.'

When I failed to respond, except to disarm the Cosworth's

security system and advise her, 'It's open,' she got in, gave a shrug so minimal I almost noticed it, and added suddenly:

'Brian's got an XJS.'

I wanted to say: Shit car, that. Instead I adjusted the driving mirror.

Isobel smiled as if to say, Yes. That's how you always adjusted your driving mirror, China. I remember.

Neither of us knew how to act. In the confined space of the car everything became meaningful; everything meaningful was dangerous; and I couldn't think of anything to talk about at all. Isobel fastened her seatbelt – staring at the mechanism for a moment as if she didn't quite understand it – then sat facing straight ahead with her raincoat folded in her lap. Occasionally she would turn her head to study a brightly lit window display. At traffic lights she peered into the dim interiors of the more expensive cars we stopped beside, as if she expected to recognize some celebrity or politician, or perhaps just some new friend she had made in Brian Alexander's company. Once I heard her say softly, 'Oh look, China.' But I missed whatever she was trying to draw my attention to, and it didn't seem to need acknowledgement anyway.

In the end I stopped trying to talk and instead of listening to the things Isobel said, concentrated on the sound of her voice. Her smell was soon mixed up with the smell of the warm car. Street lights picked out the curve of her shoulder, the long line of her arm, her fingers where they rested on the dash. I wanted to be able to remember all those things when she was gone again. In an hour, two hours, the memory would be more important than the event itself – or indeed Isobel herself. She seemed to sense that. She asked once if I would turn the heater up.

'Whose is the field mushrooms?'

'Happy birthday, Charlotte. Have a lovely evening.'

'I've got to go and buy something to make myself pretty with tomorrow: wedding.'

'Oh God.'

'What's a wedding anyway—?'

'Field mushrooms? Who's having the pan-fried field mushrooms!'

'Earth, Air, Fire, Water, Hype. Hype, the Fifth Element!'

'—just a lot of failed princesses in powder-blue lace.'

'I do agree.'

'They give you a ring with a stone on it the size and colour of a boiled sweet—'

'Field mushrooms on tapenade toast?'

'I think that's mine. Oh no. It isn't. Did I order that? I'm sure I didn't.'

'We're going to see you tomorrow evening.'

'Are you? Are we? Oh!'

'—Gavin Bryars. Sort of an anorexic Donald Pleasence, but he's actually fairly awake.'

'Alice is down in Oxford tonight.'

'Oxford?'

'She's a trustee of the Lewis Carroll Society. They're trying to raise some money. What they're trying to do is set up a centre—'

'—a sort of Lewis Carroll theme park?'

Laughter.

'It was mooted. It's been mooted.'

'*Who's having the pan-fried mushrooms on tapenade toast.*'

'What's a wedding anyway?'

'Charlotte, did you order this?'

dell 'Ugo's was hot, crowded and full of the smells of food and coffee. Isobel stared around unashamedly, drank a lot of Côtes de Rouffach, and ordered thyme muffins with glazed crab, oysters and crispy bacon. All evening the John Rocha frock added to her air of shyness and vulnerability. Against its confident lines she seemed unformed, girlish, labile. Perhaps that was the idea.

'I love it here,' she insisted, holding out her glass. 'Let's stay until they close.'

'What's that?' she said, poking at my plate.

'Chargrilled bananas, I think.'

She whispered loudly, 'China. China. That's *Muriel Gray*. No, over there.'

Suddenly she asked me: 'Do you think they'll ever get the lid back on Yugoslavia?'

I stared at her, astonished.

She stared back.

'What "lid"?' I said brutally. I said: 'Why would you care?'

'Because of all the children,' she said.

She looked down at her plate, as if this admission had disconcerted her as much as me.

I said: 'I'm sorry.'

By then it was nine or ten o'clock.

I said: 'I didn't – Look, I'm a bit jumpy . . . I . . .'

She took my hand gently.

'I know, China.'

'It's difficult,' I lied. 'Here.'

But the real trouble wasn't even dell 'Ugo's, with its freight of self-conscious TV comedians, journos and publishers. The real trouble was this: behind Isobel's voice – behind early-evening drinks and chicken hash-cake with wilted spinach – behind the whole lot of it – I had suddenly heard the received wisdom of Brian Alexander. He might have been standing behind her chair. I was filled with contempt. At the same time it came home to me with bleak clarity how being with him had 'grown her up'. That was a meaningless thing to think. But its corollary was obvious, and as the evening went on I kept getting glimpses of the pair of them together – down at Margaret Avens' cottage in Gloucestershire; visiting the Tate; and finally, of course, in the bedroom at Stepney, where the box of tissues by the bed, the scented candles burning on the mantelpiece, the satin underwear scattered on the pink carpet, would be as perfectly familiar to me as the things she murmured to herself while he fucked her.

Against the odds, dell 'Ugo's had eased Isobel's nerves; and perhaps that made me angry, too. I said:

'You aren't telling me much.'

'About what?'

'Your life,' I said.

I meant: Your life with him.

Isobel said: 'I never know how much you want to know.'

'Only that you're happy,' I said.

She reached over quickly and took my hand.

'Oh, China, I am,' she said. She said: 'I love him.' She said: 'But it isn't just that. He's going to help me to fly.'

I pulled my hand out of hers.

'You always said I helped you to fly.'

She looked away.

'It's not your fault it stopped working,' she said. 'It's me.'

'Christ, you selfish bitch.'

'He wants to help me to fly,' she repeated dully.

And then:

'China, I *am* selfish.'

She tried to touch my hand again, but I moved it away.

'I can't fucking believe this,' I said. 'You want me to forgive you just because you can admit it?'

'I don't want to lose you, China.'

'Christ.'

Towards the end of the evening, she said:

'I never trusted you. That was the problem.'

I remembered how we had been at the beginning.

'If you could hear yourself,' I said. 'If you could just fucking hear yourself, Isobel.'

She left a long silence after that.

Suddenly she said:

147

'Can't we be friends? Neither of us knows what we might want in the future.'

'You're confused, Isobel. He's your friend now.'

'Grow up, China.'

'You grow up, Isobel. People come whole. You can't just take the bits you want and throw the rest away.'

She looked across the restaurant. She blinked once or twice.

'Take it or leave it,' I said.

'If that's what you want,' she said.

I shrugged. We sat not looking at one another.

'You can't expect friendship from someone you've hurt,' I said.

'I didn't hurt you.'

'What?'

'For God's sake, China, this kind of thing happens to everybody all the time. Why do you have to make it such a tragedy?'

'I can't believe I'm hearing this.'

She pushed her chair back savagely and got up.

'It's the nineteen nineties, China.'

I didn't see her after that. I did have one letter from her. It was sad without being conciliatory, and ended: 'You were the most amazing person I ever knew, China, and the fastest driver.'

I tore it up.

'"Were"!' I said. 'Fucking *were*!'

11 · CHINA'S SYNDROME

By that time she had moved in with him, somewhere along the Network South-East line from Waterloo: Kew, East Sheen, one of those old-fashioned suburbs on a bladder of land inflated into the picturesque curve of the river, with genteel, deteriorating houseboats, an arts centre and a wine bar on every corner. West London is full of places like that – 'shabby', 'comfortable', until you smell the money. Come to think of it, almost everywhere you go is full of places like that.

Isobel kept the Stepney house. I visited it once or twice in September, ostensibly to collect my things, ended up crying in the lounge, and after an hour took away with me a compact disc I had bought her, an American fleece shirt she had bought me. Every object in that place frightened me with its potential for memory and pain. It was necessary to be careful where I looked, even among my own belongings; among hers there was no relief. On the second visit I came across the photographs Isobel's mother had given me the first year we were together. They had been kept all that time in the same old shoebox, which, faded to beige and fastened with perished elastic bands, still smelt very faintly of salt air, seaside towns. It was an object from another age. The prints too seemed older than they were, small, oddly proportioned slips of pasteboard, made to last. In them, eyes were cast down, faces turned aside, less through shyness or embarrassment – though clearly there was some of both – than in a vain attempt to look away from the sun. A strange, blanched seaside horizon transected each image. The shadow of the photographer lay oblique and truncated in every foreground, among inexplicable objects and piles of light-coloured clothing.

Out of the box they tumbled, to spill across the polished floor, dusty and a little warped as if something heavy had been thrown carelessly in on top of them a long time ago.

'Look at her,' Margaret Avens had exclaimed when she first showed them to me. 'She was a *horrible* toddler.'

That was at Cleeve Hill, the first year we were together. I still remember Margaret, in Country Casuals skirt and jumper, sitting on a wingback chair with the shoebox in her lap. Late afternoon, winter. The air outside was raw and damp. Mist crept down the hill towards Cheltenham, or, trapped by the inversions, layered itself in the growing dusk along the sides of the valley. Inside, a log fire burned up bright, slowly filling the grate with pure white ash.

Isobel was in the kitchen making scones. All afternoon I had been keenly aware of her there, moving in a kind of dreamy dance between the Aga and the work surfaces. Margaret's Burmese cats stared into the fire, or, with rapt reflective eyes, sat on the windowsill to study the wintry garden: everywhere they went, they went together. Is it possible to 'shiver with comfort'? I suppose not. But if I thought about it for a second, comfort and excitement were equally mixed in what I felt that afternoon. Comfort and excitement. Can you understand that?

'Still, she grew out of it,' Margaret said. 'They always do.' She glanced at me over the rims of her gold reading glasses. 'In fact, she really did turn into quite a nice little girl. Look.'

She offered me another print.

'Don't you think?'

I had already dismissed the dull brown bunches of hair and self-tutored smile of the ten-year-old. It was the face, I had decided, of a growing anxiety to please – a face always turned towards the nearest adult.

'Mm,' I said noncommittally.

I thought: Who wouldn't prefer the toddler?

'I love them all,' I said.

'I'm sure I'm right,' said Margaret.

This exchange has somehow entangled itself with my memory

of finding the shoebox again after Isobel left. I remember kneeling on the floor. I remember sorting the snapshots into chronological order. I remember arranging them face-down, then turning them over again, one by one. There she sat, an Isobel puppy-fatted and unassuaged, scowling out from her cluttered little territories in the sand. 'I had to be able to walk,' she had admitted to me, 'to steal toys from the beach. If I liked what I saw, I took it.' How could I ever have romanticized this monster, with its uncontrollable rages and misplaced pets? More importantly, how could I have failed to detect it, installed in the grown woman, every preoccupation intact?

I stayed all afternoon. Weak sunshine had thrown a bar of light across the varnished wooden floor. I remember how it moved across the scattered pictures, and then slowly round the room until it fell on a few dried flowers in one of Isobel's tall brass vases, isolating them from their background so that they looked like the demonstration of some well-known illusion. The visual structure of that part of the room – a corner, the table with the vase on it, some bookshelves – was subtly altered, as if it were possible to have lenses or eddies of greater depth in different parts of the same space.

By then Stepney was as bitter a memory, as irretrievable a paradise, as Cleeve Hill. I looked down at the photographs. Had Margaret Avens been warning me against her own daughter? I thought: I don't suppose I'll ever know.

I didn't go back again. I couldn't face the bedroom, with its wooden chests and paper birds. It always seemed to have filled up further with dust. Despite that I could never quite tell if anything had changed. *Had* they been in there, the two of them? Was that Isobel I could hear, whispering, 'Do you want to *fuck* me? Do you want to *fuck* my *cunt*?' Was that his answering groan? 'Say, then. *Say* you want to.' I stayed in the doorway so as not to be certain, and then – when the possibility got too close to ignore – drove back as fast as I could to Tottenham. There, sick of *Rude Dog and the Dweebs* at last, I was drinking a lot of Michelob beer, going listlessly through Choe's collection of unknown female rock singers on CD and watching Channel Four movies while I encouraged Rose Services to go down the drain.

Some films I liked better than others. I liked the beginning of *Alice in the Cities* a lot. It was such an intense replication of space and sensations: but nothing at all like standing between two mirrors. More as if these things just went on and on as you moved towards them, into them, through them. As if America really was infinite once you got past the boundaries of New York, a country in which people communicate by leaving notes for one another. They look out of windows and someone is always walking away. Someone is always asleep in the next room. They switch endlessly from TV station to TV station; and unassuagable from the very outset, unwrap sandwiches from a plastic pack. I cried all the way through *Alice in the Cities*. I wasn't sure why. But I knew why I was cheering Anthony Hopkins as *The Good Father*.

'What fucking crap,' Choe Ashton said, when I tried in a confused way to explain all this.

He had returned the day before from some New York of his own, one he wasn't prepared to relinquish to Wim Wenders or anyone else. America always put Choe in a dangerously good mood. You often found it hard to get out of him why he did the things he did. But once he started, he couldn't stop telling you about them:

'I went to Union Square, I went to Madison Avenue. Listen, I went into a *blind pig*. Fucking Tom Waits country – are you listening? People had cut so many initials in the tables they looked *carved*. It was red neon, but completely dark at two o'clock in the afternoon. But do you know what the best graffiti in the bog was?'

'No, Choe. I don't.'

'DAVE WAS HERE FROM EASTBOURNE.'

He grinned.

'You don't believe that, do you? But it's true. Fucking Eastbourne!'

He had been all over the Village, from Jane Street – which for some reason he remembered from William Burroughs, 'A dirty, furnished room in a red-brick house on Jane Street,' home of Marvin the waiter, a junkie allergic to junk – to the Cowgirl Hall of Fame, where he had eaten Frito pie and catfish fingers. He had ridden the subway to the Bronx and beyond; and convinced a taxi driver to go back and forth across the Brooklyn Bridge seven times.

'I had these fucking *sweet potato chips* somewhere else . . .' He had to stop for a minute to think '. . . I forget where. But they were fucking ace. Fucking brilliant. The best thing of all, though . . .' A broad smile passed across his face. '. . . the best thing of all was Sioux City Cream Soda. I drank five glasses of it.'

He had drunk them down, one after the other, at the Cowgirl Hall of Fame.

'I threw up after that.'

'Don't boast, Choe. Anyway, only a dickhead goes to New York to get sick on pop.'

He laughed. 'I know. What's happening?'

'I'm going bankrupt,' I told him. 'This afternoon.' I explained: 'I'm not entirely sure why.' I asked him if he'd like to sit in on the meeting, as an ex-Rose Services' shareholder. He looked at me as if I had gone mad.

'Fuck off, Mick,' he said.

'Go on, Choe, you know you want to.'

Suddenly he clapped his hand to his forehead and fumbled about in one of his jacket pockets. 'I forgot,' he said. 'I got something for you.' And he offered me a cutting, folded and furry, from some cheap DTP magazine. 'This is an East Village thing called *New Biology*: some kind of political sheet at the consumer end. More a print-out from their Web site than a magazine.'

I took the cutting and opened it. It was a brief CV.

Brian Alexander worked for some years developing patentable human cell lines for a California company called FUGA-OrthoGen; and later on transgenic farm animals under the auspices of a privatized university department known since 1989 as Agritrans Cambridge Plc whose literature boasted that it was 'one of the first companies to offer a transgenic service'. The Alexander group of clinics, in Florida, Chicago and Milan, are a partly owned subsidiary of FUGA-OrthoGen (now a transglobal with offices in Geneva and Budapest).

Dr Alexander's publications include 'New Work with Plasmids' *British Journal of Molecular Biology*, 1982: 'Firing the Genetic Bullet' OMNI, November 1994; and 'Grow Your Way to Freedom' Alexander Publications, Chicago.

I turned the cutting over. Nothing else.

'Who gave you this?'

'Is it him?' Choe said. 'It's him, isn't it?'

'Why give me this?' I said.

He shrugged.

'Let the ferret see the rabbit,' he said. 'After all, the fucker stole your tart.'

'Grow up Choe.'

It was his turn to shrug.

In the end he did turn up at the bankruptcy meeting, although his main contribution was to sit on a chair in the corner and stare appraisingly at the liquidator, who turned out to be a pleasant young man from Hither Green called Tony. So many bankruptcies were available at the moment, Tony told us. They occupied 50 per cent of his time, where once it had been 15. But he did do other kinds of work. Tony wore a Marks and Spencer suit and had trained himself to say 'I see' with a variety of different intonations, some less encouraging than others.

'I see,' he would say. 'Things are pretty bad then.'

And he would move smoothly on to the next point. As the

shortfall between the estimated and the book value of the business grew plainer, so Tony became more and more impersonal, reserved his judgement more and more. 'I see. Well, I think that's it as far as the form-filling's concerned. If I could trouble you to get those accounts again?'

'Trouble you to get those accounts?' mimicked Choe softly. 'Here,' he said. 'Let's do some blow.' He began to go through his pockets. 'Well, that's fucking odd. I'm sure I had some somewhere here—'

'Choe,' I warned him. Too late. He had made eye-contact with Tony.

'I see that we're missing my favourite nature programme, Tony, did you know that? Do you watch a lot of daytime TV? Well, this afternoon it's *The Flight of the Condom*. Have you watched that one, Tony, at all? There's some very interesting camel-fucking in that one. Ever watched two camels fucking, Tony?'

Tony shook his head slowly.

'I see,' said Choe.

'I wonder . . .' Tony began. Had he ever met anyone like Choe before? 'I wonder if—'

'Well you do,' said Choe. 'Don't you?'

'Choe!'

'You do wonder,' Choe said.

He laughed quietly to himself. '*The Flight of the Condom*,' he said.

Tony cleared his throat.

'I wonder if I could see the records of these medical waste transactions?' he asked me. 'They seem to have been the mainstay of the business—'

'We didn't actually keep records of those.'

'I see.'

I said: 'I must admit the details are a bit vague in my own mind.'

'They're a bit vague in his mind,' Choe said.

Tony thought for a moment.

'Well,' he decided, 'if the directors aren't aware of it I can often argue back to the company that it's invalid.'

'You often can, can you?' said Choe.

He laughed.

Tony looked at him. He rubbed his face. Then he asked us: 'Is there anyone who would want to pick up these assets?'

Who knew? By then, the only asset Rose Services actually had left was a 1985 BMW M3. I had bought it to race, but it was just too old to be competitive, though it had done well as a BTCC privateer for two seasons in the late eighties, coming in ninth or tenth most meetings against the team Toyotas and Vauxhalls: once even seventh. I had paid someone in Brixton to legalize the electrical and exhaust systems, put in proper seats, bulkhead insulation and a CD player, and paint out the promotional decals for RipSpeed and Demon Tweeks. But the roll cage and six-speed powertrain were still in place, the car remained quite noisy inside and it sat down into tight bends in a distinctive, predatory fashion. It was practically uninsurable.

Choe loved it.

'Coke dealer's choice,' he had complimented me the day I bought it. 'Fucking ace car.'

After Tony had gone, he looked at his watch.

'Let's get ripped and see if we can drive to Shrewsbury before the pubs close.'

'Why Shrewsbury, Choe?'

He looked at me as if I was a moron. *Because I've never fucking bin there,* he explained patiently.

'Fair enough.'

'I've got a better idea than that, even.'

'What?'

'Let's go and beat up that fucker who stole your tart.'

'Jesus, Choe.'

'Go on, you know you want to.'

'Perhaps you're right,' I admitted. But what I wanted least

was for Choe to be involved. So one evening at about seven I left him watching Channel Four News with the sound turned down; drove across town; and parked the BMW at the kerb outside Brian Alexander's clinic, which was in a postmodern block at the Hammersmith end of Queensborough Road, not far from the Broadway. Some light rain was falling. I sat with the engine running and watched the front entrance. The security staff looked back at me from behind their wraparound desk. After about twenty minutes a receptionist came out, put her umbrella up, and walked quickly off towards Hammersmith tube station. A bit later Alexander himself appeared at the top of the steps, a tall thin man, middle-aged, grey-haired, dressed in a light wool suit. He seemed worried. He looked along the street towards Parsons Green, then down at his watch. I wondered if he was waiting for Isobel; I didn't know that by then Isobel wasn't even in Britain. I was disappointed by him. 'It makes me sad to lose you, China,' she had written. 'You were the most amazing person I ever knew.'

Why did you pick this prick, then? I thought.

I wound down the nearside passenger window.

I called: 'Brian Alexander?'

I called: 'Need a lift?'

He bent down looked into the M3.

'Do I know you?' he asked.

I thought: Say the wrong thing, you fucker.

I said: 'Not exactly.'

'Then—'

'Forget it.'

He stood back from the car suddenly, and I drove off.

'What a waste,' said Choe, when I got back. 'You should have twatted him.'

He was still slumped in front of the TV. He had the remote control in one hand and a bottle of Dos Equis beer in the other.

He added, 'I would have,' and turned the sound up. He seemed to have recorded part of the news.

I said: 'Could we have less of this fucking stupid Yorkshire act?'

'You want to watch this,' Choe advised.

'Listen,' I said, 'I just went to see what he was like. OK, Choe? Is that OK with you?'

'. . . illegally dumped uranium,' said the TV.

I switched it off.

I said: 'Could you listen to me, Choe? Could you do that for me?'

I said: 'Is that OK with you?'

He stared up mildly from the sofa.

'Please don't hurt me, Mick. It's my first time.'

'Fuck off.'

I went into the kitchen to get a beer. While I was gone, Choe switched the TV on again.

'Watch this,' he said, and rewound the tape.

'Experts,' the TV said, 'have begun the delicate task of moving a quantity of illegally dumped radioactive waste from a Lancashire quarry.'

I stared at the screen – where police vehicles were moving about in confusion in the rain and mud – then at Choe.

'Choe, that's where we . . .'

He shrugged.

'Don't look at me,' he said. 'I didn't do it.'

'Removal of the drums of uranium 238, used as ballast and for balancing aircraft wingtips, was delayed this morning when AEA inspectors realized they were in a heavily corroded condition.

'A spokesman said the material could have been lying unnoticed since last year. The alarm was raised when a local scrap-metal dealer sold three drums of the waste to a Leeds processing company.'

The picture changed to security fences, falling sleet, articulated lorries reversing carefully through the late-afternoon gloom.

'When the drums were driven through *these gates* an automatic alarm sounded.'

'Jesus, Choe,' I said.

'It wasn't him, either.'

I said, 'But nuclear waste . . .'

He shook his head wearily.

'Where did you think this kind of stuff went?'

'But for God's sake, Choe. Fucking *uranium* – we never dumped anything like that.'

'I think you live on another planet,' he said.

After a moment his expression softened.

'Oh come on,' he encouraged me. 'Eh?'

He said: 'Don't be a prick all your life. Let's do some of this blow.'

'You know what upsets me most?' I asked him later.

'What?'

'You wouldn't remember him in the street,' I said bitterly. 'You just wouldn't remember that fucker's face in the fucking street.'

'Who?'

Two or three days later, I had a card from Isobel. It had been posted in Florida. The picture was an old sepia-tint of the Wright Brothers' first flight. I stared at it. Where you expected brown paper and string, a technology fumbling on the edge of Dada, you saw only hope and energy.

'Wish me luck!' Isobel had written.

As a reprisal, perhaps, I telephoned Christiana Spede.

We met in Upper Street, Islington, outside a jazz café called the Blue Saloon. 'You'll find it easily,' Christiana had assured me. But on that windy autumn night Islington was an empty, Hopper-like vault. Distracted by a handful of people round a table in the brightly lit Pizza Express, I went in the wrong direction. The Blue Saloon turned out to be on the other side of the road, directly across from Angel station. I found Christiana standing underneath its neon sign, her hands cupped round her eyes and her nose pressed to the window. She was wearing a short imitation leopardskin coat and a bright red cloche hat she had made herself. I wondered how long she had been there, peering into the deserted, unlit space.

'Hello,' I said.

'Well, there it is, then,' she said, as if we'd been together all day and this was just part of some discussion we were having. Inside the Blue Saloon, strange, futuristic metal chairs were stacked on the tables. The wind threw a handful of rain against the glass. 'Closed on Mondays', said the sign on the door; and, 'VISA'.

'Do you know,' Christiana said. 'I could have sworn it would be open?'

She looked tired and disappointed. Before leaving the house, she had applied very red lipstick with such a precision edge that by contrast every wrinkle, every slack curve of her face was accentuated. Her eyes were enwebbed, panicky. They were too direct: the eyes of a much younger woman. It was like a cruel lighting effect. Since the break-up with Choe, I realized, none of us had been in touch with her. Quite suddenly, as if the two things were connected, I had a lucid memory of her ten years before, in the Jai Krishna vegetarian restaurant on Stroud Green Road, saying of David Hare (or was it Ian McEwan?), 'He couldn't sell bananas to a monkey.' Until now I hadn't realized how fragile these kinds of pronouncements – less provocative than nervous, issued out of some passing irritability and retracted almost at once – had always made her seem.

I hugged her. Her hair smelt faintly of Neutralia shampoo.

'Come on. Let's go to Gill Wing's instead.'

'That would be nice,' she said.

Gill Wing's: flimsy petrol-blue menus, deco lights and marble-topped tables. It was a slow night. Towards the back of the room sat a couple enjoying a quiet, lethal argument over the remains of foie de veau aux anchois. 'It's not a matter of that, David,' the woman said. 'It's a matter of you fucking her on my sofa.' David, a frail, boyish-looking man of about thirty-five wearing a denim shirt under his new Gap jacket, looked bemused. 'The thing is, you never fucked *me* on that sofa, David. How do you think that makes me feel?' David shook his head. He didn't know what to think, he said. The rest of the clientele were pretending not to listen, reading that morning's *Independent*, accumulating empty cups and glasses, staring out of the window at the Hen and Chickens Theatre Bar across the road. If Upper Street had been quiet, Highbury Corner was like a grave. I would have preferred the Pizza Express, with its cheerful garlicky steam.

Christiana sat down at one of the tables near the bar. She undid the fake leopardskin coat, but kept it on. Under it she was wearing a black polo-neck top. 'Every time someone opens the door here you freeze,' she complained. She sighed, 'I don't think I'll eat anything. I don't feel hungry, do you?' She lit a cigarette.

'So,' I said. 'What have you been up to?'

She stared at me.

'What,' she said. 'Since nineteen eighty-four, you mean?'

I began to feel like David.

'I'm sorry,' she said. She reached across the table and took one of my hands between both of hers. 'China, I honestly didn't mean it to sound like that.'

I said: 'Tell me anyway.'

'Where would I start?' She blew smoke over the wine list, narrowed her eyes at something there, laughed suddenly. 'You must have been surprised when I turned up with Choe after all those years.' I couldn't think of anything to say. She shrugged. 'Or maybe you weren't.' She stubbed her cigarette out half smoked. 'Christ, China, you're hard work.' And then when, unnerved by her impatience, I still didn't reply: 'Perhaps I will eat something.'

After sausage and lentils and two or three glasses of Château Laurens, she cheered up briefly.

'I bet you didn't know I had a child.'

'Never.'

She laughed.

'Well, I did. She's eight, and her name is Vita.'

'I don't believe you.'

'She's all right, Vita is. She'll be OK.'

Vita had been born on a beach in Portugal, at six o'clock in the morning. 'She came a month early. I was performing out there. Sleeping on the beach.' I tried to imagine Christiana, alone in pale slanting light, simply giving birth there and then on the white Atlantic sand. Of course, she wouldn't have been alone. It was a seductive image all the same, full of the sound of the waves, the power and otherness of Christiana's ideas. I tried to imagine what kind of character a child born like that might have.

'Weren't you frightened?'

'No.' She lit another cigarette. 'Pour me some wine.'

'It must have been hard for you later.'

'Why?'

'To look after a child—'

'"—and have a career?" Is that what you were going to say?' She laughed. 'Jesus, China, that's what people like you always say.' She stared across the bar as if everyone in it was part of a conspiracy.

'It was easy,' she said.

I waited a moment and then, because it seemed a safe enough thing to ask, tried:

'What's she like?'

I meant: How tall is she? I meant: What colour is her hair? I meant: Are her eyes like yours?

I meant, I suppose: Does she look like you?

'Oh, Vita's OK,' said Christiana. 'She lives with her grand-mother. She does well at school. She already reads a lot. She's very independent.' She paused. She sounded almost puzzled.

162

'Vita's OK,' she repeated. 'We went all over Europe together when she was a baby. Prague. Munich. Amsterdam. She was a member of the band. Her father was a man called Gram, who thought he looked like David Bowie. He did look a bit like David Bowie when he was twenty. I still see him occasionally. He never supported her.'

Suddenly she turned her face away from me, and I saw her wipe her eyes.

'Why are you crying?'

'I'm sorry,' she said. 'I miss him.'

'Gram?'

'Oh, for God's sake, China! Are you stupid? Choe. I miss *Choe*.' She pushed back her chair and got to her feet. She pulled her coat together at the front, sniffed, wiped her eyes again. 'Look, China, I think I'll go now.'

'Christiana—'

'I'll buy you a beer, China,' she promised. 'Soon.' She tried to smile. 'Let's find somewhere quiet and really talk. Would you like that? To really talk?' She glanced at me appraisingly. 'You look as if you need to talk,' she said.

I watched her walk away.

I thought: You'd know.

12 · ICARUS FLIGHTS

Christiana ransacked north London for Turkish and Lebanese restaurants. She also dragged me to the Daquise, near South Kensington tube. 'I can't believe you've never *been* here. I can't believe you've never eaten Polish food.' Though she liked Soho she hated almost every restaurant I knew there. 'I'll drink any old muck,' she had once told Isobel over the dinner table. In fact she wouldn't. Without Choe to keep them in check her snobberies were revealed to be florid, interwoven, less inverted than reversible. She would have coffee at Pâtisserie Valerie, but not Maison Bertaux. She would go anywhere that served café latte, but edge away from me if I ordered hot chocolate and Captain Morgan rum. She really hated L'Escargot. One evening, after I had suggested Kentucky Fried Chicken as a compromise between Brick Lane and the Soho Brasserie, she said, 'We could go home and *cook*. Wouldn't you like that, China?' And then, as if making a remarkable new discovery: 'After all, it's probably cheaper than eating out.'

She lived on a curious side street in Chalk Farm. One side of it was very middle class, with flowering cherry trees, newly painted iron railings, resident parking. The other backed on to railway yards, and every other basement was boarded up. During the fifties Christiana's house had been split into two self-contained maisonettes which she had bought at auction at the height of the Thatcher boom, intending to knock them back into a single dwelling. 'Somehow it never got done. I never had the money. Mind you, I've got two of everything.' She had – although she only ever used one of each. Kitchens, lavatories, showers: all in an engaging state of disrepair. She would eye them morosely and say, 'Oh well, at least the mortgage is almost paid off.'

'Then why don't you borrow the conversion money against your equity?' I suggested.

'Oh God, don't talk about it. Put some music on instead.'

Christiana liked a lot of torch singers I had never heard of. She liked Gavin Bryars. At first I thought we had Tom Waits in common, but she only really liked *Frank's Wild Years*. If I played an old Iggy Pop track, she would always ask, 'Can you remember where you were and what you were doing when you first heard this?' She liked Laurie Anderson. Sometimes, especially on Saturday evenings, I found myself staring out at the railway yards wishing I could listen to Bryan Adams.

After we had eaten, we talked. I talked about Isobel. Christiana talked about anything that came into her head. In practice this meant that we talked about sex.

'Isobel and me . . .' I might begin, and then be unable to continue. 'I don't know how to say it.'

'For God's sake, China.'

'Things were so physical between us.'

'Of course they were. At the beginning you can't stop fucking one another, can you? It's just fuck, fuck, fuck.'

She looked thoughtful, then laughed.

'Vita's father and I found things in the bed.'

'Pardon?'

'Well, strictly, it wasn't a bed the first time, it was the toilet on an Intercity 125. Afterwards I found a perfect little wood anemone on the seat. The first time we actually slept together, a piece of straw turned up in the bed. It hadn't been there before.' She described Gram doing 'this really brilliant awed whisper', his eyes wide and naive: '"Did we *make* that?"' (Mimicking him, her own eyes widened, sly, innocent and self-conscious, and she looked about five years old.) Two days later it was half a tomato. 'He ate it,' she said, 'without a thought.' She stared into space, smiling all over again at Gram and herself, kneeling naked on the bed in some fleapit hotel in Amsterdam or Cracow, laughing over the things they had fucked into existence: a beer-bottle top, two strands of coloured wool, a small apple with woody, very sweet flesh. All her male lovers had had short names, like the names people give sheepdogs: Al, Bill, Ed. From their photographs they looked like big, dependable men, but none of them had been, much. 'Oh, Gram was a bastard. But something always caught fire when we were together. Life was never dull with Gram—'

'I know what you mean,' I began to say.

'— and then suddenly one day we went to Brighton, and nothing happened. I spent the entire afternoon remembering other times we'd been there.'

Looking east towards the town from Palace Pier, she had remembered how it floated between grey sea and sky a deep stratospheric blue, between each side of the century, real gold, buildings biscuit and cream, suspended there in the horizontal sunlight which also illuminated the seaward side of the waves before they fell and broke on the beach. She had remembered Gram for some reason shouting gleefully, 'No, it goes up your leg. Sea air is well known for going up your trouser leg.' But this time nothing like that had happened. They had walked about all afternoon. They had visited every antique shop in the Lanes. They had played an electronic motorcycle game on the pier, then hung over the railings, discovering in the low muddy swell by the stanchions two frozen-looking surfers in wetsuits. 'We caught the six o'clock train home. It was such a shock to me. Wherever we'd gone previously, something had happened to us. It was as if the very fact of us had been enough to generate a good time. Do you know what I mean? I was really quite shocked when I realized we were bored.'

'Mm,' I said.

'I've always blamed Brighton.'

'You can't tar a place with what happened there,' I thought of saying; and then, remembering how much I hated west London, went on instead, 'I didn't mean just the beginnings of things. It never went away for Isobel and me.'

'I don't think I loved him anyway,' said Christiana. 'And he certainly—'

She stopped and looked hard at me.

'It goes away for everyone, China,' she said. 'The only good luck you can have is that it goes away for both of you at the same time.' She contemplated that: shuddered. 'Relationships are so strategic. They come down to what you can offer one another.'

I looked at her.

'You don't believe that for a moment.'

'I do.'

'What about Choe?' I said.

She blinked and looked away.

'Perhaps you're right,' I said.

'No,' she said.

But perhaps she was.

Inevitably we tried to become lovers. It wasn't very successful at first. We were all arms and legs. The angles were wrong. I felt as if I might hurt her, and sometimes I had no idea what she wanted.

She said: 'Sex is very *phallocentric* for you, isn't it?'

She said: 'Is this what Isobel liked?'

She said in an amazed voice: 'You don't know my body. You don't know my body.'

'Christiana, how could I?'

But I loved her little bedroom, with its off-white walls, pale blue cupboards and single shelf of books above the narrow single bed. I loved that it had no curtains, just a raffia blind she never drew, so that all night the strange metallic halogen light from the railway yards hardened her thin, strong swimmer's body until it looked like enamel. And in the end we did get it to work, and she whispered, 'China, what are you *doing* to me?' and, 'Oh yes, oh, China, oh yes, very good, very good.' And then – to herself, but almost as if to some third party in our dark, warm transaction – 'I want to come, oh, I want so much to come.'

Except each other, we never found anything in the bed afterwards. Instead I lay tracing with the tips of my fingers the curious, raised web of scars beneath her tiny breasts, where, she told me eventually, her ribs had been laid open again and again for heart surgery.

'I was born with valve stenosis.'

At ten years old she had been admitted to hospital and offered a choice. They could replace the bad valve with an artificial one, in which case she would have to take anti-coagulants for the rest of her life. Or she could have the appropriate valve from a pig's heart. Her parents had helped her choose the latter, advising, 'It does seem more natural, dear,' only to discover that a pig's heart lasts exactly the lifetime of a pig. 'Every eight years the new valve dies and has to be replaced.' From that moment she had felt betrayed: by her mother and father, by the doctors, by her own body. Thirty years later, her sense of continuity was deeply undercut. She could be as pragmatic about this as about everything else that had happened to her, shrug and repeat, 'No expectations, no regrets.' But her heart had aged her – the anxiety, the drugs, each bout of surgery wearing her away – and sometimes she would stare at the railway lines and admit, 'It tires me out, China. It's tired me out.'

I wasn't sure what to do for her at moments like that. She didn't want comfort. I tried silence, but she didn't want that, either. In the end I stroked her scars very lightly one night and said:

'Wasn't that a bit politically difficult for you? A pig's heart?'

'China, you fool.'

She took my hand in her own and moved it down.

'I love the way you touch me,' she said. 'But there's no need to be so gentle.'

The sun shone through Christiana's kitchen window for about an hour every morning. Then it moved behind a point block until noon, when a few pale, oblique rays fell across the desk in the corner of the front room, illuminating a glass jar full of pens. That was usually the last of it until the next day. But sometimes the sunset would be reflected into the room for a minute or two by a window across the road. A ray of light fell across the empty living room on to the rosewood piano she never played – or, in the bedroom, across a pile of plain white underwear – and I shivered with the strangeness of her, the austerity of her life, her house, her furniture, both actual and emotional. In that light, even her books seemed strange. I would browse the shelves and wonder how she could reconcile Julia Kristeva with Alan Garner, or who had given her *The Earth Wire* by Joel Lane. She would be saying:

'The whole of the fifties looked like a caravan site in the rain. It looked like a bungalow on the Welsh coast.'

Or: 'Cross-Channel ferries. Don't tell me. I get sick on a flannel.'

She had the untidiness of some small animal trying and failing to make a nest. A litter of unpaid credit-card bills and music cassettes (some with the tape spilling out of them) had to be cleared off the table in the evening before we could eat. An eczema of dried soapsuds had to be wiped off the tiles behind the bathroom sink before I could wash. She was always trying to mend a broken cup with Pritt paper glue. Her kitchen smelt. A draught was enough to clear it. But as soon as the breeze dropped, there it was again, pervasive, intricate and hard to forget. Perhaps it had always been there. Costa Rica coffee grounds, the water in which pasta had been cooked, clarified butter: the primordial smell of human habitation in the London Basin.

One afternoon, in the middle of some argument I forget, she looked out of the window and said:

'The dead never answer you back.'

Christiana drove around in a down-at-heel old Citroën BX Safari. It was silver. The hydraulics leaked, and she had hacked off one of its wing mirrors and part of a plastic bumper during some disagreement with a delivery van double-parked outside a deli in Camden. I always knew when she had been out to buy groceries. The BX would be parked outside the house, one wheel up on the pavement and its lights on at two in the afternoon. She would take the shopping out of the car and then leave it in the hall, and move it item by item across the next day or so into the kitchen. A pile of vegetables would diminish by two aubergines and some sweet potatoes: the rest would remain for several hours before she went back to worry at it again. 'Don't go near that stuff, China,' she would warn me. She had forbidden me to cook the day she caught me measuring ingredients. Also, I had admitted that I shopped at Sainsbury's and had no idea how to add the water to an authentic paella.

One Friday evening, with the last of the rush-hour traffic growling up the wet hill outside towards Hampstead, and a thin cold rain in the air, I arrived to find her sitting on the hall carpet, crying silently. She was surrounded by half a dozen grocery bags and there was a brown envelope in her lap.

'Christiana!'

I took the envelope from her. She had pulled it raggedly open with her hands and then lost whatever was inside. I put my arms round her and tried to get her to her feet but she resisted.

'Christiana. What's the matter?'

She gave me a dull look.

'Tests,' she said. 'I have to go in for tests.' She pushed me away and struggled upright. 'Sorry,' she said. 'Nothing's broken.' She sat down again and moved the grocery bags about. 'I don't think I broke anything.'

'Oh, Christiana.'

'It was due a month ago, but I put it off.'

She wiped her eyes and offered me a bottle.

'Australian chardonnay,' she said. 'They describe it as "broad-shouldered". Can you believe that?' Broad-shouldered? That means it tastes like corned beef.'

'At least you won't need any dinner.'

I took the bottle off her and opened it in the kitchen and filled the two biggest glasses I could find. Then I went back into the hall and sat down next to her. The light thinned, the traffic quietened. Up and down the road people were turning on their televisions to get the news; they were making supper. Soon I could smell London Basin cuisine: frozen lasagne, microwaved chilli, the odd chicken casserole. 'I'm starving,' Christiana admitted, but she made no move to get up. We drank. We talked. 'Ever had Pineau des Charentes?' she asked. 'Unfermented grape juice with brandy, about seventeen per cent proof.' She stared into her glass. 'Actually, this stuff isn't bad.' Every time she fell silent, I asked her something else about herself. One of the things I asked her was, 'What did you do all those years we weren't speaking?'

'Oh, this and that,' she said.

She said: 'You know most of it already.' She gave me a little wry grin. 'I once spent a year fucking anyone who answered an advert in the back of *Time Out*. I was quite bi by then.'

'Bye bye then,' I said.

'Have you ever done anything like that?'

'What?' I said. 'Been bi?'

'No, you fool: put an ad in the back of *Time Out*.'

'I don't think I have.'

'Don't bother. You get this phone call, you go all the way to bloody Waterman's Arts Centre, and your date's a bloke wearing a lovat safari waistcoat with a copy of *Viz* sticking out of one pocket. He asks you if you want the couscous or the vegetarian goulash. Everyone with any youth or energy left is in the bar getting pissed, and they look at you as if you're dead, if they look at you at all, and the play is something by Eugene O'Neill.'

'I thought you liked couscous.'

'They drink a lot of Pineau des Charentes in East Sheen, China,' she said. 'I'm afraid you're grown up enough to know that now.'

'*Miaow.*'

Later, she said:

'For a while I thought Vita would be enough.'

'And isn't she?'

'Of course she is.'

'Well then, why—'

She made a little impatient gesture of the head, pursed her lips. 'Vita's going to be OK. It's not that,' she said. 'It's just ... Well, look, she's got the most beautiful voice, but she won't sing. She's got a fantastic eye and a natural hand, but she won't draw. I've tried everything.'

'She's only eight,' I pointed out. 'It's a bit early for St Martin's.'

'I know,' said Christiana.

'What does she want to do?'

'At the moment she wants to be a psychologist.'

'*What?*'

Soon we had finished the chardonnay, and I had been to the kitchen to open another bottle, and it was eleven o'clock and quite dark in the hall. After a long silence Christiana said:

'I loved the band most of all. I loved every show we ever did. We had a sixteen-wheel truck just for the lights and things. We went all over Europe and America. Vita came with us and jumped about in the audience every night. China,' she said, 'I once drove a sixteen-wheel truck into Prague at five o'clock in the morning. Look at me now.'

'You're an extraordinary person,' I said.

She sniffed and wiped her eyes.

'I know,' she said. 'I *know*. But what does that matter, when you can't have what you want?'

'Christiana, Christiana.'

'I've hardly been out of the house since he left,' she said suddenly. 'I loved him, even when he wasn't kind to me. Is that awful?' She began to cry in earnest. 'Isn't that awful? I've hardly been out. China,' she said: 'What if I'm agoraphobic?'

I held her hand and looked down at the scattered shopping. I thought of all the Turkish restaurants she had taken me to in Stoke Newington.

'I don't think you're agoraphobic, love,' I said. 'Honestly.'

She shivered.

She said: 'I was ten years old when they landed me with this. *Ten years old.*' She said: 'China, I'm cold sitting on the floor here.'

'Well let's get up then.'

'China, will you come with me to the hospital tomorrow?'

I don't believe she had ever asked anyone that before.

'Of course I will,' I said.

Understaffed and underfinanced, obscured by scaffolding, King's College Hospital expands just too slowly to detect with the naked eye along the upper slope of Denmark Hill, SE5. What funds there are have been assigned at random, so that while the School of Medicine and Dentistry is quite new, outpatients of the Maudsley drug dependency unit find themselves ringing the bell of a tired Edwardian house. None of the more modern buildings match. (Few of them even give the feel of structures finished and purposive.) The older ones seem simply unwelcoming and dull. A place with no firm boundaries, always petering out into its surroundings or into rows of Portakabins, King's has less an architecture than an oncology. The bulk of this tumour issued from the silver trowel of Edward the Seventh some time before the First World War. It is fibrous and deepseated. Corridors a stale cream colour darken to tobacco as you move inwards. There are cobwebs soft with dirt in the ceiling corners. The cracked lavatory tiles smell like the urinals of some blackened northern town four decades ago. Nothing is clean. You can't find your way. The signs at stairways and junctions use a different descriptive system to the one on your appointment form. Ask directions: heavy-duty masonry drills fill the corridors with a continual resonant grinding noise which prevents you from hearing the answer. In the end, the department you want turns out to be a cul-de-sac in which three old people wait uncertainly on tubular chairs: a cubicle behind a curtain where a few shelves curve under the weight of concertina files: a tired-looking woman who says patiently, 'Take off your jean jacket, please,' and weighs you on the digital electronic scale. At night, an occasional bus grinds past. Drunks and madmen stagger up the long incline from Camberwell Green, hoping to have A & E stitch up wounds like lips. 'I was pushed,' they claim, and laugh softly. Later they will get lost and fall down again among the builders' yellow waste chutes and stacks of Hi-Seven breeze blocks. From its vantage point on Champion Park, the barracks of the Salvation Army Officers' training school – its own walls homogenous and four-square, thick with charity, thick with good, honest funding – looks down sardonically. From up there the street seems lunar and empty, the hospital abandoned forever. But by nine next morning the local traffic is nose-to-tail again, and you can't park a car within half a mile of the Bessemer Road entrance.

'"The Changing Shape of Hospital Care,"' quoted Christiana. 'Jesus.'

We were in and out of King's for a fortnight. They lost her notes between visits. At reception they stared at her as if they had never dealt with her before. They could find nothing. Records could find nothing. The cardiac clinic was in chaos anyway – a new system, all three specialists on leave, no direction home. It was a ship without a rudder. No one could find anything this morning. 'I was here the day before yesterday,' Christiana reminded them. 'No one could find anything then, either.' She was able to point out her name on a sheet of computer output in plain view on the reception desk.

'Oh yes,' said the receptionist dismissively, 'you're on the com*pew*ter.'

'I'm going to sit here all morning,' Christiana warned her. 'If I have to.'

'You can go to radiology straight away.'

By that time it was half-past eleven. The clock in the radiology waiting room said twenty to eight. 'Ah yes, Miss Spede,' the radiology co-ordinator welcomed us. She was a cheerful woman with curly grey hair and spectacles. 'They've just rung up about you.'

'The appointment was made a week ago,' Christiana said, and turned away as rudely as she could. Later, in the waiting area, she told me: 'Last week this room was ECG reception.'

She looked around bleakly. 'It still is, for all I know.'

'Miss Spede? Miss Spede?'

'What?'

Sometimes Christiana told me:

'I don't want you with me today.'

'Will you be all right?'

'Yes.'

But she would be trembling when she returned at four in the afternoon. She wanted to be held, although she didn't know how to ask for that and could only stand awkwardly in the hall a little too far in front of me, still in her soaking wet coat, waiting until I saw what was needed.

While I sat on a tubular chair in cardiac, they put her into a copious white smock stencilled with the warning 'CAMBERWELL HEALTH AUTHORITY HOSPITAL PROPERTY'. It was designed to hang open at the back. Wearing it made her feel vulnerable and silly at the same time, the way she had often felt as a child. It was easy to imagine her wandering from corridor to corridor in this garment, tired and misdirected; returning every so often to the waiting area full of a vague anger she no longer knew what to do with. In fact she bore everything with a kind of blunt passiveness she didn't expect to share. She had been through it so many times before: and anyway was caught up, distant, filled with anxiety. If I spoke, she frowned and looked at me for a moment as if I were some hospital stranger: just someone else she didn't know.

'Pardon?'

'I said: Does it hurt?'

She shook her head.

'I just feel odd,' she said vaguely. 'You know? It's just this odd feeling.'

Suddenly her eyes focused and she looked round. In the row of chairs facing us, a baby was asleep on its back across its mother's knees, hands held in little lax fists each side of its head. On the wall above were pinned some curled leaflets and a sign saying, 'NHS prescriptions: some people get them free. Can you? If not, you could still save money with a season ticket.'

'A season ticket to hospital,' I said.

Christiana whispered. 'I hate this so, I really do.'

Outside in Bessemer Road it was raining heavily.

I looked at my watch.

'Christiana?'

'China, I—'

'Come and sit down.'

'I'm all right. What did you do today?'

'Not much.'

'China, wouldn't it be good if we could have a proper coal fire in here?

'Wouldn't you like that?

'A proper coal fire, and sleep in front of it together?'

One day she came back and said:

'Those fucking bastards in haematology. I'm not going again.'

She sniffed and wiped her nose with her hand.

'Really, China, I'm not going back this time. You know?'

I sat her down and gave her a cup of tea.

'It's Earl Grey,' I said. 'Look: we could have this done privately. I've still got BUPA, PPA, a whole bunch of stuff like that. I know it's bad politics, but . . .'

She stared at me.

'Just listen to yourself, China,' she said bitterly. 'Just fucking listen to yourself. How would that help anyone? How would that help the poor old fucker I saw this morning?'

'I don't know,' I said. 'Because I wasn't there.' I said: 'Drink your tea.'

She smiled suddenly.

'And he was such a nice old man. *Very* middle class, in a proper tweed jacket and polished brown shoes. They were old shoes, but you could see your face in them.' (Oh yes, I caught myself thinking: just the sort of old man you love, Christiana.) 'He was reading *Aspects of Antiquity* in this faded old Pelican edition.'

She burst into tears again.

'I'd rather die, China. I would.'

'What is it, Christiana?'

'He didn't hear his *name*.'

And that was all I could get out of her. The more I tried to understand what had happened in the open-plan haematology department – where two women take your sample in the waiting area itself, with all the other patients watching – the more she repeated: 'He just didn't hear his name, that's all. They said his name as if it was part of a conversation they were having. Oh, China, that poor old man.' Her anxieties had overwhelmed her at last. Whatever humiliation the old man had suffered was her own humiliation; her own sense of worthlessness in the face of King's.

'I'm not sure what you're trying to tell me,' I said. 'Won't you think about BUPA?'

'I'm not trying to fucking tell you anything!' she shouted. Then she took my hand and laid her cheek against it. 'Thank you for offering, anyway,' she said. 'You will come in with me, won't you?'

I didn't spend all my time at Chalk Farm. I wasn't comfortable there. If I found Christiana too easily irritated, I knew I was often too dull for her. Anyway, she hated to have the M3 parked outside her house. To avoid conflict, I would return to Choe's place in Haringey every two or three days, and wait until she phoned me.

'Why haven't you been to see me?'

'Because you said my car looked like a cheap stereo set.'

Choe was rarely at home. In his absence everything covered itself further with dust: the posters featuring Adjani and Huppert, Béatrice Dalle and Nathalie Baye, in films five or ten years dead – *L'Eté Meurtrier, Les Soeurs Brontë, 37C Le Matin*; the CDs of Lori Carson and the Golden Palominos stacked on the old-fashioned sideboard after being played once – 'Fucking brilliant,' Choe would say, but he soon lost interest; the piles of specialist magazines, *Photo, Vox, Motorcycle News*, subsiding day by day into yellowing fans on the carpet. Dust made rolls and mats beneath the sofa. In the kitchen there was dust thick enough to unpeel from the half-empty yoghurt cartons and unanswered correspondence.

The third of November I spent the evening watching TV. Some story of love and transfiguration, cropped into the wrong proportions for the small screen. Christiana's operation was due at the end of the week. Outside, Haringey stretched away, an endless sprawl of minicab firms, deserted bakeries, social clubs. Turn the TV off and you could hear the young Turkish Cypriots prowling Green Lanes in their Hartge BMWs and Cosworth-engined Mercedes 190s. Turn it back on and the film unrolled, passages of guilt with lost edges, photographed in white and blue light. At about half-past eleven the phone rang.

I picked it up. 'Hello?'

It was Isobel Avens.

13 · MAKEOVER

'Oh China,' she said.

I knew what had happened.

I said: 'Can you drive?'

'No,' she said.

I looked at my watch. 'I'll come and fetch you.'

'You can't,' she said. 'I'm here. You can't come here.'

I said: 'Be outside, love. Just try and get yourself downstairs. Be outside and I'll pick you up on the pavement there.'

There was silence.

'Can you do that?'

'Yes,' she said.

Oh China. The first two days she wouldn't get much further than that.

'Don't try to talk,' I advised.

London was as quiet as a nursing-home corridor. I turned up the car stereo. Tom Waits, 'Downtown Train'. Music stuffed with sentiments you recognize but daren't admit to yourself. I let the M3 slip down Green Lanes, through Camden into the centre; then west. I was pushing the odd traffic light at orange, clipping the apex off a safe bend here and there. I told myself I wasn't going to get killed for her. What I meant was that if I did she would have no one left. Traffic on the Embankment is light at that time of night. I went through it in sixth gear at eight thousand revs, nosing down fairly heavily on the brakes at Chelsea Wharf to get round into Gunter Grove. People were careful to let me through. By half-past twelve I was on Queensborough Road, where I found her standing very straight in the mercury light outside Alexander's building, the jacket of a Karl Lagerfeld suit thrown across her shoulders and one piece of expensive leather luggage at her feet. She bent into the car. Her face was white and exhausted and her breath stank. The way Alexander had dumped her was as cruel as everything else he did. She had flown back steerage from the Miami clinic, reeling from jet lag, expecting to fall into his arms and be loved and comforted. He had told her, 'As a doctor I don't think I can do any more for you.' The ground hadn't just shifted on her: it was out from under her feet. Suddenly she was only his patient again. In the metallic glare of the street lamps, I noticed a discoloration around her lips and gums. I switched on the M3's interior light and saw it was blood, sores.

'It's just a virus,' she said. 'Just a side-effect.'

She put her arms around me and sobbed.

'Oh, China, China.'

It isn't that she wanted me; only that she had no one else. Yet every time I smelt her body in the closed car my heart lurched. Alexander had made everything fucked up and eerie and it would be that way forever.

I said: 'I'll take you home.'

'Will you stay?'

'What else?'

The next morning I phoned Choe Ashton.

'Choe, it's Mick.'

'Yes.'

'I won't be at the flat for a bit.'

'Good.'

'Choe, she's back. Isobel's back.'

There was a silence.

'Choe, she's really fucked over. She needs help.'

'It's your life.'

'Choe?'

'Take care of yourself, Mick. What can I say?'

'Nothing. I'll fetch my stuff.'

'OK. See you.'

*

181

The worst thing you can do at the beginning of something fragile is to say what it is. The night I drove her back from Queensborough Road to the little house in the gentrified East End, things were very simple. For forty-eight hours all she would do was wail and sob and throw up on me. She refused to eat, she couldn't bear to sleep. If she dropped off for ten minutes, she would wake silent for the instant it took her to remember what had happened. Then this appalling dull asthmatic noise would come out of her – 'zhhh, zhhh, zhhh', somewhere between retching and whining – as she tried to suppress the memory, and wake me up, and sob, all at the same time.

I was always awake anyway.

'Hush now, it wears off. I know.'

I knew because I had been there too.

'China, I'm so sorry.'

'Hush. Don't be sorry. Get better.'

'I'm so sorry if I ever made you feel like this.'

I wiped her nose.

'Hush.'

How much had Alexander promised her? How much had she expected from the Miami treatments? All I knew was that she had flown out obsessed and returned half dead. Whatever they had tried to do to her, it hadn't worked. I had seen her last as Isobel – a bit thinner than the Isobel I loved, but Isobel none the less. Two months later, here she was: anorexic, covered in sores and open to every infection in London. I unpacked her luggage: it rustled with drugs in foil, state-of-the-art antibiotics, bizarre steroids with incomprehensible names. In the days that followed she tired easily and moved like someone in a dream. She didn't bother to dress. She walked bent forward a little from the waist, clasping her hands across her upper abdomen. She was cautious with herself, but she couldn't rest. Instead she shuffled endlessly between the bed to the window (out of which, confused, she sometimes called the name of Brian Alexander's pet cat) and the wardrobe, where she went perplexedly through the clothes she had loved before she left. I would find her stalled out on the stairs, too exhausted to go up or down. I would wake in the night to find her staring into the tall bathroom mirror like a teenage girl, half afraid, half asleep, half expectant. Can three halves make anything? Her eyes were huge with need and wonder. When she saw me looking at her over her own shoulder, her skinny hands flew together to cover the pubic mound of her image in the glass.

She didn't offer to tell me what Alexander had promised her, and I never asked. I was too shy, too angry, too jealous. Anyway, to ask would have meant using his name, and I wouldn't willingly have done that then. All I could do was look after her and hope she got well. That part was easy. I could dress her ulcerated lips and watch for whatever else might happen. I could hold her in my arms all night and tell lies and believe I was only there for her. But after a day or two she asked me, 'Will you live here again, China?'

'You know it's all I want,' I said.

She warned: 'I'm not promising anything.'

'I don't want you to,' I said.

I said: 'I just want you to need me for something.'

'Choe?'

'Yes.'

'Choe, it's Mick.'

'I didn't think it was the Queen of Sheba.'

'What?'

'My old dear used to say that: "I didn't think it was the Queen of Sheba".'

'Choe, she wants me to move back in with her.'

'Who? My old dear?'

'For fuck's sake, Choe. Isobel.'

'Ah, the Queen of Sheba. Ask yourself what she wants, Mick.'

'I don't think she knows what she wants.'

'I know what she's got.'

183

'Whatever it is, I just want her to need me for something.'

'She's got you by the cock.'

'I can't seem to care, Choe.'

'She always has had.'

'Choe, I just want to look after her.'

'Wrong.'

I was sick of Choe. America had worn off, and he was bored. I knew the signs. A general failure of his obsessions to satisfy him. Provocative behaviour in pubs. Loud music, bottled lagers, a Silver Palm Leaf pipe like a credit card designed by NASA. He grew sentimental and was attracted impulsively to animals and children encountered in the street, favouring bull terriers, foreign pedigree cats, and – especially – any bright three- or four-year-old girl turned out in pastiched adult clothes. 'Christ, I'm fucking broody at the moment. Look at that little sod. Don't you think she's perfect?' New toys appeared in the Haringey maisonette: a Power Mac 8100; B&W MATRIX 801 speakers, with kevlar cones; two silvertip burmilla kittens, whose perpetually amazed green eyes seemed the size of saucers. On the concrete hard-standing outside, the Honda CBR had been replaced by a Lotus Super 7. To start with it was, 'See this, Mick? Eighty mile an hour: not fast. But look at things this way: *it'll get there from a standing start in four seconds*. It's a fucking slingshot.' Two weeks later he was passing it in the morning without a backwards glance. Sticking his head out of my car as he thugged it through midday traffic, he would call, 'Shit bike, mate!' to anyone who cycled past on less than a Klein.

As soon as he got back from New York he had been at pains to tell me:

'All that Jumble Wood stuff: I made it up. I bet you believed me, though, didn't you?'

By then, of course, I hardly cared.

'Perhaps I did, Choe,' I said.

For no reason at all I had a sudden memory of Isobel saying

in a tired voice over the dinner table, 'Eat it then, Choe. Eat the custard.' Then a flash of Jumble Wood – the secluded little valley itself, with its sun-warmed oak and mountain ash – along with which came a strong sense of the outside world as an intimate place closed like a hand around human affairs in some way none of us could understand.

'Perhaps I did,' I repeated.

But Choe wasn't listening.

'I bet you did, whatever you say. Well, I only told you that to get you going, you know.'

I thought of the wood avens, flowering in the sun. I thought: what if the world is enchanted by us, and not the other way round?

Choe?'

'It's Mick, right?'

'Choe, I'm sick of you.'

That whole November we both needed taking care of, Isobel and me. We were as awkward as children. We didn't quite know what to say. We didn't quite know what to do with one another. We could see it would take time and patience. We shared the bed rather shyly, and showed one another quite ordinary things as gifts.

'Look.'

Sunshine fell across the breakfast table, on to lilies and pink napery. (I am not making this up.)

'Look.'

A grey cat nosed out of a doorway in London, E3.

'Did you have a nice weekend?'

'It was a lovely weekend. Lovely.'

'Look.'

Canary Wharf, shining in the oblique evening light.

In our earliest days together, while she was still working at the aerodrome, I had watched her move about a room with almost uncontainable delight. I had stayed awake while she slept, so that I could prop myself up on one elbow and look at her and shiver with happiness. Now when I watched, it was with fear. For her. For both of us. She was so thin; and hot as a child with fever. When I fucked her she was like a bundle of hot wires. I was like a boy. I trembled and caught my breath when I felt with my fingertips the damp feathery lips of her cunt, but I was too aware of the dangers to be carried away. I didn't dare let her see how much this meant to me. Neither of us knew what to want of the other any more. We had forgotten one another's rhythms. In addition she was remembering someone else's: it was Alexander who had constructed for me this bundle of hot, thin, hollow bones, wrapped round me in the night by desires and demands I didn't yet know how to fulfil. Before the Miami débâcle she had loved me to watch her as she became aroused. Now she needed to hide, at least for a while. She would pull at my arms and shoulders, shy and desperate at the same time; then, as soon as I understood that she wanted to be fucked, push her face into the side of mine so I couldn't look at her. After a while she would turn on to her side; encourage me to enter from behind; stare away into some distance implied by us, our failures, the dark room. I told myself I didn't care if she was thinking of him. Just so long as she had got this far, which was far enough to begin to be cured in her sex, where he had wounded her as badly as anywhere else. I told myself I couldn't heal her there, only allow her to use me to heal herself.

At the start of something so fragile the worst mistake you can make is to say what you hope. But inside your heart you can't help speaking, and by that speech you have already blown it.

Her dreams were uneasy. To begin with she could hardly recall them. We would wake at three in the morning to the bedclothes flung about, and find both water and medication knocked off the little African table at her side of the bed. A quiet voice had asked

her: *Why do we plant the crocuses deeper than the daffodils?* She had
woken up sweating.

'China.'

'What?'

'China, I had a dream. You and I were in a room with bare
floorboards . . .'

'Then what?'

'I don't remember.'

'Go back to sleep, Isobel.'

'No. China . . .'

'What?'

'China, you and I were in a room, and Brian was in there with
us.'

'Fuck off, Isobel.'

'No! China!'

She took my head in her hands and made me face her. She put
kisses on my mouth, on my eyes.

'China, listen, please listen. The three of us were in a room . . .'

The three of us were in a room: the two of us were fucking
her.

'I was wetter than I'd ever been.'

'Isobel, I can't deal with this.'

'No, China, please. I lay down on you and put you in me. I
looked you in the eyes. I was so wet. Then Brian knelt over us
both and fucked me from behind. China, he was so careful. We
loved each other, all of us. We were fucking in a room, and Brian
was pulling something out of my back. Whatever it was got
longer and longer. It wasn't at all painful, but I could feel it
coming out through my skin, exactly the way it feels when you
pull a hair out of your mouth. China, it was wings. When I saw
them, I just came and came.'

'China, fuck me now.'

'No, Isobel.'

'China China China.'

'Isobel, no.'

And then, to listen to her, she was a child again, and it was Christmas; and instead of her father – who was to have travelled from St Ives by train – she found a man in a wheelchair waiting for her outside the sugary-pink 'Beauty Heaven' display at Hamley's in Regent Street, where pre-pubescent manikins attended to one another's hair in a salon with walls apparently of Bacofoil. His expression was dull and puzzled as he searched the lunchtime crowds for her face. His ankles were crossed, knees apart – a posture hieratic or apathetic. An artificial hand rested on his right thigh.

'China, he was like a gate-keeper.'

Why do we plant the crocuses deeper than the daffodils?
So they won't come up and trouble our dreams.

After about a week, emerging from somewhere too deep inside her to guess at, illness took a more determined hold. To the sore throats, stomach cramps and short-lived rashes we already knew were added bouts of vomiting and diarrhoea. She could keep nothing down but mineral water. Viruses ripped through her like supernatural weather – subtropical weather, Miami weather – three distinct, low-key infections in one day, cyclical highs and lows presenting symptons from inflamed nasal membranes through arthritically swollen joints to a case of vaginal thrush that was gone in an hour. Across one rainy Thursday afternoon, her temperature reached 102, lowed-out at 93 and normalized again before five o'clock. She began to suffer constant dysmenor-rhoea. Her dreams were filled with images of self-scarification, body-horror: and, above all, failed flight. Night after night Isobel soared up from her internal runways. Night after night she smoked across the sky like an Icarus dully unsurprised by failure, to wake intact but sobbing. These flights began, like the dreams of our Stratford days, with a computer screen:

*

'Isobel, wake up.'

'What?'

'Isobel, you're OK. You're OK.'

'China, we were in a room.'

'Let me get you some water.'

'We were in a *room*, China.'

'Isobel—'

'China, I don't *want* any water. We were in a room, and everyone's work was displayed on this huge screen. China, I could see *myself* up there, I could steer myself about . . .'

Suddenly she had learned what she had to know, and she was floating up and flying into the screen to join herself 'up in the air above the world'. At first the sky was crowded with other people, she said. 'But I went swooping past and around and between them.' She let herself tumble, just for the fun of it: she rose and levelled off, her whole body taut and trembling like the fabric of a kite. Her breath went out with a great laugh.

'China, I loved it.'

But at the top of the dream her collarbones cracked suddenly with the weight of the wings. They made exactly the sound a dry stick makes when, kneeling in front of the empty grate in the morning, you break it for kindling. ('Shall I make a fire?' 'Let's have coffee first.') She never felt the pain. There was only that appalling dry domestic crack somewhere not far away from her ear: then she fell, and as she fell a paper fire burst out of her head, a fire of newspaper and sticks to melt the wings – although they continued to move cruelly and rhythmically, levering her clavicle and upper ribs out through the skin. She knew she would never make it back to the ground, which by now looked like a city – or anyway the motherboard of some vast computer – its every parallel avenue shining with silver solder. The ground, the sky and for a moment some place which was neither: it all swung in a delirious arc round her, as if her failure was necessary so that everything else could fly. Eventually, the wings began to lever out her internal organs, which bagged and fluttered in the airstream like dark-coloured washing, like tangled parachutes, making a sad, wet flapping sound. She watched them for a moment and came to the conclusion: The only way to fly is change. 'I need to lose *these* wings.' There was barely a teacup of blood.

During the fevers even her smell changed.

I would wake in the dark with my hackles raised, like a dog which has detected an intruder, to find that I couldn't recognize her. Her smell was different, her body heat was different, everything about her seemed strange. She shook perpetually, and reeked of cinnamon, yeast, water pouring over a weir. For a day I smelt her sex all over the house. Her eyes were huge, and with her face close to mine, and her hands placed on either side of my face so I couldn't look away, she breathed her newness upon me.

'China, I'm going to be sick.'

'Choe.'

'Yes.'

'It's me. Choe, she's no better.'

'Let her go to the doctor.'

'Come on, Choe.'

'Worry about yourself, Mick.'

'If you're the only person who can help someone, they become your responsibility, whether you want it or not.'

'Bollocks.'

'I believe that.'

'You fucking don't. Anyway, listen to this: HOT CARS 24-HOUR MINICAB & COURIER SERVICE. A SAFE AND CARING COMPANY. What do you think?'

'It's nice, Choe.'

'It's shite.'

'Why ask, then?'

'I'm not worried about you. You lost your touch years ago.'

'Thanks, Choe.'

'It's me I'm worried about. HOT CARS? Fucking shite. Shall I tell you why?'

'You might as well.'

'*Because old ladies take taxis too.* HOT CARS. Fucking shite. Still. I've got the office.'

The office turned out to be a narrow storefront on the corner of St Ann's Road and Green Lanes. There was a net curtain up at one window; pelargoniums and spider plants were dying in plastic pots on the windowsill of the other. 'Drivers Wanted.' Some previous tenant had painted the brickwork pink. Above it, an impressive yellow and orange sign announced: 'Domani Children's Wear'.

'They got the apostrophe in the right place,' I said. 'I'm surprised.'

On a desk pushed up against the left-hand window stood two old Akai receivers, the dispatcher's radio and an expensive plastic model of a Ferrari Berlinetta, opened up to show a tiny pristine silver engine. The bulk of the room was occupied by a half-size pool table without cues or balls, and several greasy office chairs had been arranged round the walls. The fax machine whistled, peeped and bustled to itself in a corner under a shelf made of two cheap angle-brackets and a piece of veneered softboard. In summer, air-conditioning would be provided by an electric fan, the wire guard of which was held together with brittle nicotine-coloured twists of Sellotape.

'Look,' urged Choe. 'TV and microwave.' For a moment I found it hard to tell one from the other. 'The microwave's for the drivers,' he explained. While I was trying to think of a suitable reply to that, he said: 'Fucking hell, Mick, you might be a bit more enthusiastic.'

'It's the smell, I think.'

'Awful, isn't it? Let's go out and get a beer.'

A thousand pigeons circled in the big air above the decaying

Coliseum at the junction with St Ann's. We turned on to Green Lanes and bought some pastries at Barnaby's. 'I love this street,' said Choe. 'It's the only place in London where the bakeries *smell of pepper*.' He tugged my sleeve. 'Can you account for that, Mick? I'd say you can't. I'd say you can't account for that.' On the whole, enterprise had made him a little more cheerful. 'I love these fucking Turkish women with the hooked noses, too. Don't you? Thin and nervous and full of themselves. I could eat those fuckers all night.' I wondered if he did.

Later we sat at the dispatch desk. Business was slack. Drivers came in to watch the TV and stayed. They were fattish Greek Cypriot men wearing sweaty short-sleeved white shirts; lean and vicious-looking Ethiopians in tight trousers too short for them, who drove slagged-out Volvos which smelt of cleaning fluid. The TV was black and white and kept skipping channels – as Choe said – off its own bat.

'See that?' he said. 'Christ.'

We were watching ads.

'From Bodyform towels to prawn curry in less than a tenth of a second.'

He appealed to the drivers.

'Can you believe that?'

They stared back at him emptily.

'Sure, Choe,' said one of them at last, pronouncing it as in 'Joe'.

We watched part of *EastEnders*. We watched part of a *Horizon* programme about schizophrenic perception, which led to us having an argument about what Choe called 'community of experience'.

'All that's fucked,' he asserted. 'That's all over now.' He seemed half puzzled, half aggressive. 'There isn't anything like that any more.'

He examined his own hand.

'We all go to a different wedding,' he said.

He laughed.

'You ask me, "Wasn't the bride a piece? Wasn't she a real *piece*?" No point in me answering. I don't even remember who those people are.'

'Choe, I don't know what you're talking about.'

He looked impatient.

'Every fuck you ever had with that tart of yours was separate and perfect. They don't *make* anything, those experiences. And they weren't *shared*. What do you know about what she knows? Fucking nothing.'

He looked up.

'What do you *want* to know? The same.'

Then he said:

'Do you want a job? I've got one if you do.'

He looked across at the drivers.

'None of these fuckers is any good.'

When I got back to Stepney it was late. The house was quiet. Isobel lay face-down, one long leg drawn up, in a bar of moonlight on the thick rose-coloured carpet outside the bedroom. She was naked, very white, weeping tiredly; the skin around her eyes looked bruised and dark. Waking to an empty house, she had thrown up on herself before she could get to the toilet. 'China. Where were you? I'm sorry.' The vomit was clear and almost odourless; but tonight Isobel herself had a faint, tarry, bizarre smell of bitumen and musk, which reminded me of something in childhood. I carried her to the bathroom, ran a lot of warm water into the bath and helped her in. She kept her arms round my neck as she made the awkward step over the side. Her feet slipped. I felt her draw breath nervously. 'Come on now, let go and be washed. Let's make you nice again. It's just one of your bad days. Tomorrow you'll be fine.' I looked down at her in the clear water and heard Choe say, 'That tart of yours,' and suddenly felt unreasonably angry. Her pubis, waxed to an exotic, feathery stripe, looked only vulnerable. There was no more flesh on her for illness to burn off. She seemed too long for the bath, her legs folded awkwardly to one side, her shoulders presented front-on, thin as fishbones, her head turned in profile. Every day she was easier to carry, hotter to the touch. It was as if her fevers were permanent. She was so precious to me. She was so precious.

14 · REAL WINGS

'Mick!'

'That's Choe Ashton, isn't it?'

'Fuck off Mick and listen to this. I've got it. SHOGUN CARS. *Shogun* cars! Ace, eh?'

'That's right through the other side, Choe.'

'Don't be a wanker all your life. I'm getting the sign changed.'

Isobel made progress. The nightmares eased. Her internal weather stabilized. On a good day, the state of her body frightened her less. She examined herself minutely in the mirror each morning when she woke. 'Tell me what I look like, China. No, tell me.' She greeted each new group of sores with a kind of puzzled hope – though she often seemed bemused too, as if she had expected something else. I still couldn't bring myself to ask about Miami: Isobel offered no information. When she talked, she would talk only about the flight home. 'I could see a sunrise over the wing of the airliner, red and gold. I was trying to read a book, but I couldn't stop looking out at this cold wintry sunrise above the clouds. It seemed to last for hours.' She stared at me as if she had just thought of something. 'How could I see a sunrise, China? It was dark when we landed.' Her dreams had always drawn her away from ordinary things. All that November she was trying to get back.

'Do you like me again?' she would ask shyly.

It was hard for her to say what she meant. Being thin was only part of what she had wanted. Standing in front of the mirror in the morning, in the soft, grey slanting light from the bedroom window, dazed and sidetracked by her own narcissism, she could only repeat:

'Do you like me this way?'

Or at night in bed: 'Is it good this way? Is it good? What does it feel like?'

'Isobel . . .'

In the end it was always easier to let her evade the issue.

'I never stopped liking you,' I would lie, and she would reply absently, as if I hadn't spoken:

'Because I want us to like each other again.'

And then add, presenting her back to the mirror and looking at herself over one shoulder:

'I wish I'd had more done. My legs are still too fat.'

If part of her was still trying to fly back from Miami and all Miami entailed, much of the rest was in Hammersmith with Brian Alexander. As November died into the first few cold days of December, I found that increasingly hard to bear. She cried in the night, but no longer woke me up for comfort. Her gaze would come unfocused in the afternoons. Unable to be near her while she pretended to leaf through *Vogue* and *Harper's*, I walked out into the rainy unredeemed streets. Suddenly it was an hour later and I was watching the lights come on in a hardware shop window on Roman Road.

Sometimes it seemed to be going well. I couldn't contain my delight. I got up in the night and thrashed the M3 to Sheffield and back; parked outside the house and slept an hour in the rear seat; crossed the river in the morning to queue for croissants at Ayre's Bakery in Peckham, playing 'Empire Burlesque' so loud that if I touched the windscreen gently I could feel it tremble, much as she used to do, beneath my fingertips.

I was trying to get back, too.

'I'll take you to the theatre,' I said: '*Waiting for Godot*. Do you want to see the fireworks?'

I said: 'I brought you a present . . .'

A Romeo Gigli dress from Browns. Two small stone birds for the garden. Anemones, and a cheap Boots' nail-brush shaped like a pig.

'Don't try to get so close, China,' she said. 'Please.'

I said: 'I just want to be something to you.'

She touched my arm. She said:

'China, it's too soon. We're here together, after all: isn't that enough for now?'

She said:

'And anyway, how could you ever be anything else?'

She said: 'I love you.'

'But you're not in love with me.'

'I told you I couldn't promise you that.'

We were working on the house again. Isobel wanted new floors; she wanted space and light; she wanted *height*, she said – she wanted the loft opened so she could perch up there and look out across Stepney Green towards Limehouse Basin and the Thames. She wanted a Linn proactive stereo system so she could listen to the recent Counting Crows album. One afternoon I was fitting the speaker brackets for that when the Bosch struck rotten brick, its motor racing and throwing out sparks. I looked down and saw damp orange sand pouring out of the drill-holes. Little conical piles of it were building up on the white skirting board.

'Isobel, look.'

'They lived in a sandcastle,' she announced wryly.

'The sea never quite came in . . .'

'. . . But neither did their ship.'

'Oh, it's coming in all right,' I told her. 'Don't you worry about that.'

'It's my turn with the drill now.'

'But you've had it all week.'

'China, give me the drill.'

The way I went to work for Choe was this:

'Incidentally,' he said one Monday morning, wiping condensation off the office window so that he could stare out at my car parked against the kerb in the teeming rain, 'I'm glad you kept the Bavarian iron.' He was sitting on the dispatcher's desk drinking instant coffee from a styrofoam cup. 'It's nice.'

'I'm not using it as a taxi,' I warned him.

'Has anybody asked you to? Be fair. Have I *asked* you to use it as a taxi?'

He swung round and grinned at me.

'I have not,' he said.

'Choe, I can hear you thinking a mile off.'

He put down the cup and got off the desk. 'No, Mick,' he assured me quietly. 'You only think you can.' And he offered me a yellow Post-it slip, on which he had written in his careful designer hand, 'FUGA-OrthoGen', followed by an address in SW1. I turned it over, then back again.

'So?' I said.

'So make a pick-up.'

He stared at me.

'She's a hundred-thousand a year girl since she went to the doctor, Mick.'

'Choe, leave her alone.'

He tapped the piece of paper in my hand.

'They'll tell you where to take it,' he said.

'Whatever it is.'

'Whatever it is,' he agreed.

So all through November and December I worked for Choe, which was almost like working for myself. Every trip required speed and discretion. To Eastern Europe I ferried data archived by optical drive; to Manchester, ceramic sample cases with complex electronic locks. I visited Cambridge in the middle of the night carrying an unbranded sub-notebook computer and a single transgenic mouse in its own sealed environment. My instructions were to hand both of them over at a private house. I had been given forty-five minutes to complete the trip. I settled the mouse on the front passenger seat where I could keep an eye on it, then got Choe on the cellphone. 'Have a word with this mouse,' I told him, and offered the mouse the phone. 'Ay up,

Mickey,' I heard Choe say: 'No shitting on the floor.' I rang off. The mouse ran about in its transparent plastic box, and I chatted to it. It was still alive when we arrived, though less active.

After that job I often talked to the mouse. Being away from Isobel made me feel raw and lonely; it made me angry with her again. By day I counted magpies – *one for sorrow, fuck off; one for sorrow, fuck off*. At night I listened to Lori Carson tracks and talked to the mouse.

'How's it going, Mickey?'

It was going like this: straight down a tunnel of shaking halogen light. Noise, speed, music like a second engine; something valuable on the back seat. I was often tired. Sometimes I didn't change gear for a hundred miles. Motorway signs came up a kind of living crystalline blue in the night. Above eight thousand revs, BMW engines produce a distracted whine, as if they are trying to tell you, 'Don't bother me now'; behind that I could hear the low-profile Michelins blustering and booming as they coped with strange, arhythmic changes in the road surface. The competition ride-pack made every mile seem corrugated. My shoulders ached. I wondered if it would rain. Part of me hoped it would.

'Mickey, we're up at a hundred and thirty-eight miles an hour here. What can I say? No police and right on schedule.'

I put on 'You Won't Fall'.

'Mickey, it's been real. Have a nice life.'

One Saturday morning I made a pick-up not far from home, at a discreet office near the Scandic Crown Hotel, part of a mass of new building which cuddles into the southern curve of the river at Rotherhithe. It was more like spring than winter, a cool, wide day, with a breeze off the water fluttering in the masts and rigging of the dry-docked clipper *La Dame de Serk*. I arrived too early, sat for fifteen minutes in the car, then locked it and went to see if I could find the river behind its retaining wall of film studios, local history resources and entry-level postmodern housing. A Russian blue cat sat in the middle of the sunny deserted street. 'Puss,' I called softly and, when it ran off, I followed it. Suddenly there was the smell of water and space, a sense of windy April softness in the air. Pageant Stairs. The tide was out. Rotting wooden piles led across an acre of mud towards the brown and shrunken Limehouse Reach. A gull planed overhead, banked towards Tower Bridge, a mile west and hidden by a bend in the river. Behind me, Rotherhithe Street was waking up; by then HDC Biotech had the girl ready for me.

Twenty years old and five feet six inches tall, she wore a sweatshirt and grey Levis, holed at the knee, under a dirt-glazed olive-drab parka, the sleeves of which were so long she had to clutch the cuffs continually to keep them from falling over her hands. Her hair, a dirty yellow colour, tired of being treated, fell into loose dreadlocks streaked here and there with faded purple. Her face still retained some of its adolescent fullness; her skin was still good. Her nose and eyebrows had been pierced for Camden silver rings as thin as hairs.

'What's this?' I asked the HDC people.

'Is there a problem?'

'Only that she was begging outside Turnpike Lane tube station the day before yesterday.'

'And that's a problem for you?'

'Look at her.'

Someone flipped open a mobile phone.

'Would you like an espresso,' they offered, 'while we discuss it with Mr Ashton?'

I shrugged.

'There's no need for that.'

'Fuck you,' said the girl, as if she had just noticed me. Her eyes were round and grey, very young and direct. A light cold had reddened the fleshy part of her nostril around the nose-ring and given her voice a husky edge. I told her:

'I'm not having your dog in the car.'

The HDC people looked puzzled.

'Dog?'

'The Alsatian-cross puppy on the piece of string,' I reminded them.

She laughed.

'Fuck you,' she said.

'There's no dog,' they reassured me.

'Luggage?'

'There's no luggage.'

'Fuck you.'

A good weather forecast had clogged the outside lane of the M1 with bulbous M-registered hatchbacks making a steady seventy-five miles an hour. I looked at my watch – eight-thirty – and began to pass on the left. The edge had gone off the day. Luton preceded Newport Pagnell, which gave way in its turn to Watford Gap. My passenger spent this part of the journey curled up on the back seat. She sneezed or coughed, or sang softly and tunelessly to herself and, when I tried to talk, ignored me. I watched her in the driving mirror. After an hour she sat up, stretched and said contemptuously:

'You can't catch it, you know. I'm not a pariah.'

'What's a pariah?' I said. 'Is it some kind of fish?'

'Fuck off,' she told me, and that was it for another half-hour. What she seemed to like most was watching the scenery fly past. Staring at low-lying fields, thunder clouds, rain, she showed all the unguarded delight of a child. Eventually I asked:

'Catch what?'

'How do I know? Some fucking thing. I need a Kleenex.'

I pretended to root about under the dash.

'I had some here somewhere. Do you want to steer while I look?'

'Very funny,' she said. 'I'm hungry.'

'I'll find you a McDonald's.'

'Fuck off.'

Sometimes you leave a motorway and return to ordinary human perspectives and are struck by how mad the whole thing is – the dirt, the disturbed air, the noise, the speeds people travel at. It seems inhuman and incredible, and you wonder if you'll ever manage to make yourself do it again. As we sat in a Little Chef above the motorway watching the traffic streak past beneath us, the girl said in a voice angry but puzzled, 'Most of them don't look bright enough to drive in the first place.' And then, as if the two ideas were connected: 'What would you do if you had a lot of money?'

I wasn't sure how to respond.

'How much money?'

'Enough to get everything you wanted,' she said with the exaggerated patience of a five-year-old, and looked down at the motorway again. There was a silence. Then she asked me:

'Where is this?'

'Leicester Forest East.'

'It's nice.'

We ate. She looked happier for a moment, then suddenly white and sick. 'Where's the toilet?' While she was away I raised Shogun Cars on the Vodafone.

'This job stinks, Choe. I'd rather drive veal calves to Dover.'

'Sorry Mick, I can't hear you.'

'Oh yes you can, Choe.'

'Could you say that again?'

I was still trying to talk to him when the girl came back. She seemed shaken. She sat wiping her mouth repeatedly on a paper napkin, glancing across at me every so often with an expression half aggressive, half miserable. Her face had a damp sheen. What comfort could I offer? I didn't feel I owed her anything, and Choe's bland evasions were making me angry and distracted. In the end, sick of the pair of them, I suggested, 'Have a word with this mouse, Choe,' and passed the phone over.

'Hello?' she said.

He rang off.

She wiped at her eyes suddenly.

'Why are you fucking me about like this?'

I said, 'I'm not.' I got her a packet of tissues and a bottle of Evian water and walked her out to the car-park.

'I had a lot of money once,' I told her.

She smiled for the first time.

'Oh, great,' she said. 'What did you get?'

Without thinking, I said: 'I bought a Romeo Gigli frock.'

'What?'

'Not for myself, of course.'

She stared at me in disgust.

'Being rich isn't like Christmas,' I told her. 'You just buy houses and things.' Even to me it sounded like a counsel of despair.

Out on the windy tarmac there was a real public holiday in progress: the RAC booth doing brisk business against a photographic background of wrecked and tangled Fords; two men with accordions and a plastic bucket collecting for the blind; people wandering dreamily about in front of each other's cars, treading in an ice cream or treading on the brakes, blinking in the sunshine as they tried to find 'Fuel' and get back on the road again. Their children had gone to the wrong Mondeo (metallic plum) and waited by it for twenty minutes and were still crying. They were up to here with it, they told one another: right up to here. Out on the motorway they would drive slowly and woodenly, and refuse to give up their lane. Meanwhile, a very fat woman with straggling grey hair had lost her way in the middle of the zebra crossing, a notional causeway connecting restaurant to car-park, and now stood grasping the front of her floral-print dress repeatedly, and pulling it down over her belly to reseat it. She smiled happily around until somebody came to fetch her.

The girl watched, puzzled as a Martian, then said: 'They're thick and they love it. It's such a revenge for being alive, isn't it? To be thick and in the way.' Waiting for me to unlock the BMW she added:

'What sort of shit car is this anyway? They said I'd get a limo.'

It was my turn not to talk.

Leicester preceded Nottingham, which gave way in its turn to Mansfield, where the clouds, as they say, opened. The traffic slowed, curdled across all three lanes, then, finned with spray and blinking its hazard lamps, went nose to tail at twenty miles an hour into the rain. The sky was dark, the motorway silver: cold air filled the car. The girl looked out. She tucked her hands into her armpits and curled up so tight she barely occupied half the rear seat. Every so often she shivered briefly, like a wet dog. At Rotherham I took the M18 east and then the A1(M) which I intended to follow to Edinburgh. Doncaster, Pontefract, York, said the roadsigns: A630, M62, A64. Despite that, I soon found we were heading into unmarked territory. The girl sat up abruptly. She pushed back the cuff of her parka to reveal a gold Breitling Chronomat.

'Where are we?'

'Darlington,' I said. 'We've just passed Scotch Corner. You can go back to sleep: we won't be there for another two or three hours.'

'Yes we will,' she said.

'What?'

'Take the A68.'

'Too much local traffic to be any quicker.'

'Are you stupid?'

'Let me explain. I was hired to drive. You were hired to sit in the back.'

'You are stupid,' she said.

She shook her head. 'Look, *we aren't going to Edinburgh.* OK?'

The Vodafone rang.

I answered it. Choe's voice said: 'Where are you, Mick?'

I told him.

'Good,' he said. 'I thought you'd be there about now.'

'Choe, there's a problem.'

'It's not ours, Mick. Do what she wants.'

'Choe, what's going on?'

'There's no problem, Mick,' he said.

He rang off.

Perhaps half an hour later we were pushing into the raw North Pennine hillsides above Consett. Tired and withdrawn, the girl rested her cheek against the nearside rear window and watched the summit of Bolt's Law, axle of our shallow north-western sweep, shredding the rainclouds. 'Turn left here. And now right.' She kept us in the valley of the South Tyne, which on a wet day is the bleakest, most useless place you've ever been: groups of sodden pedestrians plodding along in the grass beside the road, empty petrol stations and tea-rooms, the watery glint on the long pathways between vanished Roman settlements; then suddenly a glimpse of Hadrian's Wall like excavations for a new Sainsbury's. 'Now right again. Now stop. Stop here.' She had me pull into a gateway somewhere on the edge of the Spadeadam Forest. Behind us, the valley spread out to where Crag Lough lay like a mirror in the grey light; beside us, a steep tussocky drop into the Irthing. It was raining steadily. Mist breathed out of the trees to meet the low cloud. The road curved away gently uphill between drystone walls and dense stands of conifer. I could see a lay-by six hundred yards ahead, and in it a black car much bigger than mine.

The girl said: 'I change rides here.'

She got out and slammed the door. The BMW was filled briefly with a smell of woodland and damp bracken.

I wound my window down.

'I hope you live long enough to get what you want,' I called after her.

She sneezed. Without turning round she said:

'I wouldn't wear a Romeo Gigli dress if I was paid to.'

'Frock,' I said. 'I think you say frock.'

'Fuck you.'

She walked slowly and tiredly away up the hill, stopping once to massage the small of her back, the way a pregnant woman often will. Five minutes later the car ahead left its position in the lay-by and coasted silently down past me. It was long and black, and awkward to drive in a Northumberland lane: a Moscow car covered in chrome, as American as a Dead Kennedy playing card. *Zil 117*. I saw the girl's tired smile, I saw her hand lifted to me. I saw Ed Cesniak sitting beside her in one of his plum-coloured suits, and I saw him grin across at me. I saw how much room they had between them on the cheap leather seat.

Well, I thought: At least you got your limo.

In my dreams I soon catch them. White faces stare back at me down all the narrow lanes. 'Your driver's no good,' I tell them. Trying to get away from me, he has put the power on too hard and come out of the turn in radical oversteer. 'Your car's no good either,' I say, watching it wallow on its diplomatic-grade shocks: but I don't think they can hear me. I stick to them like shit all the way across country to Preston, where they turn south on the M6. It is beginning to get dark, squalls of rain are blowing almost horizontally across the road. Suddenly the Vodafone chirps. It's Choe.

'What are you doing, Mick?'

'Oh, hi Choe,' I say. 'I thought you couldn't hear me?'

'Mick, Ed says you're tailgating him at a hundred and ten miles an hour. He says he's not worried but he thinks you might get hurt.'

'Does he now?' I say. 'Would he like his wing mirror ripped off?'

I slip the M3 a bit closer and switch the halogens on to main beam. I switch on the fog lights. I switch on anything else I can find, including Lenny Kravitz, making his way with a kind of psychotic self-control through 'Mama Says'. The driver of the Zil raises his hand to cover his interior mirror, brakes heavily and swerves back into the middle lane. I go up on his nearside, wind my window down, stick my head and one arm out into the airstream and grin at him.

'I tell you what, Choe,' I shout into the Vodafone. 'Do you bet

I can? Rip it right off?' It's getting hard to speak to him if I want to steer as well.

'Mick, stop that!'

'Do you bet me?'

Choe says quietly: 'The girl wants you to leave them alone, Mick.'

'The girl doesn't know what she fucking wants. And what are they going to do with her when they've finished with her, Choe? Dump her on the Lancashire waste tip with all the other used rubber gloves? Remember that tip, Choe?' By then we are down at eighty miles an hour and the Zil has hustled me on to the hard shoulder. I say: 'I'm sick of these fuckers, Choe.' I brake irritably, drop a gear and get eight and a half thousand revs, all in the same gesture; and in that gesture depart. At a hundred and forty I am still trying to accelerate.

Nothing like that happened, of course: or ever will. The Zil and its occupants are long gone in the dirty rain, en route to Budapest or Zurich. Who was screwing who? Did the girl have herself kidnapped? Or had HDC Biotech intended to sell her to Cesniak all along? How far was Choe involved? When I got back to Shogun Cars it was late; everything stank of kebabs. I leant over the dispatcher's desk and told him, 'I'll drive a cab from now on.'

'Whatever you want, Mick.'

'She was a live host. She was a live host.'

'Fucked if I know what that *is*, Mick,' he said puzzledly. 'Do you?' He pretended to look through the paperwork. 'They told me it would be an "industry executive".'

'I'll drive a cab from now on.'

'Whatever you want.'

Because minicab work requires a very specialized vehicle I bought a Mercedes 230TD with 110,000 miles on the clock, equipping it with 'No smoking' signs and a Magic Tree air-freshener ('You'll find one in every car'), despite which its blue-grey nylon upholstery soon soaked up the smell of ocakbasi, sweat and patchouli oil. A powerful heater kept the inside too warm. I practised asking, 'Where do you want to go?' in a voice of neutral exasperation; driving with my eyes fixed on something in the top left-hand corner of the windscreen, especially at complex junctions; and repeating the words 'King's Cross' as if I had never heard them before. I liked night work because there was no pressure from other motorists. I could encourage the Merc amiably out on to some vast empty interchange in Tottenham Hale or Harlesden – where the wet tarmac and tall buildings looked like another country inhabited by another race of people – and take time to misread 'Neural History Museum' on a torn and flapping poster under a bridge. Wherever you are in London at two in the morning, there is always someone coming out of a late shop reaching into a brown bag of groceries. 'AH. FORKEY,' the dispatcher will say suddenly and very loudly: 'Is anyone near Colyton Road? FORKEY: Colyton Road, anyone do me Colyton Road? GRON,' and be lost in a burst of static. Then all is quiet again.

I got home from these night rides feeling at the same time rested and lively, to make espresso on the stove; load the dishwasher with Cuisinox cookware and the washing machine with Hanro knickers; wipe the kitchen top, upon which Isobel had been spilling milky tea all day; and at last go quietly upstairs to tidy her clothes and watch her while she slept: or talk if she was awake. 'China,' she would whisper in delight; 'Hello, China,' as if I had been absent for months – expected back, like a child from boarding school or a husband from a business trip: but not so soon. She might be reading: Camille Paglia one night, Françoise Sagan the next. (Her tastes yawed. She could always mix a paragraph of a self-help text called *The Road Less Travelled* with two or three of Baudrillard, *The Evil Demon of Images*. It was disconcerting.) Sometimes she took my hand tightly in hers; and sometimes she seemed so pleased to see me I couldn't look into her eyes. One morning I came in and found her convulsing.

She had fallen off the bed, pulling the quilt with her and knocking down the African table again. Barleywater and drugs had gone everywhere. Isobel was lying on her back looking startled and panicky. Sweat ran off her. She couldn't speak, but she could grunt, and anyway everything was there in her round white staring eyes – fear, confusion, loneliness. I wondered if she could see me: I knew she could. Her spine arched and relaxed, arched and relaxed, quite slowly, in a way that had nothing to do with her. She seemed most of all to be trying to convey that: *This is nothing to do with me.* At the crux of each spasm I could hear her teeth grind with the effort of denying it. She had wet herself. The smell of her, breathing from every pore and aperture on a long, languorous swell, changed from moment to moment: ammonia to sloe gin, expensive shoe cream to cheap banana milk. I bent over her there in the dark room, not quite knowing what to do, while Isobel unpacked herself, like a Victorian medium, of these ghosts and ghost-locations: the smell of a zoo; the smell of a tidal pool; moist earth, torn leaves and uprooted sticks; stale bread; bruised grass in a wedding marquee; plastic and frankincense; fennel, fenugreek and burnt cork. Beneath that, deeper, more bodily odours, oils, waxy secretions, bloods and fluxes, things glandular and hidden. I didn't know what was happening. Was Isobel *remembering* puberty? A wet dog on the White Downs? The miasma of old tobacco in some deserted hotel lounge? It was as if the Alexander treatments had unsettled old emotional sites within her, so that they flickered and flared up. Suddenly the convulsion let her go, dropped her at my feet without a gesture and walked away. Her eyes widened, brightened, as if they had seen something preternatural, closed again: and she was able to speak. 'No. They wait here for people,' she insisted, trying to warn both of us about something. 'China! The screen! We can fly!' I bent over her to listen. She choked on a plug of mucus and writhed away from me. 'No! Oh no!' She changed her mind and held out her arms like a toddler for comfort, and when I recoiled, because she reeked like a mare on heat, could only wail: 'Oh China.' I picked her up and put her back in bed. Her body was rigid, slippery to touch, fantastically hot, hotter than a human being should ever be. She smelt of lemon, and something glutinous beneath – albumen, or perhaps semen, caught at the point of drying; then, briefly, milk from a dandelion stalk broken on a late spring day. With that, all the tension went out of her. 'Have me, Brian,' she said, in a clear, sane voice, a voice almost conversational: and slept. I was left trembling in the growing light, tears of rage and misery running down my face. Whatever Brian Alexander had promised her, it wasn't this. I saw with a sudden hopeless clarity that whatever either of us had promised her, it wasn't this.

15 · HI-PAD LONDON

Jealousy is malarial because:

It recurs.

It is unpredictable in both frequency and ferocity.

It causes you to hallucinate.

Nothing you think or predict or imagine, no conclusion you reach in a condition of jealousy, can be trusted. Jealousy builds a housing project of logic from a single brick. What can you do? Wander the ramps and serviceways of your private Broadwater Farm like any other puzzled debt collector. Every floor looks the same. Knock on the right door and there is a sudden tense silence inside. You want something from the occupant, but you no longer understand what it is, let alone how to get it.

Isobel had passed the crisis, and now improved daily. Her skin began to heal. All her different fevers broke. She collected her medication together, took it to the bathroom and arranged it on the shelves, where it could gather dust. Her appetite increased, and she put on a little weight.

'Work days now,' she ordered me. 'Work days now, China. I want to do cooking again.'

'Shall I hire a video tonight?'

'Yes. Get *Moonstruck*. No, get *Three Colours White*.'

'I'll get them both.'

'Bring popcorn. Bring lots of popcorn.'

'I thought you wanted to cook.'

'Bring Maltesers.'

When I got back, she was frying chicken livers for pâté, stirring them with a wooden spoon held at arm's length.

'Isobel, what are you doing?'

'Standing well back, in case I see them.'

'What did you think about at work today?'

'Nothing much.'

'China, you must think about something.'

'Not really.'

'China, tell me.'

'I drove around imagining you in a hospital smock.'

'Oh yes? That's what you do all day, is it?'

'Yes. It was open at the back. "HOSPITAL PROPERTY" was stencilled on the front of it in red, in case someone stole it.'

'Why would someone want to steal that, China?'

'They might want to steal you.'

'And why would they want to do that?'

'They might. Anyway, in the end, you and I met—'

'Oh, we met, did we?'

'—in some dusty little consulting room with a filing cabinet and a desk, which you bent over almost immediately.

'*Bent over?*'

'I was a doctor—'

'Of course you were. *Bent over?*'

'Well, that's cheered you up a bit,' I said.

Half-past three in the afternoon. Pink clouds over the trees round the communal garden. The crows complain from their perches on top of the flats across the road. The sky is greying away from blue. In ten minutes it will be grey with a greenish tinge, a much flatter, less illuminated, colour, like the difference between the scales of dead and living fish. A breeze gets up and moves the branches of the London plane outside our house. A dog yelps, running in circles on the darkening grass. It is a neatly clipped Old English sheepdog, barely more than a puppy, whose favourite game is to run three or four times round a thick group of shrubs, then turn round and run three or four times in the opposite direction. It is happiest if another dog will join in, but content to run in any case. Eleven lights come on, one above the other, on the eleven landings of the apartment block. One drowsy fly, woken perhaps by the brief sunshine earlier in the day, buzzes and taps at the sash window. The block of flats, the trees, the Victorian houses on the other side of the square, are now silhouetted against the sky, completely black.

I stare out. I hear her in the room behind me. I wait for the right moment. I say:

'Are we back together again Isobel?'

'I do love being with you, China.'

It wasn't enough.

'She never makes an effort, Choe. I make all the effort.'

'I told you, Mick.'

'She won't come an inch towards me.'

'She's got you by the cock.'

'It's not that, Choe.'

How can I admit this?

I was terrified that, recovered, she wouldn't need me.

A mild winter made London intimate and cosy. The residential streets seemed to become narrower, the brickwork warmer. I knew it was nearly Christmas when I dropped a fare in Camden and the whole of Inverness Street market smelt of Christmas trees. Vanloads of them were coming in, with shouts and palaver as the drivers tried to manoeuvre in the confined space between the stalls in the afternoon gloom. By then, Isobel and I were shouting at one another late into the night, every night. I slept on the futon in the spare room. There I dreamed of Isobel and woke sweating.

You have to imagine this:

The Pavilion, quite a good Thai restaurant at the corner of Rupert Street and Shaftesbury Avenue. Isobel orders beef panang. 'Can I have a red curry as well? Would that be really greedy?' she asks me. And, before I can answer: 'I'm going to.' She gives me a jacket wrapped in birthday paper. She leans across the table. 'Ally Capellino, China. Very smart.' The waitresses, who believe we are lovers, laugh delightedly as I try it on. But later, when I want to buy Isobel a red rose, she says, 'What use would I have for that?' in a voice of such contempt I begin to cry. In the dream, I am fifty years old that day. I wake thinking everything is finished, even my life.

Or this:

Budapest. Summer. Rakoczi Street. Each night Isobel waits for me to fall asleep before she leaves the hotel. Once outside, she walks restlessly up and down Rakoczi with all the other women, waiting for Ed Cesniak to pick her up and take her back to the decaying courtyard off Damjanich and there discover that beneath her beige linen suit she has on grey silk underwear. She is always hot. She cannot explain what has failed in her life. I wake and follow her. All night it feels like dawn. Next morning, in the half-abandoned *Jugendstil* dining room, a paper doily drifts to the floor like a leaf, while Isobel whispers urgently in someone else's voice:

'*It was never what you thought it was.*'

Or this:

Isobel and I were in a room with bare floorboards, and Brian Alexander was in there with us.

Appalled all over again by their directness, astonished to find myself so passive, I would struggle clear of dreams like this thinking, What am I going to do? What am I going to do? It was always early. It was always cold. Grey light outlined a vase of dried flowers on the dresser in front of the uncurtained window, but the room itself was still dark. I would look at my watch, turn over and go back to sleep. One morning just before Christmas I got up and packed a bag instead. I made myself some coffee and drank it by the kitchen window, listening to the inbound City traffic build up half a mile away. When I switched the radio on it was playing Billy Joel's 'She's Always A Woman'. I turned it off quickly, and at eight o'clock woke Isobel. She smiled up at me.

'Hello,' she said. 'I'm sorry about last night.'

I said: 'I'm sick of living with the two of you. I can't do it. I thought I could, but I can't.'

'China, what is this?'

I said: 'You were so fucking sure he'd have you. Four months later it was you crying, not me.'

'China—'

'It's time you helped,' I said.

I said: 'I helped *you*. And when you bought me things out of gratitude I never once said, "What use would I have for that?"'

She rubbed her hands over her eyes.

'China, what are you talking about?'

I shouted: 'What a fool you made of yourself.' Then I said: 'I only want to be something to you again.'

'I won't stand for this,' Isobel whispered. 'I can't stand this.'

I said: 'Neither can I. That's why I'm going.'

'I still love him, China.'

I was on my way to the door. I said:

'You can have him then.'

'China, I don't *want* you to go.'

'Make up your mind.'

'I won't say what you want me to.'

'Fuck off, then.'

'It's you who's fucking off, China.'

This time I had some cardboard boxes delivered by a firm in Camberwell, packed all my stuff up in them and drove them across the river in a Luton van. I threw away the things she had bought me. When she asked, 'But don't you want any of the photographs?' I shrugged. 'What would be the point?' I asked her. She looked down at her feet. She was crying silently. 'I just thought you might want to keep some of it.' She left the room and came back with two prints we had bought in New Orleans; a ceramic bowl from Tenerife in which she had piled clementines to remind us of the sun. 'I thought you might want these. You did like them.' She brought me the brand new steam iron and stood there holding it awkwardly in front of her, her thin wrists trembling with the weight of it.

'This is yours, anyway.'

I returned to Haringey and unpacked in Choe's spare bedroom. 'Unpacked' is a misleading word. There were things there I had never got round to taking with me when I moved back in with Isobel – a small shelf of unread books; an ironing board and a lot of wire coat-hangers, one with a pair of easyfit Levis folded over it; a carrier bag from the Conran Shop. There was also a stove-top espresso maker still in its packaging. I stacked the boxes on top of one another until they made a kind of Alamo round the cheap futon. They were big, stout boxes, thirty inches on a side, stamped QTY 20PCS GW 15.5 KGS. Suddenly I couldn't see the point of opening them. Neither did I look back much on the life they contained, the one I had planned with Isobel. 'Nostalgia's first meaning is the yearning for a lost home,' claims Jonathan Meades. I was beginning to get used to living out of my own head, like a sales rep out of a suitcase. There were no curtains at the window, so I hung my jackets up there instead. They faded steadily in the light. The boxes loomed over me. GW 15.5 KGS, I read: HI-PAD LONDON.

Choe hardly acknowledged my arrival. Preoccupied and irri- table, he talked long-distance on the telephone far into the night. Bulky packages were delivered for him by bike messenger in the afternoon when he was out. He borrowed the BMW and when he brought it back, sometimes two or three days later, the footwells were littered with plastic cups and half-eaten food and it smelt somehow of Eastern Europe. Plumes of grey mud, hardened to concrete and full of pinkish salt crystals, had sprayed up from the front wheel arches to customize its side panels. He lost interest in the minicab business, and promoted the wife of one of his drivers to dispatcher – a fat woman with thick red creases in her elbows, who wore her hair in a kind of black crocheted bag, ticked the pages of *Puzzler* magazine with a leaky biro and drank sachets of flavoured hot chocolate all day. A handwritten notice appeared in the window, next to 'DRIVERS WANTED'. '*Customers not known to this company,*' it said, '*will pay their fare before they get in the cab.*' On his rare visits to the office Choe spent the afternoon staring disgustedly at the TV.

'Just fucking look at that.'

This time, it was Isobel who wrote the letters. Shortly after I moved back I received a notecard with a Picasso dove on it. 'This is my favourite card,' she wrote. 'I hope you like it too.' Soon, she was writing every other day. 'I miss the way we used to wake up together,' she finished one letter; and began the next: 'Do you remember when we went to Windsor and got a boat, and you laughed because even though it rained I kept saying, "Aren't we lucky. Aren't we *lucky.*"' (I did. If I closed my eyes I could remember clearly the way she had trailed her bare feet in the water, laughing delightedly as the little yellow boat, its outboard droning like a toy, bobbed in the wake of a larger one. I remembered the humid late-summer air; willows 'like a jungle,' as Isobel described them, on the south bank; a man swimming with his two dogs from a tiny sandy beach; lightning far down the Thames towards Staines. I remembered being astounded by the simplicity of her joy in these things.) 'Well we were, China. We were lucky. And I miss the fun we had.'

She seemed confused. 'I love Brian,' she wrote, and only a paragraph away in the same letter: 'It's you I love now. Please come back.'

'No thanks,' I replied.

What did I care if Isobel was sad? I was bankrupt, fifty years old and living near Tottenham with a sociopath. I couldn't quite understand why she was hurting me like this. Perhaps she didn't know that she was hurting me. It wasn't really something I could tell her. It wasn't really something I could tell Choe either. 'You can get a tart anywhere,' he said. His patience was gone. 'Just shut up about her.'

'I've got to talk to *someone*, Choe.'

Two or three days later Isobel began telephoning.

'China? I'm not very well.'

'Phone the doctor,' I said. I left a careful pause, then advised: 'That's what I'd do.'

She took this in.

'But would you come and stay? Just until I feel better?'

'I don't think I want to do that,' I said.

'China, I think it's started to work at last.'

'What has?'

'The Miami treatment. China, I don't know what to do if it's started to work.'

'Phone the doctor. He'll be pleased.'

There was a silence. I was going to hang up when she said:

'China, can't we be friends?'

'Friends is one thing. This is another. Either you want him or me.'

'Nothing's ever that simple,' Isobel said. She sounded empty and depressed.

'Yes it is.'

There was a pause.

Suddenly she said: 'I haven't been in touch with him anyway.'

My heart seemed to shift painfully in my chest.

'Why don't you leave me alone?' I said, and put the phone down.

'If it rings again,' I told Choe, 'I'm not in.'

He stared at me incuriously. Then he shrugged and said, 'I'm surprised the fucker's still connected. I haven't paid the bill.'

Christmas. Central London. Traffic locked solid every late afternoon. Light in the shop windows in the rain. Light in the puddles. Light splashing up round your feet. I couldn't keep still. Once I'd walked away from Isobel, I couldn't stop walking. Everywhere I went, 'She's Always A Woman' was on the radio. Harrods, Heal's, Habitat, Hamleys: at each stop Billy Joel drove me out on to the wet pavement with another armful of children's toys. I even wrapped some of them – a wooden penguin with rubber feet, two packs of cards, a miniature jigsaw puzzle in the shape of her name. Every time I saw something I liked, it went home with me.

'I bought you a present,' I imagined myself saying. 'This fucking little spider that really jumps:

'Look.'

Then quite suddenly I was exhausted. Even if I had wanted to go somewhere for the holiday I wouldn't have been able to: Choe had the BMW, and was pushing it through the night to Switzerland on a simple, face-bursting fuel of crystal meth and adrenalin. Christmas day I spent with the things I'd bought. Boxing day, and the day after that, I lay in a chair staring at the television. Between shows I picked up the phone and put it down again, picked it up and put it down. I was going to call Isobel, then I wasn't. I was going to call her, but I closed the connection carefully every time the phone began to ring at her end.

I wondered if I should go and visit Christiana Spede.

Once I had the idea, I felt as if I would lose my nerve unless I carried it out there and then. I left the house quickly. Halfway to the tube station I ran back, wrapped the wooden penguin with rubber feet and put in a card saying, 'Merry Xmas. I hope it all turned out well.' I went out the second time via the corner off-licence, where I bought two bottles of a nice California chardonnay, 1991.

Turnpike Lane, King's Cross, Chalk Farm. The stations were deserted and cold: tiled and dirty, forsaken, far underground. Sudden winds; those ads for bestselling books and designer underwear; an aluminium beer can rolling and dancing at the bottom of a completely deserted escalator. Braided cables a wrist thick lined the tunnels, yellow, violet, green. Tired middle-aged schizophrenics, retreating from quality lives in the Home Counties, haunted the lower platforms with their dogs and bags of clothes. As I passed, an educated look sprang from nowhere into their eyes, and suddenly they were talking loudly to themselves on various disconnected topics – the KGB; Oxford; change. At Chalk Farm the lifts were out of order. In the street it was raining heavily. I turned up my coat collar and stepped out with reluctance.

Chalk Farm was deserted. Rain dripped from the shiny black branches of the flowering cherry outside Christiana's house. I rang her doorbell. After a minute, I knocked. I felt certain she was in. I knocked again, then knelt and shouted through the letterbox:

'Christiana! It's Mick Rose.'

Nothing.

'Merry Christmas.'

After a moment, I thought I heard a second-floor sash window sliding up, and then a quiet voice saying: 'Fuck off, China.' But there was no one there; and when I stood back on the wet pavement, I could see clearly that all the windows were dark and none of them were open. Street light flared back at me when I raised my head, like the light reflected off someone's spectacles. I felt slightly dizzy. I stepped backwards off the kerb and into cold water. It seemed a long way down. I said, 'Christiana?' A train made its stealthy, thoughtful grinding noise as it rolled in a slippery haze of halogen light along the rails behind the house.

'Christiana?'

No answer.

After a while, I pushed her present through the letterbox, tearing the wrapper only a little; arranged the bottles of wine on the doorstep like an eccentric milk delivery; and walked back to Chalk Farm tube.

*

There were less than two days of December left to run when Choe returned from Europe. He was dressed in Thierry Mugler slacks and a white dress shirt. He hadn't shaved since he left the house on Christmas Eve. The speed had worn off but he still couldn't seem to settle. He walked nervously about the flat as if it belonged to someone else, picking his own things up and putting them down again like someone who didn't approve of them very much and was wondering who might buy stuff like that. 'Fucking shit people, the Swiss,' he repeated several times. He wanted to talk, but was clearly reluctant to allow himself; in the end all he would say was, 'I get so fucking tired of this. You know? If people deal, they deal, that's all there is to it.' We had pizza delivered. He sat at the kitchen table, eating American Hot with his fingers and finishing a case of Budvar he had opened in the car on the way back. Over the last three months he had let his hair grow, and now wore it pulled back from his forehead into a short, oily pigtail, which gave him a brutal look. The fluorescent light, though, revealed him as haggard and tired. I was shocked to see grey hairs in his stubble.

Much later that night I decided for some reason I would phone Isobel again. I would have it out with her this time. I would tell her just what a shit I thought she had been. Her Miami postcard – with its naive injunction, 'Wish me luck!' – was propped up on the dusty side table in front of me as I dialled. I let the phone ring fifteen times; pressed the redial key and let it ring twenty: but no one answered. I replaced the receiver, waited five minutes and dialled again. Nothing. Whenever that happens, I think of a long hallway, old-fashioned wallpaper, a smell of lavender floor polish, an old black Bakelite telephone with a dial. I don't know why. Outside, three steps down into the deserted street, it is raining steadily. Upstairs the rooms are neat but untenanted, full of very large furniture. All unanswered telephones ring in this space. I put the handset down and stared for some minutes at Choe's collection of used theatre tickets, BFI tickets, receipts from Waterstone's and Murder One for novels by Harry Crews,

James Crumley and Tim Willocks. Some dusty paperclips and pencils in a jar. An unopened packet of incense sticks. Then I went into the kitchen, made a pot of espresso and drank it while I watched an *X Files* rerun on TV.

'Fuck,' I said.

Suddenly I wanted to hear her voice. I was filled with an unreasonable fear for her: but more than anything I just wanted to hear her voice.

I said, 'This fucking phone.'

Choe, who had been aimlessly cutting lines on a mirror while he soaked Europe off in the bathtub, came part of the way into the room and leant on the door frame looking at me. I was already dialling again, letting her phone ring four or five times, then dialling again.

'I'm worried, Choe.'

He shook his head.

'One thing or the other, Mick,' he said tiredly. 'Sort her out or leave her alone.'

I looked at my watch.

'I'm worried about her,' I said.

'I'll drive you over there,' he offered.

I stared at him in surprise.

He shrugged.

'What the fuck,' he said: 'I get to drive the heap again.'

He said: 'Hang on a minute.'

When he came back he was sniffing and wiping his nose. He had got dressed in his black Levi 620s, now glazed with dirt along the front of the thigh; sixteen-hole DMs with red laces; and the old cap-sleeve T-shirt which best showed off his hard little shoulders and rose tattoo. On the way out he picked up a nice Comme des Garçons jacket.

He said: 'Good deed for the day.'

So that was how we came to be in Stepney in the early hours of a wet New Year's Eve, full of fancy foreign lager and some quite decent blow Choe had picked up outside a *routier* on his way through France to Zurich. We talked about Isobel. I said everything I always said. Choe said everything he always said. Then he surprised me by adding, 'I've always fancied her. But I suppose you knew that'; and ended up weirdly:

'You want to dump her, Mick, and get someone nearer your own age.'

At the time he was chopping down through the gears to leave the A102 for Victoria Park. Engine noise batted back off the dark buildings, *oom, oom, oom*, then fell away behind us down the empty streets, as if it was after all possible to leave yourself behind in this life. I stared at his face, underlit by the dashboard instruments, further from understanding him than I had ever been.

'You what?' I said.

Imagine this:

Two a.m. The house was quiet.

Or this:

I stood on the pavement. When I looked in through the uncurtained ground-floor window I could see the little display of lights on the front of Isobel's CD player.

Or this:

For a moment my key didn't seem to fit the door.

Imagine this:

Late at night you enter a house in which you've been as happy as anywhere in your life: probably happier. You go into the front room, where street light falls unevenly across the rugs, the furniture, the mantelpiece and mirrors. On the sofa are strewn a dozen colourful, expensive shirts, blue and red and gold like macaws and money. Two or three of them have been slipped out of their cellophane, carefully refolded and partly wrapped in Christmas paper. 'Dear China,' say the tags. 'Dearest China.' There are signs of a struggle but not necessarily with someone else. A curious stale smell fills the room, and a chair has been knocked over. It's really too dark to see.

Switch on the lights. Glasses and bottles. Food trodden into the best kilim. Half-empty plates, two days old.

'Isobel? Isobel!'

As if in answer, I remembered her voice on the telephone, whispering:

'I think it's started to work.'

The bathroom was damp with condensation, the bath itself full of cold water smelling strongly of rose oil. Wet towels were underfoot, there and in the draughty bedroom, where the light was already on and Isobel's pink velvet curtains, half-drawn, let a faint yellow triangle of light into the garden below. The lower sash was open. When I pulled it down, a cat looked up from the empty flowerbed: ran off. I shivered. Isobel had pulled all her favourite underclothes out on to the floor and trodden mascara into them. She had written in lipstick on the dressing-table mirror, in perfect mirror writing:

'Leave me alone.'

16 · THE SIGNS OF LIFE

I found her in one of the bigger blanket boxes. When I opened
the lid, a strange smell – compounded of blood and beeswax,
pot-pourri, vomit and whisky – filled the room. To fit herself in,
Isobel had curled up, scrawny and foetal, with her head pillowed
on one hand, in the pained attitude of a thirteenth-century peat-
burial. Beneath her was a litter of brochures ('The Alexander
Clinics Welcome You'; 'How We Can Help; Grow Your Way to
Freedom!'), Polaroid snapshots and sodden tissues. She was
clutching an empty Jameson's bottle. She had torn the waxy
machine-varnished covers off the brochures and then thrown up
on them. The photographs were all of Isobel (seen arranging
flowers at the Peckham flat; perched smilingly on a slab of rock
at St Govan's Bay, while the great waves broke not twenty feet
from her; caught drinking milky coffee in a pink towelling robe
with a row of hand-washed Marks and Sparks cotton knickers
drying on the radiator beneath the window behind her – that
was a very early one). She had discarded two cans of Gillette
shaving foam, an old-fashioned safety razor of mine and some
spare blades. She had slit her wrists. But first she had tried to
shave the nascent feathers from her scalp, upper arms and
breasts, hacking at the keratin until her skin was a mess of
bruises and abrasions, indescribable soft ruby scabs, ragged and
broken feather sheaths like cracked and bloody fingernails.
Miami. In a confused attempt to placate me, Isobel had tried to
get out of the dream the way you get out of a coat.
She was still alive.
'China,' she said.
Sleepily, she held up her arms. As she moved, the down of
twenty different birds puffed up out of the blanket box into the

air around us like grey smoke. It fell back into her wounds and clung there, turning red. For a second I was breathing it. It was as if a quilt had burst in my face, and I was breathing feathers. They had a strange odour, musty yet exotic, dry but full of musk. For a fraction of a second I felt as guilty as if I had smelt the private smell of someone I hardly knew.

Suddenly I heard wings. They were soft and distant. They were close and panicky. They seemed to circle the room, then fade.

'China.'

Here at the Alexander Clinics, we use the modern 'magic wand' of molecular biology to insert avian chromosomes into human skin-cells. Nurtured in the clinic's vats, the follicles of this new skin produce feather-sheaths instead of hair. It grafts beautifully. Brand-new proteins speed acceptance. But in case of difficulties, we remake the immune system: aim it at infections of opportunity: fire it like a laser.

Our client chooses any kind of feather, from pinion to down, in any combination. She is as free to look at the sparrow as the bower bird or macaw. Feathers of any size and colour!

THE ALEXANDER CLINICS WELCOME YOU

Isobel, poring over these brochures in nicely appointed waiting rooms in Miami and west London, had chosen for her breasts muted weights and shadings of grey into pale turquoise, grey into pink, worked in the body feathers of lovebirds and parakeets. On her upper thighs, she had decided, the base grey would darken to a browny charcoal she had picked from a tufted duck; and then into the dense black pubic stripe. Across her shoulders and along the backs of her arms she had opted for a sheaf of primary flight feathers from the biggest birds in the world, set in such a way as to mimic the wings of a peregrine falcon half-folded for the stoop. Finally, to cup her head like the hands of some exotic lover, the curved main coverts of Contamini's desert owl.

The design team were disappointed.

Running new graphics software on an office Mac upgraded to three gigabytes of RAM, they had used an ordinary Wacom tablet and 20-inch display to match the cobalt blues and iridescent greens of mallard speculum to a dense metallic black lifted from the African starling. A tall and bizarrely proportioned figure, all bars and chevrons, stared at Isobel out of the monitor – Twenty-First-Century Transgenic Woman. Isobel stared back with contempt.

'It looks like a car.'

They tried again. A riffle through the current issue of *Harper's* unsettled them, though they did like what they saw. In response they split the difference between Gaultier and *animé* art, assembling a short skirt and two-stripe crop from the greasy-looking primaries of a South American vulture.

'No,' said Isobel.

'There are some amazing things here by someone called Wendi Hoey—'

'No.'

'It's "deconstructivist fashion".'

'No.'

'We could try this—'

'Not on me.'

'Or this—'

'No.'

When they weren't doing couture they liked facts. 'Twenty-five thousand feathers on a swan,' they informed her. They explained filoplumes. They explained structure: 'Under high magnification the barbs themselves look almost like tiny feathers.' At lunch she overheard them telling one another how, where the eyes of the predator tend to look only forward, those of the prey can see all around and above. They were impressed by extremes. 'Really big lifters,' they would boast, 'like Canada geese . . .' as if they had once shaken hands with some. They offered her a kind of stole made from ostrich feathers. They offered the long unbarbuled plumes, soft and trailing, of Count Raggi's bird of paradise.

Later she would complain:

'They were idiots. This wasn't a *frock*. It was my life, and they wanted me to look like Sarah Bernhardt.'

In fact they were only postgraduate biologists in the storefront of a new technology, a bit dishevelled by success. They liked Isobel, though her diamond gaze and outright sexuality had frightened them at first. They admired her. But they were always having to be off to weekend conferences in short-sleeved shirts, chinos and blazers: so in the end they taught her how to use the Mac. She loved it. It was as if all along her dream of flight had been a dream of sitting in front of this machine. She had an immediate sense of *déjà vu* (she said): brushed a key. A million red and blue parrots burst out of the digital forest into the morning air. She touched the Wacom tablet with the pen and looked up just in time to watch a million colours wash across the screen. She toyed with lory and macaw, oriole and crimson rosella: discarded them. She scanned in her favourite photograph of herself – Isobel shown meditative in a Monsoon dress as exotic as the Guiana jungle in 1595 – stretched and tugged it into the strangest shapes, reinventing herself as wren; as swan ('Come and live with me and be a swan!'); as Lady Amhurst's pheasant. It was, in a way, the happiest time of all: that hinge or pivot in your life at which it seems you can have everything, that precarious moment of delight before the fall into choice. She was in the studio thirteen hours at a time. If she looked up from the screen she could see Miami stretching away, night and lights and water. Suddenly she yawned. It was midnight and she had had nothing to eat since lunch.

She always wound up with her original idea.

'I want this,' she told the design team. 'I really do.'

The team had hoped for a platform. They had hoped for a showcase, something that would demonstrate the breadth of the technique.

'I want this.'

Half of them were in love with her anyway; and the other half were in love with fashion.

'It's nice,' they said.

Feathers of any size or colour! But the real triumph is elsewhere . . .

Designer hormones trigger the 'brown fat' mechanism. Our client becomes as light and as hot to the touch as a female hawk. Then metabolically induced calcium shortages hollow the bones. She can be handled only with great care. And the dreams of flight!

HOW WE CAN HELP.

Telling me about herself as a child, watching guillemots and black-backs hover and dip against the grey sea light, Isobel had once said:

'How I hated it all.

'I willed myself away. I didn't know where, just anywhere.'

And then:

'At least the gulls could get away.'

What had she wished, a seven-year-old thinned by growth and ambition, blown about after school by the blustery winds of Aire Point? To be as free as the father who had brought her into the world at Sennen Cove only to maroon her in the same gesture, in that small ice-cream business – in that world of small business – and who now, easily released by his adulthood, flew like a bird every Wednesday in a toy Cessna from a toy aerodrome near St Just? What fantastic resentments a seven-year-old must bear. What did she promise herself, watching the gulls brace themselves against the sky then turn impassively out to sea and let the cold air slip by them? What did she dream, running down the hill with her arms outstretched in a classic bank-and-turn? Whatever it was, she never banked on this . . .

A gull needs a keel. A gull is a machine for levering the air. Something must anchor the huge packs of muscle that operate

229

its wings. Gulls need an armature, complex and Victorian, and inside they must look much as the turkey does, a curious cage of bone, stripped and bared after Christmas dinner.

This is not to mention a beak.

Isobel had none of these things. Oh, her heart beat three hundred times a minute. In those days she ran hotter than any other human being. And she looked so beautiful and eerie in her plumage. But despite all that she was a thinnish woman of the Thatcher middle classes who liked to have an income of between fifty and a hundred thousand pounds a year. Alexander had made her resemble a bird. But underneath the cosmetic flourish, the DNA treatments, the Miami cut-and-splice, she was still Isobel Avens. Whatever he had promised her, she was only Isobel. Eventually she would shop again at Harvey Nichols.

Engineered endorphins released during sexual arousal sim-ulate the sidesweep, swoop and mad fall of mating flight, the frantically beating heart, long sight. Sometimes the touch of her own feathers will be enough.

GROW YOUR WAY TO FREEDOM!

Whatever he had promised her, she could never have flown.

Some events take language away from you. The pieces of the world settle into a shape that won't be said. It is a kind of vertigo. The endless panic bubbles up but it doesn't seem to show. I stared down into the blanket box. After a long time I managed to pick Isobel up and carry her carefully down the stairs. Then I was running across the pavement towards the M3, and Choe was blinking muddledly at the sight of her, throwing the nearside rear door open and beginning to say, 'Christ, China.'

I couldn't get her into the seat. Her arms and legs were everywhere, pivoting loose and awkward from the hips and elbows. I didn't panic until then.

'Isobel, you'll have to help . . .'

'China.'

'What, love? What?'

'China.'

She could talk but she couldn't hear. Blood ran into my shirt where she had put her arms round my neck. I slammed the door behind us. Choe started the engine.

'Drive,' I urged him.

He looked surprised. Then he said mildly, 'OK Mick.'

At that the BMW seemed to slither away from the kerb of its own accord, fishtailing out into the empty arcade-game of Whitechapel, where we began to pass the scattered traffic on either side at eighty or ninety miles an hour. Some radio station I didn't know was playing the protracted, formal opening of the old Who song 'Baba O'Riley'. Choe turned up the volume. Suddenly London was falling away from us at odd angles, as if it had achieved the topological values of a Vorticist painting. Lumbering taxis, wry hoardings, white faces of pedestrians fearful on traffic islands splashed with halogen pink, rushed upon us and were snatched away in the nick of time.

'Yes,' said Choe to himself.

He had the carbon-fibre front seat set right forward and his face up near the windscreen. Driving was a physical thing for Choe. Cars loathed him, I now saw. He never let up. They always had to be forced. They had to be contained somehow between his hands and feet, held in a vice constructed out of revs and brakes, revs and brakes. They always had to be driven on and held back both in the same moment, the same gesture. Choe ground his teeth and, purple in the face from coke and aggression, aimed his cars like guns, from hazard to hazard.

After a bit he asked in a conversational voice, 'Where we going?'

'Oh, *come on*, Choe.'

'Honest question, Mick. Be fair.'

Something took his attention and silenced him for a while after that. I sat in the back with my arms round Isobel. I talked to her but she didn't answer. 'Do you remember the time we stayed in St Ives for Christmas, and to cheer me up you bought me a pushalong duck, with rubber feet that flapped?' I kept catching glimpses of her in weird neon shop lights from Wallis or Next or What She Wants, lolling against my chest with her mouth half open. She knew how bad she was. She kept trying to smile up at me. Then she would drift off, or cornering forces would roll her head to one side as if she had no control over the muscles in her neck and she would end up staring and smiling at the back-seat upholstery whispering:

'China. China China China.'

'Isobel.'

She passed out again and didn't wake up.

It was twelve minutes since I had found her. We were nearly there.

I said: 'Can't you get a move on, Choe?'

'Fuck off Mick,' he said.

After a moment he added matter of factly: 'I've lost it, I'm afraid.'

A late taxi had forced him to brake in a turn. Instantly the rear-wheel drive was all over him, flicking the back end around so fast we could almost see it catching up. Three in the morning, New Year's Eve: Hammersmith Gyratory. The piers of the flyover loomed above us in wicked orange light, stained grey concrete plastered with anarchist graffiti and torn posters. The M3 waltzed sideways towards them, ballistic at last, a car glad to be out of Choe Ashton's hands. I curled my body over Isobel's, trying to cradle her head. G snatched her away from me. G for gravity. G for the gravity of things. I could hear Choe repeating 'fuck' in a monotone: 'Fuck, fuck, fuck, fuck.' We tipped the kerb, tripped over our own feet, and began a long, slow roll like an airliner banking to starboard. We hit a post box with an extraordinary noise, like someone stamping on a cardboard box. The BMW jumped in a startled way and righted itself. Its offside rear suspension had collapsed. Uncomfortable with the new layout, still trying to get away from Choe, it spun twice and banged itself repeatedly against the opposite kerb with a sound exactly like some housewife's Metro running over the cat's-eyes on a cold Friday morning. Something snapped the window-post on that side and broken glass blew in all over Isobel Avens' peaceful face. She opened her mouth. Thin vomit came out, the colour of tea: but I didn't think she was conscious. Then she said, quite clearly: 'I went too far, China. I went too far.' Until that moment everything had seemed to happen in slow motion, some Hollywood choreography featuring an obsolete BTCC racer which dismantles itself to the long, romantic, yet interrogative guitar lines of Joe Satriani's 'Always With You, Always With Me'. Now, things came back up to speed again. Hammersmith Gyratory, ninety-five miles an hour. Choe dropped a gear, picked the car up between steering and accelerator, and shot out into Queensborough Road on the wrong side. The boot lid popped open and fell off. It dragged along the road for a minute, then went backwards quickly and disappeared.

'Christ, Choe.'

'Not many cars would do that.'

'China.'

Draped across my arms, Isobel was nothing but a lot of bones and heat. I carried her up the steps to Alexander's building and pressed for entry. The entryphone crackled but no one spoke. 'Hello?' I said. After a moment the locks went back.

Look into the atrium of a west London building at night and everything is the same as it is in the day. Only the reception staff are missing, and that makes less difference than you would think. The contract furniture keeps working. The PX keeps working. The fax comes alive suddenly as you watch, with a query from Zurich, Singapore, LA. The air-conditioning keeps on working. Someone has watered the plants, and they keep working too, making chlorophyll from the overhead lights. Paper curls out of the fax and stops. You can watch for as long as you like: nothing else will happen and no one will come. The air will be cool and warm at the same time, and you will be able to see your own reflection, very faintly, in the treated glass.

'China.'

Upstairs it was a suite of open-plan offices – health finance – and then a suite of consulting rooms. Up here the lights were off, and you could no longer hear the light traffic on Queensborough Road. It was two-fifty in the morning. Choe got into the consulting rooms and then Alexander's office, and ranged about breaking things, while I walked up and down with Isobel in my arms, calling:

'Alexander?'

No one came.

'Alexander?'

Someone had let us in.

'Alexander!'

Alexander's desk, an oiled sweep of top-end hardwood, was stacked with computer printout and brochures. 'For fuck's sake Choe,' I called. 'Stop that and come and help me here.' We swept everything off on to the floor and tried to make Isobel comfortable by folding my coat under her head. 'I'm sorry,' she said quietly, but not to me. It was part of some conversation I couldn't hear. She kept rolling on to her side and retching over the edge of the desk, then laughing. I had picked up the phone and was working on an outside line when Brian Alexander came in from the corridor. He had lost weight. He looked vague and empty, as if we had woken him out of a deep sleep. You can tear people like him apart like a piece of paper, but it doesn't change anything.

'Press nine,' he advised me. 'Then call an ambulance.'

He glanced down at Isobel. He said:

'It would have been better to take her straight to a hospital.'

'Shall I twat him one, Mick?' Choe said.

I put the phone down.

Isobel woke up, saw Alexander, and put her arms up imploringly to him. '*Brian*,' she said. She threw up again. 'Sorry.'

I rubbed my eyes.

'Just talk to him, Choe,' I said.

Choe took Alexander's arm and, murmuring, 'This is a really nice suit you've got on,' guided him over to the window. There he continued, 'See that? The traffic is really bad tonight.' Alexander looked at Choe, then down at the sleeve of his own suit, and then out of the window at the BMW, half up on the pavement with smoke coming out of it. Choe said: 'You've got to agree that's a perfectly good car, haven't you? Well, look, I just *stuffed* the fucker into a post box.' He smiled reminiscently. 'Drugs and classic oversteer. The two best things in the world.' He added, as if he was discovering it for the first time: 'Mick's a wanker but he knows a good car.' Without taking his eyes off the doctor, he reached round behind him with one hand and picked up a copy of 'The Alexander Clinics Welcome You'. 'And another thing,' he said. 'What's all this crap?'

'Leave it, Choe,' I told him. 'That's not the point.'

'No, be fair, Mick. Let him explain himself.'

He waved the brochure in front of Alexander's face, in such a way that it fell open at random. Alexander, under the impression he was being invited to read the paragraph which began, 'Here at the Alexander Clinics,' misunderstood him comprehensively.

'Oh, that,' he said. 'Grafting turned out to be unnecessary. It was a very early idea. Do you know anything about this? Genome mapping was the difficult thing. By the time we'd done sufficient mapping to give us a vocabulary of fifty or a hundred birds, someone had found a way we could simply punch the new genetic material directly into the patient's cells, tethered to regulatory sequences which switched the correct ribosomes on only in hair-follicles. We had no trouble, even with the hormones.'

He shrugged.

'Grafting was just expensive and unnecessary. We left it in the brochure because the patients are already familiar with cosmetic surgery.'

He produced a faint smile.

'Molecular biology excites them, but it makes them feel less comfortable.'

He stared at Choe. Choe stared back.

'For fuck's sake,' Choe said. 'I said, you know, ex*plain*.'

He pulled Alexander's face quickly down towards him and butted it. A long dollop of blood shaped like a very streamlined dumb-bell shot out of Alexander's nose, turned over once or twice in the air, stretching elegantly, and landed on the arm of Choe's beige Comme des Garçons jacket.

'Fuck,' said Choe.

'Choe!'

'How am I going to get this off, Mick?' Choe appealed.

I stood between them and gave Alexander a wad of Kleenex for his nose. Wiping blood across his face so that it left an oblique brownish smear, fading where it reached the dark granulated skin above his cheekbone, Alexander focused shakily on me. I had been moving things about for him since the old Astravan days; since before Stratford. And if I was just a contract to him, he was just some writing on a job sheet to me. He was the price of a 1985 competition M3 on to which I had had someone bolt a Garrett turbocharger. He blinked.

'I know you,' he said. 'You've done work for me.'

'But you did this,' I reminded him.

I got him by the back of the neck and made him look closely at Isobel. Then I pushed him against the wall and stood away from him. I told him evenly: 'Now I'm glad I didn't kill you when I wanted to.' I said: 'Put her back together.'

He lifted his hands.

'I can't,' he said.

'Put her back together.'

'This is only an office,' he said. 'She would have to go to Miami.'

I pointed to the telephone.

I said: 'Arrange it. Get her there.'

He examined her briefly.

'She was dying from day one anyway,' he said. 'The immune system work alone would have killed her. We did far more than we would normally do on a client. Most of it was illegal. *It would be illegal to do most of it to a laboratory rat.* Didn't she tell you that?'

I said: 'Get her there and put her back together again.'

'I can make her human again,' he offered. 'I can cure her.'

I said: 'She didn't fucking want to be human.'

'I know,' he said.

He looked down at his desk; his hands.

He whispered: '"Help me to fly. Help me to fly!"'

'Fuck off,' I said.

'I loved her too, you know. But I couldn't make her understand that she could *never* have what she wanted. In the end she was just too demanding: effectively, she asked us to kill her.'

I didn't want to know why he had let me have her back. I didn't want to compare inadequacies with him.

I said: 'I don't want to hear this.'

He shrugged.

'She'll die if we try it again,' he said emptily. 'You've got no idea how these things work.'

'Put her back together.'

You tell me what else I could have said.

I lived in a hotel on the beach while it was done. Miami. TV prophecy, humidity like a wet sheet, an airport where they won't rent you a baggage trolley. You wouldn't think this listening to Bob Seeger. Unless you are constantly approaching it from the sea, Miami is less a dream – less even a nightmare – than a place. All I remember is what British people always remember about Florida: the light in the afternoon storm, the extaordinary size and perfection of the food in the supermarkets. I never went near the clinic, though I telephoned Alexander's team every morning and evening. I was too scared.

Infections were racing through her again as her immune system went down block by block. Contamination from bacterial soups employed in the original treatments had filled her with fragments of a strange or damaged DNA. Her blood was a junkyard of proteins. In addition there were problems with the engineered hormonal chemistry. Most of the bird hormones had one or two more amino acids than their naturally occurring counterparts: some had as many as ten. Worse: because they had been manufactured on human robosomes, they all had radical differences in topology. It was a language problem. Unable to make sufficiently fine grammatical distinctions, or indeed fully separate signal from noise, Isobel's biology, unsure what kind of animal it might now support, was spiralling into total metabolic collapse even as it tried to understand the new messages raging through it. Intubated and strapped down, she fluttered and thrashed like a sparrow trapped in a room; or lay still, breathing at some impossible rate.

One day the team were optimistic, the next they weren't. They seemed like children to me; smooth yet aggressive: full of themselves. 'You want to call in a veterinary?' they asked one another every morning. 'Ha ha, ah ha ha ha.' But in the end I knew they had got involved again. They were intrigued by the chemistry, excited by its implications. They were going to stabilize her. She was going to have what she wanted. They were going to do the best they could for her, if only because of the technical challenge. All I needed to do was wait.

In your early forties the summers rush past. Before you know it, November has ended everything. By contrast the winters seem long and dreary. Then in your early fifties, winter begins to rush past, too. You are just settling down to endure February when you notice buds on the trees: it's March, and if the air is still cold and northerly, well, the sunshine is warm. Two kinds of subjective time have suddenly meshed like gears. The first kind is an illusion of acceleration – the older you get, the smaller a proportion of your life a single summer becomes. The second kind is an illusion of duration – the sense we have that something unpleasant takes longer to pass than something pleasant. Once these two kinds of time have equalized or changed gear, waiting for anything becomes much easier.

Isobel slipped in and out of the world until the spring. But she didn't die, and in the end I was able to bring her home to the blackened, gentle East End in May, driving all the way from Heathrow down the inside lane of the motorway, as slowly and carefully as I knew how, in my new off-the-peg 7 Series. I had adjusted the driving mirror so I could look into the back of the car. Isobel lay awkwardly across one corner of the rear seat. Her hands and face seemed tiny. In the soft wet English light, their modified bone structures looked more rather than less human. Lapped in her singular successes and failures, the sum of her life to that point, she was as calm as I had ever seen her.

About a mile away from the house, outside Whitechapel tube station, I let the car drift up to the kerb and stop. I switched the engine off and got out of the driving seat.

'It isn't far from here,' I said.

I put the keys in her hand.

'I know you're tired,' I said, 'but I want you to drive yourself the rest of the way.'

She said: 'China, don't go. Get back in the car.'

'It's not far from here,' I said.

'China, please don't go.'

'Drive yourself from now on.'

If you're so clever, you tell me what else I could have done. All that time in Miami she had never let go, never once vacated the dream. The moment she closed her eyes, feathers were floating down past them. She knew what she wanted. Don't mistake me: I wanted her to have it. But imagining myself stretched out next to her on the bed night after night, I could hear the sound those feathers made, and I knew I would never sleep again for the touch of them on my face.

EPILOGUE · IN JUMBLE WOOD

A kind of paralysis gripped me whenever I thought about Christiana Spede. In the end it was she who got back in touch. She returned two books I had lent her with a little note written carefully on the brown-paper wrapping. It was an act of language, an invitation to treat. Her operation, she said, had been successful; and she was recovering well. Would I send back the denim jacket I had borrowed in October? I would. I was curious. 'Did you feel it would be *inappropriate* to put your note inside the package?' I enquired carefully. 'Or did you just forget?' She replied on a postcard of Chagall's *Garden of Eden*, in which it is Adam who tempts Eve with the apple:

'I wasn't sure you'd want to hear from me.'

It could easily have rested there, but one thing led to another, and we met at Camden Lock on an unseasonable Sunday afternoon in May. It had been raining for a week. Under a sky marbled lead and silver the markets had reverted to type – stalls flimsy and bricolaged, sheets of heavy-gauge plastic flapping madly in the wind, the tourists wincing and ducking away. A pair of lace gloves blew down a crowded aisle and adhered, disfigured, to the muddy cobbles underfoot. No one noticed. 'Sorry,' a jeweller told us shortly, when Christiana asked to look at some little turquoise and silver ear-rings, 'I'm closed.' So we walked up to Inverness Street and ate at the Mimico Bistro, now defunct. Among the middle-class adolescents and Spanish tourists, an old lady in a thick maroon woollen coat was eating fried eggs, carefully dipping chips into them one by one.

'Look at that,' said Christiana. 'There's something about the way old people eat, even when they're greedy. Do you know what I mean, China? Dignified, and with a steady concentration.'

'I'm an old person,' I said.

All this time we hadn't touched.

'Christiana—'

'Camden is still worth it because of that,' she said.

Suddenly she looked away and blinked. Her hand came out and held mine across the table.

'China?'

'Christiana, I—'

'I couldn't understand what had happened,' she said. 'I felt totally alone.'

Suddenly I got up and went round to her side of the table. She scraped her chair back and started to get up. We embraced awkwardly, and then she pushed me away. She laughed. I must have looked terrified.

We live together now, although perhaps 'together' is the wrong word. We turned the Chalk Farm house back into separate dwellings. Christiana kept the garden and her little bare blue and white bedroom looking out on to the railway. I thought about it for a while, then hired a design partnership to do my half. They put in a Japanese cedar bathtub, Seimatic worktops, ARCO taps by Hansgröhe; floors of Douglas fir. By the time they'd finished, it was austere yet sensual, Pawson-like (though I couldn't afford Pawson himself). Less a home than a clean slate. Christiana hates it. While her snobberies are no longer those of the woman I knew in the early eighties, they present as political even when their content is domestic. Sometimes she will admit grudgingly, 'At least it's an easy place for you to keep clean.'

We have separate entrances and telephone accounts and grocery bills. We are careful with one another's privacy (which she calls 'space'). Even so, things are sometimes bad between us, and when they are she remembers how I abandoned her to King's College Hospital, and she says:

'You turned out to be a bigger bastard than Choe in the end.'

I never respond to that. What can I tell her? That in forgetting her I remembered Isobel, as if they were two halves of the same woman? That to me, then, it was as if one woman had gone into hospital and immediately, in a single fluid, seamless movement, returned to convalesce? As if she had entered by the front door at King's and come out by the back door of the Alexander Clinic, Miami?

'A much bigger bastard, China.'

What can I say about Choe Ashton?

During Isobel's second term in the Miami clinic I had taken a week off here and there to set up a new business, flying back steerage from Miami. By then, I suspect, I already knew that I wasn't going to be there for her when she came out; that whatever I did now I would do for myself. They still remembered me in Soho. Fifty years old and full of a visible – if at times undependable – energy, I was able to borrow enough to get back into the production side: ads, corporate videos, pop promos. After I walked away from Isobel in the spring, it was easy to immerse myself in that. It was hard work, and I felt too empty and distanced from everything to want to get involved with Choe again. But I did go looking for him on one of those trips back, and I did find him.

Haringey, late April: 10 a.m., and I was walking down towards the Salisbury Hotel. The rush-hour traffic had diminished to a trickle and the morning queues were in the Cypriot banks. There had been an early frost, but now bright sunshine was spilling into the slot of Green Lanes, pouring off the grimy buildings and splashing on to the exotic vegetables stacked outside the Turkish shops, some of which had been closed for barely eight hours. (This brought me a quick, aching memory of Budapest: paprika and flowers in the open markets, then Dohany Street east of the synagogue, ablaze with morning light. You stand dazzled, almost afraid to cross the road; then, looking north up Klausal, catch a glimpse of scaffolding, trees, Klausal Square in a resplendent haze. Happiness and beauty are the worst things you can

243

have in a life, because you never forget them. They go on and on ambushing you, presumably until you die.) Ten minutes later I was outside the minicab office. The locks had been changed at Choe's flat. Choe hadn't returned my calls. Shogun Cars had responded with a disconnected tone. Now I saw why. A fire in the night, and Choe's enterprise had burnt to a shell.

There were scorch marks on the pink walls above the empty casements. Parts of the roof were open to the air. The first floor had fallen through into the minicab office. Blackened, eroded beams barred the doorway. But I ducked and shoved my way in and stood in a puddle of water in the middle of the room and tried to locate the dispatcher's desk, the filing cabinet, the pool table. Not much left to see. It was cold and dark in there, yet somehow comforting, and I stood for quite a time feeling grateful that nothing was required of me. Then beneath the acidic smells of charred wood and melted plastic, the residue of burnt petrol, I caught a faint, stale reek of something else. I heard a stealthy noise; looked up in anxiety. Pigeons. Pigeons had already moved in from the abandoned cinema across the road to breed. They shifted their pink, mangled feet awkwardly among the rafters high up.

'Don't do that,' I begged them.

Then Ed Cesniak, who'd been standing at the edge of the room all along, coughed and said:

'Hi, Mick.'

'Jesus Christ.'

I remembered his face as pale. Now, as he stepped out of the shadows, it was a white on the edge of green – an albescent, almost radiant green. I felt an extraordinary fear and stepped back.

'Mick, Mick,' he said softly, as if to calm me.

'My name's China.'

'Hey, China,' he said. 'Look, whatever you do, don't feel scared. You were only the driver. You weren't involved. We know you weren't involved.' He laughed. 'Even Choe wasn't really involved,' he said. He looked round at the devastated office. 'Pity about this. It was a nice little place.' He shrugged. 'Look,' he said, 'tell Choe, "No hard feelings." He won't be hurt. But he should stay away for a while.'

He pushed up his cuff to look at his Breitling Chronomat.

'Hey,' he said. 'I'm late. Look, it was good to see you, China. Sometime soon, yeah?'

He held out his hand.

'Where's your Walkman, Ed?'

He smiled.

'Choe liked that more than anything, didn't he? Robert Johnson.'

A long black car drew up quietly in the street outside. Ed picked his way with care over the puddled TV, the bubbles of silver metal that had been cable and chassis of the microwave oven, all the gluey, melted rubbish of Choe's ambition, over the threshold and into the bright April light. 'Do you all need a *lift?*' he called back. 'I'm going west. Or is it east?' he asked himself. When I told him no, he raised his hand goodbye; then, changing his mind suddenly, turned to speak again. The light caught his eyes and made them so blank, so empty, so very transparent that I could see right through to the imp bottled in there. That imp; it's never so much the other person's ego as something escaped from our own. Some residue of personality we never wanted to acknowledge which slips over to people like Ed and, suddenly able to be honest about itself, becomes a real goblin.

'The Walkman was for Choe,' I heard him say. 'All for Choe.'

Someone told me Choe had moved to Chiswick; someone else that he had left Britain altogether. One day in July I got a call from him.

'Hello?'

'Don't be a prat, Mick.'

'Choe. Nice to hear from you.'

'You could get your head stuffed in a litter bin just for talking to me.'

'It was you who phoned,' I pointed out.

'I'm not kidding, Mick.'

'I know, Choe.'

I said I would like to talk anyway.

'Can you get up here?'

I said I could, and we arranged a meeting. He was living in his home town again. *I fucking hated that place*, I remembered him saying; and wondered how he could be getting on there. 'Does that seem like a good idea?' I asked. 'Given how you felt?'

No answer.

He rang to cancel the arrangement three or four times. Each time it was back on within an hour or two. First I was to meet him at a pub called the Bear's Paw. Then, if I was bringing a car, the place where he lived – though he seemed reluctant to give me its address. Finally he agreed to be in the town-centre car-park at one o'clock the next day. He was distracted, I thought by fear, although I see now it wasn't that. He seemed to have forgotten about Isobel, because once or twice he asked me:

'How's your tart, Mick?'

I drove up in Christiana's battered Citroën Safari, leaving the M1 at Sheffield and following the Snake Pass west. At that time of the year the moors seem burnt and derelict in the sun. Then you look into the deep little cloughs that run away up into the peat and you see how full of trees they are – green oaks, green turf, yellow tormentil, silver water running over stones. From its summit the Snake slipped back down through a series of tight hypnotic curves to farmland. I turned south and took the A6 for a few miles, and the next thing I saw was a tall steel chimney, elegant as a rocket, towering above the rows of do-it-yourself warehouses and light chemical plants which had moved in on the quarry companies in the late eighties and now lay calm and exhausted under the sun, caught between boom and bust.

Otherwise it was Choe's nightmare: Woolworth's, Sainsbury's, the record shop, the bus station. *Only the recently dead use a bus station*. I found him sitting on the broken-down brick wall of the car-park, kicking his feet in the sunshine. His jeans were rolled up to show off a pair of paint-splattered workboots. He had shaved his head, then let the hair grow two or three millimetres so that the bony plates of his skull showed through, aggressive and vulnerable. I thought he was nervous, but bored and lonely too, as if he had been sitting on his own all morning. He seemed reduced, as if the town had already done its work on him, peeling him back along his own lifeline to first display and then dismiss every self-reinvention since adolescence.

He jumped off the wall when he saw me.

'Where's the car?' Then, realizing that the BX was mine: 'Jesus Mick, what's this? It looks like a fucking minicab.'

'Where to, mate?'

'Look Mick, I really meant that about the litter bin.'

'Ed sends you his love.'

'Oh yes?'

'Let me see if I can get this right. He says he could swallow you with a glass of water, but he won't. He says to tell you, "Don't be a wanker all your life, Choe."'

Choe grinned wanly.

I said: 'I think that was it.' I said: 'Does that sound about right?' I said: 'So where do you want to go?'

'When I was young,' he said, 'my parents kept chickens in a hutch in the back garden.' He watched a woman carry two supermarket bags across the car-park and stand by the door of her little red Corsa as if she expected someone else to come and unlock it for her. 'They named a chicken after each of us. Then they served them up for dinner, once or twice a year.' He blinked up into the sun. 'Alan, Andy, Edie, Choe,' he recited. 'I got mine at Christmas. Do you believe that?'

Well, do you believe that? I thought. He had asked as if my answer was important to him – as if it might help him under-stand the way he had seen the world since.

'No, Choe. I don't.'

'I really like housewives,' he said. 'Don't you?'

247

'Where do you want to go, Choe?'

'Jumble Wood.'

I stared at him.

'Are you sure?'

'I live there now mate. It's where I live.'

'You'll have to direct me.'

At its southern edge the town petered out into a labyrinth of narrow lanes between tall, honey-coloured gritstone walls. The road would dip suddenly into a valley, turn two hundred degrees, then lift up to some empty, open little bit of land with a wind-farm on it. Blind junction followed blind junction, each marked by a white, abandoned-looking pub. Soon I had no idea where I was. But summer had brought the flowers out; horses were up to their knees in moon-daisies in every field. The verges were fat with clover and cow parsley. The foxgloves were like girls. Thick clusters of creamy flowers weighed down the elders, and wherever I looked there were wild roses, the most tremulous pink and white. Every field's edge was banked with red poppies. That would have been enough – fields of red poppies – but among them, perhaps one to five hundred, one to a thousand, there were sports or hybrids of a completely different colour, a dull, waxy purple, rather sombre but fine.

'Stop here,' ordered Choe.

A quiet road of stone three-bedroomed houses, mature horse chestnut trees and neat, rather unimaginative gardens bright with stonecrop, pelargoniums and lobelia, curved up and round to oak woods suspended on the lip of a steep little gritstone scarp. It was much as I remembered it. If the roadway looked in need of repair, that rather added to its comfortable quality; if the woods looked a little dustier, they were just as tangled, just as secretive. Birds were flocking in the hot blue air above the trees, dipping, sweeping, hovering; a coherent, noisy wheel of gleaming white specks.

I turned the ignition off. The Citroën dieselled briefly into silence.

'Gulls,' I said. 'They're seagulls.'

'This car sounds like shit, Mick.'

'It's French, Choe. That's how they sound.'

He got out.

'It's crap,' he said. 'That's how crap sounds.' And then: 'Jumble Wood.'

When you got closer, you saw he had fenced it in with chain link. There were tall, heavily padlocked gates of galvanized metal, big enough to admit a truck, and from there a raw-looking lane, surfaced with limestone chippings and lit at night by halogen lamps on concrete standards, had been cut through the wood. The sign on the gate, green letters on a white wooden board, had originally read: 'SHOGUN SERVICES'. Some local child had added a T to the first word.

'Shotgun, eh?' boasted Choe. 'Shotgun Services, that's me.'

'Choe—'

'Come and have a look.'

Jumble Wood was still meditative. But now it was full of small black flies too. Dust thrown up by days and nights of contractors' traffic had greyed the bark of the oaks, which seemed suddenly dwarfed and contorted in the face of it all. An oppressive breeze rustled through branches strung with heavy-duty electrical conduit. We walked up the hill in silence, Choe smiling and grinning at me, while the seagulls circled above something perhaps two hundred yards in front of us, crying rawly into the heated afternoon air. At the geological divide, where millstone grit gave way suddenly to limestone, the trees had been bulldozed out of the way. We stood and looked across to the spot where Choe's fat girl, his green woman, had come up from out of the earth.

'What do you think, Mick?'

The dump had almost filled the little valley. It was the usual stuff. Grey earth and burst cardboard boxes. Cascades of used pippettes, gel-loading tips and sample combs. Empty nucleotide phials with poster-coloured lids as bright as toys for very young children. A Lego of transparent plastic trays and cheerful red flipper racks. Puddles of run-off solvent, detection-reagents and electrophoresis gels. It was stuff that would glow in the dark. It was carbon tetrachloride, a rainbow in your head at night, hallucinations like the dimples in oil. It was the diamondy glitter of smashed borosilicate glass, the remains of a consignment of flasks with characteristic blue polypropylene caps. Where the wood avens had grown, someone had got rid of a dozen plastic dustbins stuffed with computer output, now sodden, caky and unreadable – though I picked out the words 'microfiltration zones'. Where Choe had fucked the green girl and, panting, sealed her with his adolescent kiss, a small rusty-yellow bull-dozer rested hull-down among heavy-duty waste tubs sealed 'Burn Without Opening'. The trees that remained were leafless, decorated with nests and tangles of biohazard tape, or strips of polythene floating like good-luck charms in the hot breeze. As I watched, a flimsy white plastic bag drifted past at eye level, turning over and over on itself, expanding and contracting like some formless, slow-moving creature of the sea, until it became tangled in the upper branches of a sycamore. Even then it seemed to have achieved, rather than death, development: as if it might settle down now for some years to sift the wind for food, produce spores, change shape, and only then die.

'I come here a lot,' Choe said vaguely.

He waved his arm.

'Look at those fucking gannets.'

Thinking perhaps that he had thrown them something, the circling gulls dipped and veered abruptly in their flight.

'They could wait forever.'

'They're big strong birds,' I agreed.

He stared at me.

'I'm fucking scared of them,' he said.

'I thought you were scared of nowt.'

He laughed.

'Come and have a beer.'

About four hundred yards down the track he had bulldozed a

little clearing in the oak wood and that was where he lived, in an old green caravan about thirty feet long, sitting askew on a broken axle and deflated tyres. Moss grew from its aluminium window frames, but there was a good Honda generator at the back, and a brand-new satellite dish beside the door. Inside – though a disturbing light filtered in through the oak trees, as of a storm always approaching but never arriving – I found it quite comfortable. Refrigerator, microwave and telephones were installed at one end; at the other a gigabyte Mac on a cheap white stand, more phones and five Sony TVs bolted into the kind of display rack popular in bars in the mid eighties. He had brought his Harry Crews collection with him from Haringey. He had books by Robert Stone, Jayne Anne Phillips and Harold Bloom. He had a shelf of *Internet* magazines and novels with titles like *Snowcrash*. Where he slept, I couldn't see. Perhaps he didn't sleep.

'What's on TV?' I said.

He picked up a remote control. All five screens sprang silently into life. They showed: poor-quality video images of the Titanic – anchor chains, winches and capstans which resembled nothing so much as shots of some heavily moulded ceiling discovered in a country house; a live mouse with a full size human ear growing out of it; Isobel Avens' face in close-up, her lips making the word 'China' over and over again; the credits of a film called *Leningrad Cowboys Go America*; and a single magpie, which seemed to wear its wings like an iridescent cloak, flapping up in slow motion from a grass verge into a hedge.

One of the pictures changed and the rest stayed the same. Then the rest changed, and nothing was the same.

'Is that a prophecy?' I asked.

Choe shrugged.

The refrigerator was full of bottles. I took one out and opened it. Choe already had one.

'I bought a case of this,' he said.

'Giraffe beer. Ah.'

'Why drink anything else?'

'Why indeed.'

We sat down and watched the TVs for a while. Eventually, when he realized I wasn't going to say anything, Choe got up and switched them off. He was desperate to get my attention. 'The thing is,' he said, making a gesture intended to include the caravan, Jumble Wood and the waste tip he had made of it, 'that the whole world's going to be like this soon.'

'Choe. How clever of you to guess that.'

'At least I can live with it, Mick. You were just a fucking hypocrite all along.'

I began to turn away, but he got hold of my sleeve. 'A fucking hypocrite all along.' He wanted me to be angry with him because he had spoilt the valley; he wanted me to be angry with him because he couldn't grow up. Neither of those things seemed to be the issue any more. 'Mick, I only told you all that stuff about the girl to get you going,' he said. 'Really. None of it was true. I never believed it.' He nodded back in the direction of the town. 'I lived down there, and I used to come here just to get away. Just to sit on a Saturday afternoon. Have a wank. You know.'

'Do you think I care?' I said.

He looked upset and ran out of the caravan. I drank the rest of my Giraffe beer and smashed one of the TV screens with the empty bottle. It was getting late by then. I went out. Horizontal sunlight gilded the tops of the oaks, and Choe was back at the tip. Twenty or thirty herring gulls had gathered shrieking above him, and he was throwing stones at them with single-minded ferocity. It was some time before he noticed me.

'These fuckers,' he said. 'They can wait forever.' He rubbed the inside of his elbow. 'I've hurt my arm.'

'They only live a year or two, Choe.'

He picked up another stone.

Whatever he says now – and whatever you and I might think – something happened to Choe in Jumble Wood when he was young: something that centralized itself in his life so thoroughly that for over twenty years, puzzled, charmed and frustrated, he was compelled to return there yearly on the anniversary of the event. In doing so he reassured himself less perhaps of the green woman's existence than of his own.

I imagine him standing there all afternoon as the sunlight angled across the valley. Seen in the promise of that light, the shadows of the sycamore saplings are full of significance; the little crag still resembles a white church. Behind him, on the gritstone side of the divide, the wood is hot and tranquil and full of insects. He rests his hand on the rough bark of an oak. He appeals to whatever lives in that place, or at least in that part of his heart, 'Bring her back. Bring her back to me,' only to be hurt time and again by its lack of response. Then one day, tiring of the long wait, and finding himself in a position to do something about it, he buys the valley and buries it forever. To understand how completely Choe jumped ship on his own dream is to understand the confidence which Isobel Avens maintained in hers.

For a time I didn't dream at all. This wasn't entirely Isobel's doing, though I suppose she made my life a dream in itself, one so surprising and gracile that until I lost her I was always moving from moment to moment, incident to incident, in a kind of warm seamless daze. I never wanted anything until Isobel. I've not really wanted much since.

ACKNOWLEDGEMENTS

Thanks to:

Paul McAuley for advice on molecular biology and the genetics industry. Mistakes – deliberate or otherwise – are mine, not his;

Malcolm Edwards and Liz Knights; also Jane Johnson, Robert Kirby, Richard Evans, Jo Fletcher, and Gordon Van Gelder, without whose efforts the book would have stalled out;

Judith Clute and John Clute, Ellen Datlow, Chris Fowler, Simon Ings, Adam Lively, Clare McDonald, Philippa McEwan, Jim Perrin, Sara Sarre and Alex James (also Joseph and Oliver), and Nicholas Royle, for all their encouragement, hospitality and heavy-duty first aid.